HOW MUCH I LOVE

MIAMI NIGHTS SERIES, BOOK 3

MARIE FORCE

How Much I Love
Miami Nights Series, Book 3
By Marie Force

Published by HTJB, Inc.
Copyright 2021. HTJB, Inc.
Cover Design by Kristina Brinton
Ebook Layout: E-book Formatting Fairies
ISBN: 978-1952793103

The Miami Nights Series

Book 1: How Much I Feel *(Carmen & Jason)*
Book 2: How Much I Care *(Maria & Austin)*
Book 3: How Much I Love *(Dee & Wyatt)*

CHAPTER 1

DEE

*I*s it possible to go into hiding when everyone knows where you are? Asking for a friend. Well, that's not true, and we all know it. I'm asking for myself because I'm in a mess of my own making. There's no other way to put it. I had revenge sex with one of the groomsmen at my cousin's wedding, and for months he's been texting cute little daily notes that I find myself looking forward to with far more excitement than I should have for a supposed one-night stand.

Wyatt is coming back to Miami to interview for a job here and wants to see me again. File that under things that *weren't supposed to happen* when I decided to get busy with a man *who doesn't live here*. Meanwhile, my ex—and the subject of the revenge sex he doesn't know I had—is texting me, pleading for a chance to make things right.

Did you follow all that?

In case you're wondering, I'm not that girl. I'm not the one who juggles the boys and giggles when she gets too much attention or has sex with men she isn't in a relationship with.

I. Am. Not. That. Girl. I assure you I'm not judging that girl. I've been envious of her in the past, how she could bed-hop, having all the sex without the stress of dealing with a "boyfriend."

I've had one boyfriend, and once upon a time, before he lost his mind and married someone else, I expected to marry Marcus. Somehow, he ended up married to a woman we now refer to as "the skank."

Too bad he didn't see fit to break up with me before he got married.

Semantics.

I didn't see any of this coming, and it flattened me. Marcus *married* someone else. My sister, cousin and I have no idea if his *wife* deserves the name we've given her, but what does it matter? She married *my* Marcus, and she'll never be anything other than "the skank" to us.

For a long time after I heard he got married, I blamed myself. I was the one who desperately refused to move back to Miami after we both attended college there, and for a while, he was a good sport about it. But six months after he left New York, he said we needed to see other people. So that's what we both did for a few years, not that I "saw" that many people.

About eighteen months ago, he reached out to tell me he'd made a big mistake letting me go and could we try again? Since I hadn't met anyone I loved more than I loved him, I said okay, but I kept our reconciliation between us—and the cousin I lived with, who was the only one in my life who knew we were back together.

Marcus flew up to see me every other month, made sure we talked every day and said all the right things about supporting my dreams and loving me enough to let me spread my wings.

After he suddenly married someone else, though, I began to wonder if he got all that supportive shit from Hallmark cards at the local CVS.

My phone buzzes with a text. I make the mistake of glancing at it to find that Marcus is begging me—*again*—to call him.

Did I mention the skank dumped him, and he's been telling people that the biggest mistake he ever made was letting me get away? I heard about *that* two days before Carmen's wedding five months ago, now.

Thus, the revenge sex with one of her husband's grooms-men, an incredibly sexy doctor from Phoenix who rocked my world in more ways than one.

I experienced actual rage when my sister, Maria, and cousin Carmen gently broke the news that Marcus was apparently in some sort of regret tailspin regarding me and how our relation-ship ended. Oh, and he's still in love with me and never stopped loving me. Even then, I hadn't told them that we'd recently reconciled, and as far as I knew, we'd still been together when he married someone else.

You got married, I'd scream if I returned one of his hundred calls over the last few weeks and months. *What more is there to say?* And yes, I know I should block him. I just haven't gotten around to that yet. Stop judging me.

He has regrets. Whatever. How soon into his "marriage" did he regret leaving me after six on-again-off-again years without so much as a *conversation?* He let me hear through the formidable Miami-to-New York grapevine that my *boyfriend* got *married. To someone else!*

So yeah, call me crazy, but I'm not in any great rush to make him feel better by calling him and talking it out. He can screw himself. Was he thinking about me when he *married* her? When he had sex with her? When he let me hear about his "marriage" from other people?

And you wonder why I'm in hiding in my new apartment. A couple of months ago, I inherited the garage apartment at home owned by my aunt and uncle from my sister, Maria, who moved in with her fiancé, Austin. She managed to grab the golden ring with a great guy who came with a beautiful daughter named Everly, whose life Maria saved when she donated bone marrow to Everly.

Maria met Austin a year after the transplant, when they were finally allowed to talk to each other, and fell madly in love one email and text at a time. Austin is a star pitcher who'll be playing for the Miami Marlins next season. He took a lesser deal than he could've gotten elsewhere so he could live in Maria's town.

Now that's a real man who steps up for the woman he loves, and I couldn't be happier for them. They're adorable together, and Everly is a sweetheart. Maria hit the jackpot, and I'm a nasty cow for being jealous that my sister and cousin have it all figured out while I hide out, hoping the whole world will just go away and leave me the hell alone.

Of course, with my mother battling breast cancer and me being back in Miami to help take care of her, I can't hide out for long. My brothers Nico and Milo are in charge of dinner for my parents tonight, so I'm able to stay in my bunker for a while longer.

I watch mindless TV and try not to think about what I'm going to do about Marcus's nonstop texts, or Wyatt, the one-night stand, trying to score a second night, or my mom's illness, or anything other than which of the Property Brothers is going to win their latest Brother vs. Brother challenge.

I need a real job beyond waitressing at the family's restaurant. At nearly twenty-eight, I'm living in an apartment owned by one aunt and uncle while working for another aunt and uncle. Not where I thought I'd be at this age, that's for sure. I need to go to New York and get my stuff out of my cousin Domenic's apartment. I need to get a freaking life. That's the bottom line.

My phone buzzes again. I swear to God, I'm this close to blocking Marcus. But this text isn't from him.

It's the weirdest thing how I can't stop thinking about what a great time I had at my buddy's wedding. I never expected to meet the sweetest, sexiest bridesmaid in the history of sweet, sexy bridesmaids.

God, it's from Wyatt, the first one-night stand of my life. At least, I *intended* it to be a one-night stand. He has other ideas.

Coming to Miami this weekend to hang with Jason and Carmen before my interview at Miami-Dade on Monday. Any chance I might run into you while I'm in town?

I have a systemwide meltdown as I read and reread his texts. Why had I given him my number, anyway? Oh, right, because I refused to leave with him from the wedding, so we exchanged numbers so I could sneak into his hotel like a dirty secret.

"Ugh," I say to the walls. "How can this be happening? Why can't everyone just go away and leave me alone?" I like being alone. Being alone makes it so someone I expected to spend my life with, only to find out he didn't picture his life with me at all, can't hurt me.

I never again want to put myself in a situation where something like that can happen. By keeping to myself, I can avoid that kind of drama—and that kind of pain. Yes, I see that my sister and cousin have found great guys who make them deliriously happy, and I'm glad about that. They both deserve all the happiness they can find. Carmen went through hell after her first husband, Tony, a police officer, was shot and killed on the job when they were only twenty-four. It took a long time for her to come back from that and take a chance on love again with Jason.

And Maria… her ex cheated on her while they were living together, turning her life upside down. Then she met Austin, who lived in Baltimore when they were first together, and they did the impossible—made a long-distance relationship work until his baseball season ended. He came to Miami for the off-season, and now they're engaged.

It's all worked for Maria and Carmen. But I'm under no illusions that's going to happen to me, too. My illusions, such as they are, were shattered when Marcus married *her*. There's no coming back from that kind of betrayal, especially since he didn't even have the decency to let me know it was over between us *before* he married her.

At first, I laughed at Domenic, the cousin who sat me down and very gently told me he heard Marcus got married. How could that be? I laughed at the foolishness coming from Dom. "Marcus is my *boyfriend*," I said. "He wouldn't *marry* someone else." I angrily accused Domenic of spreading rumors that weren't true. I told him I'd seen Marcus a month ago, and everything had been fine. There was no way in hell he got married.

But he did. And realizing the "rumor" was true was the single most devastating moment of my life until a few days later, when I miscarried the baby I hadn't even known I was carrying. That was worse than what Marcus did, but not by much. After the miscarriage, I holed up in my room in the apartment Dom and I shared in the city and refused to come out, except to use the bathroom.

Domenic threatened to call my parents, which finally got me to come out, to eat something, to return to the land of the living. Still, I was a shell of my former self over the last year as I walked through life like a zombie while I tried not picturing the man I loved living and sleeping with another woman.

Naturally, I had to stalk them online, which is how I learned that the skank is a stunning blonde with big boobs. Why couldn't she be a troll? At least then I could live with him marrying down. But from everything I've seen of them together, he married up, and that hurts worst of all. He threw me over for a stranger who's prettier than me, not to mention her boobs are twice the size of mine.

Ugh, what am I doing reliving this shit? What's the point?

Before I can answer my questions, the phone rings with a

call from Marcus's sister, Bianca. I decline the call. I don't want to talk to her any more than I want to talk to him.

A minute later, Bianca texts me. *Please take my call. It's an emergency.*

For crying out loud. Why can't people just leave me alone?

The phone rings three times before I take the call.

"Dee?" Bianca sounds frantic. "I've been using Marcus's phone to reach out to you, but you're not responding. He... He's in the hospital, Dee. He was found unresponsive this morning and is in the ICU."

My heart drops into my stomach. I don't want to talk to him, but I don't want him to be sick. "What's wrong with him?"

"They don't know. The doctors think maybe he took something."

"What're you saying?"

"*I don't know*, Dee! I just don't know. He's really sick. Can you come here?"

There was a time when the thought of him being sick or in need would've had me running out the door to get to him as fast as I possibly could. That time is in the past. "I'm sorry. I can't."

"Dee! He could *die!*"

Tears fill my eyes, but I battle through the emotional firestorm, determined to look out for myself even when everything in me still wants to go to him. "I'm sorry. I'll pray for him, but I can't come there. I just can't."

The phone goes dead.

Before I have a second to process that Bianca has hung up on me, someone is pounding on the door.

"Open up, Delores." My sister calls me that only when she means business—or is spoiling for a fight.

I haul myself off the sofa and unlock the door for Maria, who comes barging in like she owns the place. Just because she lived here before me doesn't give her barging rights.

"What the hell, Dee? Mommy called me at work today to ask

me why she hasn't seen you in days, and I told her I had no idea because you were supposed to take dinner to them this week."

"Nico did it. We switched weeks." I return to my spot on the sofa that used to belong to Maria until she moved into Austin's mansion and didn't need it anymore. I also inherited her bed, dresser, TV and coffee table.

"I went by the restaurant, but they said you weren't working tonight. What's going on with you?"

"Nothing and this is Sofia's weekend. We alternate, as you know."

"I can tell just by looking at you that something's up. You always do this when the shit hits the fan."

"What do I do?"

Maria sits next to me on the sofa. "Go into hiding."

I fixate on the enormous diamond ring on her left hand. I feel like an asshole for being jealous of what she has with Austin —a beautiful man, a beautiful little girl, a beautiful home and a stunning engagement ring. She's the best person I know and deserves every good thing. "I'm not hiding."

My phone chimes with a new text. I'm almost afraid to look. It's Marcus—or I should say, Bianca. *I can't believe how selfish you're being.*

Now *I'm* selfish? How rich is that? I should've asked her how long he's been in the hospital so I'd know when he last texted me himself. They're going to blame me for this somehow. I didn't respond to his texts, so he did something stupid and dramatic. Did he do it to get my attention?

I've almost forgotten Maria is there. I glance at her, wishing I could keep this to myself. But that's not how things work in my family, which is one reason I was so eager to move to New York in the first place.

"Marcus is in the hospital."

"Why?"

"I don't know. Bianca said he took something he shouldn't

have, and she's trying to guilt me into going there. He was blowing up my phone, and I was ignoring him, so I guess now it's my fault he's in the hospital."

"She *said* that?"

"She said I'm selfish for not going there."

"No, you're not. You owe him nothing."

"You and I know that, but she sees it differently. If he dies, they're going to blame me."

"Let them. You know the truth of what he did to you."

Maria doesn't know the half of it. No one does. Then I'm sobbing. She moves closer and puts her arms around me. I'm furious because it shouldn't hurt this much after all this time.

"I'm so sorry, Dee. He's an asshole for doing this to you—and so is she."

"There's more to what happened than you know." I wipe the tears from my face and decide to tell her the truth. Maybe if I say it out loud, I can finally get some peace.

"Tell me," she says, giving me her full attention.

I realize it's been a while since I had my sister's full attention. Between her ass-kicking job as a nurse at the free clinic and her new life with Austin and Everly, I hardly see her.

"Six months before he got married, Marcus and I had gotten back together—or so I thought."

"*What?* You guys were *together* when he got *married?* Are you *kidding* me?"

I shake my head. I wish I were kidding. "We were keeping it low-key and working on our issues. I'd just seen him a month before, and I thought he was coming back the following weekend."

She stares at me, incredulous. "This is unbelievable."

"I found out he'd gotten married on a Friday. The following Monday, I had a miscarriage."

CHAPTER 2

DEE

*N*ow someone else knows, and I'm not sure how to feel about sharing something that's been such a raw wound for more than a year.

"Oh *God*, Dee," Maria says, her eyes filling with tears. "Why didn't you call me? I would've come!"

"I didn't want anyone to know. I didn't want him to know."

"He didn't know you were pregnant?"

I shake my head. "I was going to tell him the next time we were together in a couple of weeks. But then… Everything fell apart. He got married, and I lost the baby. I lost them both within four days."

"Wait… Was this the week last winter when you weren't answering anyone's texts, and everyone was calling Dom to find out what was wrong with you?"

Nodding as I wipe away tears, I say, "I told him I had the flu."

"Yes! That's what he said. You had the flu. Why didn't you tell me? You know I would've come. Carmen would have, too."

"I couldn't. I was... It was so awful, Maria. *So* awful. And when I came home for Carmen's wedding, and you guys told me he was telling people he wanted me back..."

"That brought it all up again."

"Yeah. He's been relentlessly texting me. I was thinking about blocking him when Bianca called to tell me he's in the hospital."

"You should've blocked him. He has no right to do this to you. No right at all."

"He said he's sorry for what he did, that he fucked up and didn't mean to hurt me."

"He didn't *mean to hurt you*? What the hell did he think would happen to you when he *married* someone else?"

"Especially when I had no idea he was even unhappy. The last time he came to New York, we had the best time. We went to Coney Island and saw a show, and..." A sob comes from the deepest part of me. "Everything was *fine*. I asked him to give me six more months in New York before I moved home, and he was okay with that. I don't understand what happened, Maria. And I want to understand. I really do."

"What will change if you know the why of it?"

"I don't know. Maybe nothing, but I can't figure out how we went from that great weekend to him married to someone else in the span of a few weeks. After I lost the baby, my doctor asked me if there was anyone she could call, like the baby's father, and I just word-vomited the whole ugly story to her. That led her to test me for STDs, which was the ultimate humiliation."

"Jesus, Dee."

"It all came back negative, but still... It was horrible."

"I'm so sorry you went through something like that alone."

"There was nothing you could've done." Thinking back to those unbearable four days makes me ache like it just happened when it was more than a year ago. "I've been kind of a mess ever since, and when I came home for Car's wedding, and you guys told me what he was saying..." I shake my head, thinking about the conversation we had in the limo the night of Carmen's bachelorette party. "I couldn't believe what I was hearing."

"From what Bianca told us, he's legitimately remorseful."

"I don't care! Where was that remorse when he was marrying her? I hadn't heard a single word from him in a year until you guys told me what Bianca said. What do I owe him?"

"Nothing," Maria says firmly. "You owe him nothing at all."

"I've been spinning for five months since the weekend of Car's wedding."

"Which was the same weekend we found out Mommy is sick."

"Right." Our mother was diagnosed with stage three breast cancer in October and had a double mastectomy with reconstruction in January. She's undergoing treatment now, and the four of us, as well as our extended family, have rallied around her and my dad. I came home to Miami for the wedding and never went back to New York.

She pushes my hair back from my face. "I have an idea."

"What?"

"Come to my house for a few days. Hang out by the pool. Play with Everly. Drink wine with me. We'll get you through this rough patch."

"You don't need my sad-sack self underfoot in your happily ever after."

"Oh, hush. I'm inviting you. I want you to come. You'll have your own room and bathroom, and you can hide out whenever you want to be alone. I can't bear the thought of you sad and alone here. Come on. It'll be fun."

I'm tempted. Maria's house is bonkers, the most amazing house any of us have ever been in, and since I don't work again until Tuesday, I've got nothing better to do. "Are you sure you don't mind? I'm not very good company right now."

"I'm sure. I want you to come."

"What about Austin? He has better things to do with his season starting than deal with a grumpy future sister-in-law."

"He won't mind, either. I promise. He loves you. You know that."

I drop my head into my hands, so she won't see how her kindness has wrecked me. I've been so alone with my feelings about Marcus and what he did and losing the baby for so long that it's a relief she knows the whole story now.

She puts her arm around me. "It's going to be okay, Dee."

"Are you sure I shouldn't go to the hospital?"

"I'm positive. I'll call Bianca and tell her to leave you alone."

"You don't have to do that."

"I know, but I'm going to anyway. Pack a bag, and let's go to my place. We'll order Mexican takeout and drink margaritas. It'll be fun."

My phone buzzes with another text, and before I can check it, Maria grabs it, probably preparing to run interference for me with Marcus's family.

"Um, who's Wyatt?"

I grab the phone from her, dying to know what he said this time. "Just a friend." I take it with me into the bedroom and immediately check the text.

I just hope you're ok. Write back to tell me you're still out there. Hello? Dee? Come in.

I smile at his silly text and write back. *Alive and well.* Even if that's not exactly the truth.

Go out with me when I'm in Miami this weekend. Say yes. Please? I can't stop thinking about you.

I'm in absolutely no condition to be considering his invitation, but I find myself clinging to his offer like a lifeline. He can't stop thinking about me. In truth, I can't stop thinking about him, either, and maybe a night with a man who makes me feel good about myself is just what the doctor ordered—pun intended.

I reply before I can talk myself out of it. *Yes.*

He writes back right away. *Tomorrow night?*

Ok.

Where should I pick you up?

I'll meet you at Giordino's parking lot at seven-thirty. We'll figure out a plan from there.

See you then. Can't wait.

I can't wait, either. A sexy guy with a crush on me is just what my fragile ego needs to recover from what Marcus did to me. Maybe another hot night in Wyatt's bed would help things, too. It took me days to recover from the first one. I had aches and pains in places I'd never ached before, which showed me something else—that Marcus wasn't very good in bed. He'd certainly never tended to my needs the way Wyatt did. He discovered needs in me I hadn't even known I had, and I walked around in a daze for weeks after the wedding.

And then he began texting me, continuing something that was supposed to have been one and done. As I pack a bag to hang out with my sister's family for the weekend, I include my sexiest black dress and a pair of come-F-me heels I bought for the wedding festivities but didn't end up wearing.

My life is a big fat mess at the moment, but Wyatt can't wait to see me tomorrow night. That makes me feel a thousand times better than I did before I agreed to see him. Not that I'm putting any eggs in his basket. He's a fling, and that's all he'll ever be.

In the other room, I hear Maria on the phone, her voice raised. "She doesn't owe him a *goddamned thing*, Bianca. After dating her for years, he *married someone else* and didn't even have the decency to tell her. He let her hear that from other people. We're sorry he's in the hospital, but you need to stop this guilt-trip shit with Dee right now, or you and I are going to have a problem."

Yikes. Don't screw with my big sister.

Thank God she's taking care of that. I can't bear to have Marcus's family think this is my fault in some way. What did I ever do besides love him with my whole heart, which he crushed without a single look back until his "marriage" went bad? Then he was all about me again. To hell with that. To hell with him.

I'm moving on.

WYATT

I'm an asshole. There's no other word to describe someone in my situation looking for more from a woman who was supposed to be a one-night stand. If only that one night hadn't been so freaking awesome, I would've moved on by now.

But memories of the incredible day and night I spent with Dee have plagued my waking hours and many of my sleeping hours, too. I wake up hard and horny and ready to go, realizing I've had yet another dream about my sexy bridesmaid. It's not for nothing that I'm going back to Miami for the weekend after hearing from my friend Dr. Jason Northrup that the hospital where he works has an opening for a cardiothoracic surgeon.

Before I went to Jason's wedding, I wasn't thinking about changing jobs, but now that's all I seem to think about when I'm not reliving the hottest night of my life.

The flight from Phoenix to Miami lands ten minutes early and taxis to the gate. I used the in-flight Wi-Fi to make plans with Dee, and ever since she said yes, I've been flying higher than thirty thousand feet.

Which brings me back to how I'm an asshole for wanting another night with her. I have my reasons for not getting involved with the women I date or sleep with, and I'm usually pretty disciplined about sticking to my own rules when it comes to these things. But everything about Dee is an exception to my rules. She's smart, funny, gorgeous and sexy as all hell, and what's best about that is she doesn't even know how hot she is. I loved seeing her partying with her sister, brothers and cousins, and witnessing their close bond firsthand.

There's a refreshing innocence to her, especially when she admitted to me that ours was her first one-night stand. How cute is she? I've had more one-night stands than I can count, but that's by design. It wouldn't be fair to drag someone else into my reality. I know that, and yet I'm elated that Dee has agreed to see me tomorrow night.

I'm definitely an asshole.

Another thought occurs to me, and I'm not sure if I need to check with her or not, but hey, any excuse to talk to her…

Do you care if Jason and Carmen know we're going out tomorrow?

She doesn't write back until I'm in an Uber on my way to Jason's place in Brickell. *It's very difficult to keep anything private in my family, so I guess it's okay if they know. I'd rather they NOT know we already spent time together if that's all right.*

No problem. I get it. Any chance we can eat at Giordino's? That's the other thing I haven't stopped thinking about since the wedding weekend.

Sure, I can make that happen.

Something else to look forward to. Just landed in Miami. Can't wait for a great weekend.

When is your interview?

Monday morning. What're you doing tonight?

Hanging out with Maria and Austin at their place.

I'll see what J&C are doing, but maybe we'll connect later. Hope so.

She responds with a thumbs-up.

I hope that means she wants to see me as much as I want to see her. What is it about her that makes me feel like a teenager in the throes of a first crush? Maybe it's because I never got to crush on anyone when I was a sick teenager. I barely left my house or hospital room. I'm making up for lost time with Dee.

I text Jason to let him know I'm on the way to his place. I wish I'd gotten a hotel now that I have plans with Dee tomorrow night, but Jay would've had a fit if I hadn't stayed with him this weekend. He's excited I'm interviewing for a job at the hospital where he and his wife work.

Jay responds right away. *Can't wait to see you!*

I met him in medical school at Duke, which was the first time I ever lived away from home. When we weren't studying, I was a bit wild during those years, and Jay assigned himself to be my wingman, making sure I didn't do anything stupid or dangerous. I'll never forget the freedom of those years, the fun, the laughs, the friends, the hard work. Those were the greatest years of my life, and Jay is one of the best friends I've ever had.

When he asked me to be in his wedding, I was thrilled and honored. After what he went through in New York with his crazy ex, I was so happy to hear he found someone great in Miami. And once I met Carmen, I was even happier for him. She's awesome, and her family is, too. Their restaurant... *Holy shit.* Best food I've ever eaten in my life. I can't wait to eat there again tomorrow.

I've almost forgotten I'm here for an interview. The job feels secondary to the other "attractions" in Miami. I call up the one photo I have of Dee, a candid from the wedding, taken by the official photographer. Jay sent it to me, not knowing anything about what happened between Dee and me after the wedding, and I've looked at it hundreds of times since then.

She was so incredibly sexy in that dress that I was hard for her from the first time I saw her coming toward us in the wedding party processional. When she took hold of my arm to walk down the aisle after the happy couple said, "I do," her touch sending a charge through me, all I wanted was to get to know her. We had the best time that day, dancing, talking and laughing.

My phone chimes with a text from my mom. *Saw you landed. Hope you're safe.*

For God's sake. She kills me. I know how she worries and why she worries, but sometimes her hovering is just too much. I'm a thirty-four-year-old surgeon, and my mom still checks on me like she did when I was a sick teenager. Wait until she hears I'm thinking of relocating to Miami. She'll lose her shit—and probably come with me. She'd live with me if I'd allow it. That is *not* going to happen.

Did you remember your meds?

Yes, Mother. Relax. All is well.

I want to remind her I'm a *doctor* who knows all too well what'll happen if I don't stay on top of my meds. But I don't remind her of that. She went through hell with me and never left my side through the worst of it. I'd never say anything other than "thank you" to her, even when she's driving me to drink with her hovering.

She tells me that someday I'll understand when I have kids of my own, but that's not going to happen. I'm not bringing kids into this world when I won't be around to raise them. The thought of them losing me in some dramatic, traumatizing way makes me shudder. But that's not something I've come right out and told my parents. I walk such a fine line where they're concerned.

"Hey, man," the Uber driver says. "We're here."

I realize I zoned out and had no idea the car had come to a stop. "Thanks so much." I grab my bag from the seat next to me and get out of the vehicle. Standing on the curb, I text Jay. *Here. What's the secret to getting in there?*

Coming down.

I'm waiting outside the main doors when I see Jay come off the elevator, smiling widely. He's wearing basketball shorts and a tank top and looks nothing at all like a world-class neurosurgeon. After giving me a one-armed bro hug, he takes my bag as we head for the elevator.

I want to tell him he doesn't have to carry my bag, but old habits die hard.

"Glad to see you, buddy," Jay says. "I was so stoked when I heard a cardiothoracic spot is opening up at Miami-Dade. I said to Carmen, I've got to get Wyatt back here, *stat*."

"Thanks for thinking of me."

"Of course I thought of you. You're the best of the best, and we'd love to have you here with us."

"Well, *you* would, but Carmen might not be too happy if we get up to our old ways."

"Ha! She knows I'm thoroughly domesticated these days."

We get off on the seventh floor, and he leads the way to his place, where the door is propped open.

"Carmen, Wyatt's here!"

Jason's pretty wife comes out to hug me. "Great to see you." She has the same dark hair and eyes, olive-toned skin and curvy body that Dee has. Dee is taller than Carmen but not as tall as her sister, Maria.

"You, too. Thanks for letting me crash on your sofa this weekend."

"We're happy to have you anytime. Can I get you a drink?"

"I got you some of that lemon seltzer you like," Jay says. "I'll get it for you."

"We have stronger stuff than that," Carmen says.

"Thank you, sweetheart, but I don't drink."

"Oh, okay. Sorry."

"No worries." I don't drink. I don't smoke. I don't eat red meat. I don't do caffeine or anything that might endanger my fragile health. The good news is I never got the chance to develop a taste for booze before my doctors put it on the list of forbidden substances.

Jay pours the seltzer for me, a glass of wine for Carmen and mixes a cocktail for himself. We take our drinks outside to their awesome patio that overlooks Biscayne Bay. The spring air is warm but not oppressive like it is in the summer, or so Jason told me.

Carmen goes back inside and comes out with a charcuterie platter that the three of us enjoy while we catch up. I stick to the cheese, crackers and fruit, while they enjoy the salami.

"How was the honeymoon?" I ask, even though I already know they had a blast in Turks and Caicos because I'm friends with them on Facebook.

"It was awful." Jason grins at his wife. "We hated it."

"Worst trip ever," Carmen adds. "So bad we're already planning to go back for our first anniversary."

"You have to get to one of the all-inclusive resorts," Jay says. "You'd love it."

"I'm sure I would," I tell him, even though I have a lot of other things ahead of that on my bucket list. And yes, I have a list. You would, too, if your life expectancy was as shitty as mine is. I want to drive cross-country. I want to go to Paris. I want to spend a month in Italy and travel from north to south to see as much of it as possible. I want to spend a month each in London and Dublin. I want to go to Australia and New Zealand. I want to write a book about being a heart patient who becomes a cardiothoracic surgeon. I'm well aware I might not get to do any of it, but I do have a list.

Carmen's phone chimes with a text. "Maria is asking what we're up to and if we'd like to come over for drinks and takeout."

"I'd be up for that if you are, Wyatt. You probably remember from the wedding that Carmen's cousin Maria lives with Austin Jacobs, the pitcher who recently signed with the Marlins. Their house is *sick*."

"Sicker than this?" I gesture to their stunning view.

"Way sicker than this," Jay says.

Of course, I want to go. Dee will be there. But I try to play it cool. "I'd be down with it. Whatever you guys want to do is fine with me. I just need to grab a quick shower."

"I'll get you some towels," Carmen says.

Thirty minutes later, we're on our way in Carmen's car to Austin and Maria's place. I'm looking forward to seeing this so-called sick house, but more than anything, I can't wait to see Dee. I think about texting her to tell her we're coming, but I figure she knows by now.

I wish I knew how she really feels about seeing me again, if she's anywhere near as excited about it as I am, and then I again feel like a complete and total jerk for being so excited to see her. I remind myself over and over again of the rules I've set for my life. There's no reason for me to take someone else down with me when I go—and I will go sooner rather than later. That's just my reality.

"Oh shit," Carmen says, reading something from her phone while Jay drives.

"What's wrong?"

"Maria texted me. Dee's ex, Marcus, is in the hospital. They think it could be a possible suicide attempt."

I sit up taller, tuning in for intel about Dee.

"Is that the guy who married someone else?" Jay asks.

"Yeah, he's the only guy she's ever dated. They were together —on and off—for years."

And he *married* someone else? *What the fuck?* I want to know more. I want to know everything, but I bite my tongue so I won't pepper Carmen with questions. Thankfully, Jay is curious, too.

"I never heard the full story, only that you guys recently got word that he broke up with the wife and wants Dee back."

Oh, hell no. No fucking way is he getting her back. *Easy, cowboy. The rules, remember? Fuck the rules.*

21

"Yeah, Maria and I told Dee the night of my bachelorette that he was telling people he wanted her back. We waited until we could tell her in person. The news blindsided her, to say the least."

Interesting. So, Dee found out her ex wanted her back two days before Carmen and Jason's wedding. My stomach twists a bit at that news as it occurs to me I might've been some sort of revenge-rebound one-night stand. I don't like the way that thought lands. Was she using me to get back at him? As disappointing as that might be, it makes a certain kind of sense, seeing as I was her first-ever one-night stand.

Carmen is texting up a storm with Maria. "Mari says that Marcus's sister has been trying to get Dee to come to the hospital, but she won't go."

That's my girl.

Whoa, rein it in, man. She's not your girl. You had sex with her, which was probably revenge sex for her.

Whatever, it was the best I've ever had, and I want more of it and her—revenge or not.

"They're making her feel seriously guilty, but Mari is telling her she has no reason to be guilty. Marcus up and married someone else just over a year ago, and Mari is telling me that she and Marcus were trying to put things back together, which I didn't know. He got married a few weeks after he'd had a regular weekend visit with Dee in New York. He knew she was planning to move home in six months and apparently couldn't wait. I remember how flattened Dee was after we heard he'd gotten married. It was awful being here when she was far away and so upset."

My heart aches for her as I wonder how long they were together.

"How long had they been together?" Jay asks.

I want to kiss him for doing the heavy lifting for me.

"On and off for six years! After they went to college in New

York, she wanted to stay, and he didn't. He wanted to come home to Miami. He was our cousin Domenic's friend in high school. That's how he and Dee met. Anyway, they made it work for six months and then decided to see other people because the long-distance thing wasn't working for them. But from what Mari tells me, they'd been back together for months when he got married. God, that makes it even worse than it already was!"

"That's horrible," Jay says.

I couldn't agree more. Carmen will never know how thankful I am for this insight into Dee or how helpful it is as I try to understand this woman who has me so captivated.

"And when he married the skank, as we call her, he let Dee hear about it through the grapevine, which is just complete bullshit."

"Is the wife a skank?" Jay asks.

Once again, I want to thank him. It's like our brains have melded or something.

"Who knows? We've never met her. We just call her that because she married Dee's boyfriend."

"To be fair, he was the one with someone else, not her," Jay says.

"Oh, we know that, but it doesn't matter. To us, she's the skank."

I love these people and their loyalty to each other. It's refreshing to be around a family that would, quite literally, take a bullet for each other. Not that my family wouldn't, but we're not tight like the Giordinos are. I chalk that up to the years I spent in the hospital while my brother and sister enjoyed a somewhat normal childhood, albeit as normal as it can be when one sibling is in and out of the hospital and often one step away from death.

A critically ill child tends to consume a family, forcing the parents to focus all their attention on the sick kid to the detriment of the other two. My brother ended up with drug issues that he's since beaten, and my sister got pregnant as a teenager, but my parents don't know that or how she had an abortion.

The impact of my illness on my family was enormous. I wonder all the time if I might be closer to my younger siblings if my struggles hadn't dominated our lives for the better part of a decade.

We're driving through a nice part of Miami, lots of palm trees, colorful flowers and lush landscaping that's in contrast to the stark, desert topography in Phoenix. Usually, I'd be interested in the scenery, but all I can think about is Dee and what her ex put her through, what he *continues* to put her through.

"Why are they saying it was a suicide attempt?" Jay asks.

"I guess his blood indicated high levels of something."

That's called a tox screen, and it was probably the first thing they did when he arrived at the ER.

"Is he going to live?" Jay asks.

"Sounds like it. I texted my friend Angela, who's close to Marcus's sister, Bianca, and Ang says he's awake and talking but not offering any insight into what happened or why. Ang says they think it was because he was trying to talk to Dee, and she was ignoring him."

Good for her. I'm unreasonably proud of her for standing up for herself with this guy, even if it occurs to me once again that I have absolutely no business flirting with her, or whatever you want to call what I'm doing with her. She's had more than enough heartbreak. She certainly doesn't need more, and I'm a heartbreak waiting for a place to happen.

Literally.

I sag into my seat, disappointed to realize I ought to do the right thing and step back from her before it gets messy. We had a great time after the wedding. That night was, truly, one of the best nights of my life. It's going to take a lot to top how I felt being with Dee. I ought to tell Jay thanks for arranging the interview for me at Miami-Dade, but I'm going to keep my job in Phoenix.

Dee is better off with me on the other side of the country, far enough away that there's no chance of me breaking her heart. The thought of taking that necessary step back is depressing as all hell. It's been a very long time since anything excited me more than the idea of more time with Dee has. I had a "girl-friend" a long time ago, back when I was sick. We were twelve and met in the hospital. She ended up dying from our shared ailment. I mourned her for a long time while I continued to fight for my own life. I often wonder why she died and I got to live, even if I'm living with a ticking clock that makes me painfully aware that time is short and every minute counts.

Later, I was so busy in college and med school and catching up on all the fun I never got to have as a kid that I sort of skipped the "relationship" phase of the maturity process.

I've been more about the touch-and-go, emphasis on the *touch*, followed quickly by the *go*. That's how it was supposed to have happened with Dee, but here I am back in Miami, inter-viewing for a new job. All because of a one-night stand that knocked the cover off the ball.

Speaking of knocking covers off a ball, Austin's place is as insane as Jay said it was, and I can't wait to see the inside of it. I follow them in, trying to play it cool when I feel anything but. They're obviously regulars here, know the lay of the land and where to find the residents.

"Hey," Austin Jacobs says, giving Jason a bro hug as they clasp hands.

I met him at the wedding, but I'm still a bit starstruck to be in the presence of a Cy Young Award-winning pitcher of his stature.

"You remember my friend Wyatt from the wedding, right?" Jason says.

"Sure do. Good to see you again, Wyatt."

I shake his hand. "Likewise. Congrats on signing with the Marlins."

"Thanks. It's good to have it settled."

I read about him signing for eighty million for four years so he could stay in Miami with Maria, when he could've gotten much more from another team. I have to give him credit for having his priorities straight when most people would've followed the money, no matter what.

A little girl comes running into the massive family room, her hair wet and her feet bare. She's wearing a pink nightgown, and her cheeks are rosy. "Dada! Don't wanna go to bed!"

Austin scoops her up into his arms and kisses her cheek. "You never want to go to bed. If it was up to you, you'd never sleep."

"No sleep."

"*Yes* sleep."

"Wyatt, I think you met my daughter, Everly, when you were here for the wedding. Ev, this is Uncle Jason's friend Wyatt."

When I waggle my fingers at her, Everly gives me a shy smile before burrowing into her daddy's chest.

Maria comes into the family room with Carmen and Dee. Maria's shirt is wet, probably from giving the little one a bath. My gaze is immediately drawn to Dee, and the first thing I notice is that she looks pale and tired. Is that because her ex is harassing her and staging a suicide attempt to try to get her back?

I don't joke about suicide. I've seen far too much of it in my career for it to be anything other than tragic. I heard just enough about her ex in the car to suspect he staged the attempt as a desperate cry for her attention. I want to tell her to stay strong, to not give in by going to see him, but if I did that, I'd have to confess that I know about him and what he's put her through.

I'd rather she tell me that herself.

Wait, what happened to five minutes ago in the car when we were going to take a step back because she's already had enough heartache?

That was then and this is now. Dee is in the same room with me, and it takes every ounce of willpower I can muster not to go to her, put my arms around her and tell her she has no reason to feel guilty about what her ex did. I force myself to stand still, even when her dark-eyed gaze connects with mine, and I feel like I've been hit with defibrillation paddles. And yes, I know what that feels like, and this is just like that—a shock to my entire system.

"Good to see you again, Wyatt," Maria says.

"You, too. Hey, Dee."

"Hi, Wyatt."

"Drinks," Austin says. "We need drinks."

"I'll do that while you tuck in the monkey," Maria says, kissing Everly.

The little girl's head is resting on her dad's shoulder, where I suspect she makes herself at home quite often. Everly appears to be a perfectly healthy three- or four-year-old, which must be a relief to her dad and everyone who loves her after the ordeal of her illness. I love how Maria met Austin after donating the bone marrow that saved Everly's life. What an amazing story that is.

After Austin takes Everly off to bed, Maria whispers something to Dee as she looks at me.

Dee shrugs in response to whatever her sister said. "Maybe. Maybe not."

The sisters share an intense look before Maria goes to make the drinks. We take them outside to a huge patio that has a fenced-off pool and hot tub surrounded by palm trees, flowering bushes, potted plants and subtle lighting. What a setup they've got right on the Intracoastal Waterway.

"This is beautiful," I tell Maria when she joins us, bringing chips, salsa and guacamole.

"I wish we could take credit, but it was like this when Austin bought it."

I'm happy to see the fence around the pool. I'll never forget the child who drowned in a backyard pool during my ER rotation, how hard we tried to save him and his parents' anguish when we were unsuccessful. I still think about that child and his parents.

"Where'd you go, Wyatt?" Jay asks, grinning at me as I realize all eyes are on me.

"I'm thinking about pool fences and how wise it is to have one with a child in the house."

"That was nonnegotiable for us," Maria says.

"I was also thinking about a child we were unable to save during my ER rotation. You never forget those cases."

"I had one of those, too," Jay says, frowning. "A two-year-old girl. Dreadful."

"You hear about it far too often around here," Maria says.

"In Phoenix, too." I notice Dee is looking at me, which makes me feel like a fifth-grade boy about to kiss the girl he likes during a game of spin the bottle. Yeah, seriously. I'm in major crush mode where she's concerned. She's wearing a black shirt with the shoulders cut out, tight jeans that hug her delicious curves and high-heeled wedge sandals that show off a coral-colored pedicure.

She's wearing her shiny, curly dark hair down around her shoulders, and her brown eyes are fringed with extravagant lashes. I remember thinking at the wedding that her eyes were stunning, but tonight, they convey sadness and stress. Probably because of what her ex did and the guilt that has to be eating her up, even if it's not her fault.

I wish so badly I could tell her that, but I abide by her wishes to keep our secrets from the others. If I say something, I'll give away that we know each other better than we've let on. We were paired up at the wedding, but that wasn't any big deal. Until it was.

We talk about Mexican takeout, and when Carmen and Jason go with Maria to get more drinks and use the bathroom, I take advantage of the moment alone with Dee. "It's so good to see you."

"You, too," she says with a shy smile.

She wasn't shy after the wedding. Not even a little bit. Is she embarrassed by that now? I really hope not.

"Are you okay? You're quiet."

"I've had a rough day."

"I'm sorry to hear that." I want to tell her I know what happened, but more than that, I want her to tell me about it herself. "Anything I can do?"

"No, but thank you for asking."

"You want to hang out later?"

"I, um, I'm not sure I can do that. I'm staying here."

I cock a brow at her. "Do you have a curfew?"

"No," she says, smiling.

"Come pick me up at Jason's. We'll go for a ride."

She glances toward the window, where we can see the others inside, gathered around Maria.

"Live dangerously." I send her a goofy smile that I hope she'll find charming or adorable or maybe both. "Pick me up."

"Text me when you get back to their place."

The words are no sooner out of her mouth than Maria returns with Austin and her phone, which she passes to Dee to pick what she wants from the restaurant. "Their enchiladas are to die for."

"Sold," I say when Dee has the phone. "Will you add chicken enchiladas for me?"

"Yep." She orders for both of us and then hands the phone back to her sister.

"What'd you get?" I ask her.

"Same thing. Their enchiladas are so good."

"Everything I've eaten in Miami is *so* good."

Her face turns bright red, and *oh shit*. I realize she thinks that means her, too. Well, it does. Of course it does, but I didn't actually mean *that* when I said it. I start to laugh, and I can't stop no matter how hard I try.

Before I know it, she's laughing, too, and everyone else is looking at the two of us like we're crazy. Maybe we are. All I know is I like being with her, and I want more of her.

CHAPTER 3

DEE

I cannot believe he said that! He's laughing so hard, he can't breathe, and he's taken me down with him. The sheer outrageousness of the comment broke the tension that has filled me since I heard about Marcus being in the hospital.

"Um, what'd we miss?" Carmen asks, her shrewd gaze darting from me to him and then back to me again.

"Do *not* repeat that," I say to Wyatt.

He wipes tears off his face as he sends me a dirty grin. How can one man be so incredibly gorgeous? He reminds me of Patrick Dempsey at the height of his Doctor McDreamy-ness, with wavy dark hair, blue eyes and a smile that lights up his face. And, apparently, a filthy mind. Although I sort of already knew that…

I can't believe I slept with this man, had dirty sex with this man—*three times*—and no one knows that but the two of us. It's not like me to keep something like that from Maria and Carmen, but for some reason, I just never got around to telling them. Now, he's back and asking me to go for a ride with him later tonight and see him tomorrow night, and there's no way I'm going to be able to keep whatever this is with him hidden from them for much longer.

We were raised by mothers and grandmothers who are experts at extracting information from unwilling parties. Any of us can sniff out a scoop with the tenacity of a bloodhound, and judging by the way the two of them are watching us as we enjoy our inside joke, they're on the scent. Maria has already asked me if he's the Wyatt who was texting me earlier.

It's not that I'd care if they know, but for some reason, I want to keep him to myself for a bit longer. I try not to pay too much attention to him as we eat the delicious enchiladas that Austin insisted on treating us to and sip margaritas. I only have one, because apparently, I have to drive later.

Wyatt sticks to seltzer like he did at the wedding. I'm not sure why he doesn't drink. We never talked about it, but now I wonder.

My phone chimes with a text from Bianca. *He's conscious. Not that you care.*

I'm relieved to hear Marcus is awake and hopefully going to be all right. I respond to her. *I do care that he's all right, but I'm not coming there, and I'm not going to see him. If you can make him understand that, you'd be helping him move on.*

"Everything all right?" Maria asks.

"Marcus is awake."

"That's good news."

"I told Bianca to let him know I'm not coming there, and she needs to tell him that."

"Good for you. That's the right thing to do."

I can feel Wyatt watching me, probably wondering what we're talking about. "A friend of mine is in the hospital."

"Sorry to hear that."

"We, um, we might've talked about it on the way over here," Carmen says. "Wyatt knows what's going on."

"Ah, okay, then you know he's my ex, and he might've staged a suicide attempt to get my attention."

"I do know that, and I'm sorry he put you in that position."

"Did they also tell you how he married someone else when he was supposedly still with me?"

"They might've mentioned that."

So he knows my entire deal. That's just great.

"He's a fool."

The way he says that, not to mention how he looks at me as he says it, means so much to me. "Thank you."

"He's the *biggest* fool," Maria says. "He had *Dee*. What the hell was he thinking *marrying* that skank?"

"I'm sorry that happened to you, Dee," Austin says. "It was his loss."

I already love my future brother-in-law, but now I love him even more. "Thanks. It's in the past now. I'm sorry he's in a bad place, but I keep telling myself it's not my fault. He made his choices."

"He made the *wrong* choice," Carmen says. "He was lucky you ever gave him the time of day."

"You guys are good for my dented ego."

"Your ego shouldn't be dented," Wyatt says.

He may as well have just told them we've already slept together.

Maria and Carmen are intrigued by the vibes he's putting out.

"How long are you here, Wyatt?" Maria asks.

"Just until Monday night this time. I'm interviewing at Miami-Dade on Monday."

"What kind of doctor are you?" Austin asks.

"I'm a cardiothoracic surgeon."

"I don't even know what that means," Austin says, laughing.

"Don't worry," Wyatt says. "I don't have much of a fastball."

I love the way he downplays his skills by complimenting

Austin. That earns him big points with me, not that he needs them. He's already batting a thousand. Haha, good baseball analogy.

"I specialize in heart and lung surgery as well as other thoracic, or chest, organs," Wyatt says.

"And my head just exploded," Austin says.

"Jason can fix that," Wyatt says, grinning.

He's adorable, funny, smart as hell and sexier than any man has a right to be. The more time I spend with him, the more I like him. And I already liked him a lot before tonight.

"So you've been thinking about relocating to Miami?" Maria asks.

"I hadn't been, but after I was here for the wedding, I started thinking about a change of scenery." He glances at me, but I pretend not to notice.

Maria and Carmen most definitely notice.

"Then Jay mentioned the opening at Miami-Dade, and here I am. Miami is looking better to me all the time."

"I love it here." Jason smiles at Carmen. "It's the best place I've ever lived."

"I love it, too," Austin says with a goofy grin for Maria. "My favorite place in the whole world."

"The scenery is rather spectacular," Wyatt says.

And we're fooling no one. My face is so hot that I wonder how my skin doesn't blister.

"Dee, how would you feel about showing me around while I'm here?" Wyatt says. "I've only ever been to Miami for the wedding. I didn't get to see much on that trip."

"That's a fantastic idea," Carmen says. "Dee knows Miami inside and out. She'd be the best tour guide you could ever have."

"And it would give Dee something to do besides stew over what's happening with what's-his-name," Maria adds. "I love this idea."

"We can take you to see the ballpark sometime if you're interested," Austin says.

"I'd love that," Wyatt says. "Thanks."

"Sure. Let me know when you'd like to do it."

"I'll leave that up to my tour guide," he says, giving me a side-eye, probably to determine whether I'm angry with him for recruiting me to show him around.

I'm not angry. I'm thrilled that he asked and gave me cover with my sister and cousin. I can't stand having everyone up in my business, which is the number one reason why I stayed in New York for so long. Long before I left for college, I'd gotten tired of my family knowing my every move before I even made it.

I can't wait to show him my city. Maria is right that I know this town, and I love every wonderful, diverse corner of it. That I get to spend extra time with him is a bonus. I like him a lot, which is an interesting development, seeing as I thought I'd never see him again after the one night we spent together.

But now he's back, and he came because of me, which is a rather lovely lift for a girl with a dented ego. I need to be careful, though. He's only here for the weekend, and who knows if he'll get the job or even actually move if he does? It would be too easy to get caught up in a sweet guy who looks like a dream and is a god in bed, too.

"You want to go now? We could check out some of the clubs in Little Havana you told me about last time I was here."

I snap out of my memories of what it was like to be in bed with him to realize he's just asked me out right in front of the others and is waiting for me to reply.

"Sure, that sounds fun." It sounds like more fun than I've had since the night I spent with him five months ago. I glance at Maria, who's watching me intently, looking for the rest of the story. If only she knew… "As long as I'm going back to Little Havana, I may as well stay at my place tonight."

"Whatever works," Maria says, her eyes glittering the way they do when something excites her.

If I didn't know better, I'd think my sister is giving me a firm push into bed with the dreamy doctor.

"Will Everly be upset if I'm not here when she wakes up?" I've developed a fun aunt-niece bond with Maria's future step-daughter, and I'd hate to disappoint her.

"I didn't tell her you were sleeping over. I figured we could surprise her in the morning."

"We'll do it again soon." To Wyatt, I say, "I'll just grab my stuff."

"Take your time. I'm not going anywhere."

Ignoring the inquiring gazes of the others, I go into the guest room to gather my belongings. I'm not at all surprised when Maria and Carmen follow me.

"Holy shit, *he's totally into you*," Carmen says. "He hasn't taken his eyes off you all night."

"Don't make it into something. It's just fun." I toss the few things I unpacked into the turquoise Vera Bradley bag Carmen gave me last Christmas and zip it closed.

"I told Jason that something was up with you two at the wedding," Carmen says.

"There wasn't. That was also fun. We had a good time together."

Maria takes me by the face. "Tell me the truth. Is that *all* it was? Fun?"

"Yes," I tell her as I roll my eyes. It was fun. That's the truth.

"Jason was surprised that Wyatt's interested in the Miami-Dade job," Carmen says. "Now it's starting to make sense to me."

"You're jumping to conclusions," I tell her.

Carmen lets out a happy squeal. *"How exciting would it be if you met someone because of my wedding?"*

"You guys, please. Don't do this. I'm still dealing with every-thing with Marcus."

"No, you're *not*," Maria says emphatically. "You have nothing to do with what's going on with him."

"He tried to *kill himself* because I wouldn't take his call."

"That's not why he did it," Maria says. "He did it because he's messed up his life all on his own, and now that it's blown up in his face, he's sorry for what he did to you. Where's the big apology been for all this time? He never once said a word to you until the skank left him. He doesn't get to come back after the fact with regrets. What happened today had *nothing* to do with you."

"She's right, Dee," Carmen says. "You can't take that on. He fucked up, and he knows it. This is about him, not you."

"Still… It was shocking, and I'm reeling over it. I'm not in a place for this to be anything more than a fun weekend with a new friend. Please don't go crazy over it or tell the family."

"We won't say anything," Carmen says, "but you should bring him to Sunday brunch. He loved the food at the restaurant."

"I'll see what happens."

Carmen hugs me. "Have fun. Go crazy. Let your hair down."

"My hair is already down," I say, laughing.

"You know what she means," Maria says. "You were in a long relationship that ended badly. If anyone needs a fun rebound, it's you. Go for it."

"I'll take that under advisement. Can I go now, ladies?"

"Do you need condoms?" Maria asks with dead seriousness.

"I'm going now. Bye!"

I walk out of the bedroom toward the foyer, where the three men are engaged in animated conversation while they wait for us. Jason and Austin have become great friends. They golf and fish together and hang out every chance they get. Naturally, Carmen and Maria are thrilled about that, and I'll confess to having felt, more than once, like a fifth wheel around the four of them. They get together often and always include me, which I appreciate. But this is the first time I haven't felt like an extra among their happy foursome.

Wyatt evens things out, and when he directs a warm smile my way, the flutters in my belly are a sign that the excitement of the others is having an impact on me.

Slow your roll, girl.

"Ready?" Wyatt asks.

"Yep." I hug Austin and Maria. "Thank you for dinner."

Wyatt shakes hands with Austin and hugs Maria. "Thank you. The enchiladas were awesome."

"Did you give him a curfew, Jason?" Carmen asks, delighted with her joke.

"No later than midnight, young man," Jason says sternly.

"Don't wait up, Dad," Wyatt says as he follows me out of the house. "Phew, tough crowd. Are they watching us?"

"Probably, but I'm not looking."

"I see what you mean about not being able to do much without your whole family involved."

"There was that one night…"

"Ah, yes, that one night." His hand finds my lower back in an innocent gesture that makes my entire system go haywire. "Want me to drive?"

"You're the guest. You don't have to."

"I don't mind."

I hand him the keys and stash my overnight bag in the back seat.

He gets in and adjusts the driver's seat to fit his much longer legs.

I direct him on how to get out of the neighborhood and onto the highway that will take us back to Little Havana. "What do you feel like doing?"

"Whatever you want."

"We could take a walk, get a drink or hit a club."

"All that sounds good to me." When we're on the highway, he

looks over at me. "Was it okay for me to ask you out in front of everyone?"

"It was fine."

"Did your sister and cousin pump you for info when they went after you?"

"What do you think?"

Smiling, he says, "What'd you tell them?"

"Not to overreact. Nothing to see here."

"Nothing at all?" he asks, crooking an eyebrow.

"Nothing they need to know about."

He moves his hand from the shifter to my thigh. "Do you know how hard it was to pretend like I barely know you in front of your family?"

The heat of his hand may as well be a branding iron as it sets off a systemwide reaction that has my most essential parts tingling in awareness of him. "How hard was it?"

"*So hard.*"

Suddenly, we're no longer talking about pretending in front of my family.

"I've thought about you and that night so much since the wedding," he says. "Have you?"

"Here and there."

"Are you lying?"

"Maybe a little." I don't want to talk about Marcus, especially not with Wyatt, but I want him to know how messed up I've been lately. "It's been a rough couple of months."

"Because of your ex?"

"That and my mom has been receiving treatment for breast cancer. She had a double mastectomy in January, and now she's having chemo."

"I wondered why you ended up staying in Miami after the wedding."

"How did you know I did that?"

"Instagram."

"Ah… so you've been stalking me?"

"Following. That's different from stalking."

I like knowing he thought of me so much after the night we spent together that he cared enough to find me online and wondered why I didn't go back to New York after the wedding.

"So are you staying here, then?"

"That's the plan. At some point, I have to go to New York and get the rest of my stuff. My cousin, who I lived with there, is going to sublet my room. I can't go back there as long as my mom is sick."

"How's your mom doing?"

"The chemo is kicking her ass. It's been rough. It's hard to watch her suffer."

"I'm sorry she's going through that and that you are, too."

"She's a trouper."

"She's lucky to have her family supporting her. Are you bummed about New York?"

"Not really. I was planning to move home this year anyway. I just moved up the timeline a little. What about you? What's up with applying for a job here?"

"I liked Miami when I was here for the wedding. I've lived in Phoenix most of my life, and I'm ready for a change. When Jay mentioned the opening at Miami-Dade, I figured why not?"

"Can I ask you something, and will you tell me the truth?"

"Sure."

"You're not applying because of me, are you?"

Smiling, he says, "Not specifically because of you, but knowing you live here definitely makes me more interested in the job than I would be if you weren't part of the equation."

"I'm not really in a good place for, well, anything."

"Neither am I." He sounds sad for some reason.

"Oh, well. Okay, then. I know why I'm in a bad place, but why are you?"

"Things are just weird right now with the possibility of

changing jobs, moving cross-country. I'm not sure what's going to happen."

"You'll get the job."

"How do you know that?"

"They'd be crazy not to hire you. Aren't you board certified in your specialty?"

"I am, but how do you know that?"

"You're not the only one who did some stalking."

CHAPTER 4

WYATT

*H*earing her say that she checked me out online makes me happier than I've been in... well... ever. Not only did she think of me after our night together, but she went so far as to search for me. I just hope she didn't stumble upon my whole story. "What else did you find out about me?"

"I only read your bio on the hospital's website and found out you've published a lot of articles about cardiothoracic surgery and have become a nationally recognized expert and speaker in the area of supporting patients through life-threatening illnesses."

I've put my personal experiences to work in my career, constantly emphasizing the need to treat the whole patient, not just the part of them that's malfunctioning. "That's a big interest of mine." I'm incredibly thankful she didn't dig any deeper than the hospital website.

"It's something that's badly needed. My mother's oncologist is considered one of the best there is, but he's got no personality whatsoever. He doesn't seem to appreciate how terrifying this is for her and us. He's very matter-of-fact about life-threatening things."

I wince hearing that. I've known far too many doctors who are like the one she describes. "It's a challenge to train doctors to be experts in medicine *and* how to manage the wide variety of needs that each patient has. Not to mention the family's needs."

"He always makes me feel like a jerk for bothering him when I have to call about something. Usually, I let Maria deal with him because she's a nurse—and it's better if I don't talk to him. I'm afraid I'm going to tell him what I really think of him."

That makes me laugh as I imagine her ripping the oncologist a new one. "Maybe you ought to tell him what you think. He might need to hear it."

"I can't. I'd be too afraid of my mother not getting the care she needs and deserves. But I really want to."

"You can tell me anything you need to say to him. Standing offer. Call me when you want to scream at him. I'll always listen."

"You're busy enough with your patients. You don't need some random woman in Miami screaming at you about someone who isn't even your patient."

"If that random woman is you, I need that."

"All this flattery is going straight to my head."

"I couldn't wait to see you again." *Way to play it cool, man. Remember how it wouldn't be fair to let her or any woman get too involved with you? Remember that talk we had before we saw Dee? Yeah, I remember, so fuck off.* I held firm to my resolve until she walked into the room at her sister's house, looking sexier than any woman has a right to look, and just that quickly, I forgot why this isn't a good idea.

Maybe we could have this bonus weekend before I go back to reality. Who could be hurt by one more weekend?

If the ache in my chest at the thought of not seeing her again is any indication, I could be hurt. And so could she. This weekend has to be it. It just has to be. To encourage anything more would be grossly unfair to her—and myself. "Can I ask you something?"

"Sure."

"Do you feel like going out, or would you be up for going somewhere that we can be alone?"

She's quiet long enough that I begin to worry I've misjudged her.

"Let's go to my place."

MARCUS

I screwed up so bad. My parents and sister have been hysterical since I woke up. I feel awful that I upset them. I can't believe Bianca told Dee they suspect I tried to kill myself. I didn't. Not consciously, anyway. I took a few Xanax to calm my nerves, forgetting about the vodka I'd had earlier, and apparently, the combination nearly killed me.

That wasn't intentional. I don't want to die before I can make things right with Dee. She's the only thing that matters to me.

I've been hiding my alcoholism from her for years now. That got easier when I moved home from New York. But my drinking is the reason I ended up married to someone else. It's the reason I broke the heart of the only woman I've ever loved. I barely remember that night in Vegas or how I ended up married to one of the women who hung out with me and my boys.

I came to the next day with a blonde in my bed, a ring on my finger and the worst feeling I've ever had in my life when I began to fill in the blanks from the night before.

Dee.

She was my first thought then and is my first thought now. She's been my first thought every day since I brought this disaster down on both of us. I need to talk to her, to tell her I don't blame her for any of this. That's my fear, that Bianca will have laid a guilt trip on Dee that she doesn't deserve. She hasn't done anything wrong. No, this is all my fault.

I should've listened to the family and friends who pleaded with me to get help before something awful happened. They were worried about me killing someone by drinking and driving, which I've never done. So that didn't happen, but something else did—I broke the heart of my one true love, and now I'm desperate to fix that.

Bianca left my phone charging on the rolling table next to my hospital bed. I reach for it, find Dee's name in my contacts and compose a text.

I didn't try to kill myself. No matter what Bianca said, that's not true, and if she tried to make you feel guilty in any way, I'm sorry. None of this is your fault. I fucked up, and there's stuff I need to tell you, things you have a right to know. Could we please talk?

The text shows up as delivered but not read.

I'm staring at my phone, trying to will her to read the message, when yet another doctor comes into the room. What now? I've already been poked and prodded every which way. What's left?

"Hi, Marcus," the dark-haired woman says. "I'm Dr. Stern, the psychiatrist on call. You can call me Justine if you'd like."

The word *psychiatrist* makes me groan. "I didn't try to kill myself. That's not what happened."

She takes a seat next to my bed. "What did happen?"

"I mixed Xanax and booze by accident. I didn't think about what the combination might do. It was a mistake, not a suicide attempt."

"Your family was pretty upset, from what I'm told."

"My sister pushed the panic button when she came to check on me and couldn't get me to wake up. I feel bad I upset them."

"Why would they assume you tried to take your own life?"

45

"Things have been messy lately. Really, really messy."

"How so?"

"Do we need to go through all this?"

"If you want to be discharged. I need to be confident you're not going to harm yourself if I sign off on your release. So how about you tell me what's been so messy lately?"

"My wife left me."

"I'm sorry to hear that."

"No, it was a good thing."

"Is that right?"

I nod. "We were never meant to be married. That was a mistake."

"You married someone by mistake? How'd that happen?"

"I was drunk. We were in Vegas. She was there. One thing led to another, and I woke up married to the wrong woman."

"Who was the right woman?"

"My girlfriend, Dee. She's the one I love, the one I've always loved. We were together for years before we broke up, but we were putting it back together when this happened. She was in New York, and I was in Miami, but things between us were good. Until I fucked up, anyway, and since then, she doesn't take my calls or respond to my texts."

"How did she react when you told her you married someone else?"

"I'm not really sure."

"She didn't hear it from you?"

"No, and I regret that. She absolutely should've heard it from me, but what was I supposed to say to her? Oh, by the way, I got lit last night and woke up married to my friend's sister Ana, which *wasn't* supposed to happen."

"Okay, so you got married by accident. What happened then?"

"We came home to Miami. Ana moved in and wanted it to be a real marriage."

"And in the meantime, you're thinking about Dee, who's not taking your calls or answering your texts. Is that right?"

"I thought of her every minute of every day that I was married to Ana."

"Did you sleep with Ana?"

That question makes me uncomfortable. "I guess."

"You guess? Did you or didn't you?"

"We were married."

"So while you were pining for Dee after having broken her heart by marrying someone else, you were having sex with your new wife. Do I have that right?"

I squirm under the intensity of her gaze. She wants to stab me on behalf of women everywhere, and I don't blame her. "You have it right. I'm not proud of how I behaved, but you should know I've never done anything like this before."

"Marry someone who isn't your long-term girlfriend?"

"Yes," I say through gritted teeth. The doctor is starting to annoy me. "I've come to realize I have a problem with drinking."

"What're you doing about that?"

"I haven't done anything yet."

"What're you waiting for?"

"I don't know."

"Do you think a near-fatal incident that resulted from mixing Xanax and alcohol might be the impetus you need?"

"Maybe."

"This is no joke, Marcus. If your sister hadn't become concerned when she couldn't reach you, you might've died."

"Yes, I know."

"And that wasn't your intention? To end this suffering you've been going through by overdosing?"

"It wasn't my intention. I don't want to die. I just want to fix things with Dee."

"I think you need to accept that isn't going to happen."

"How can you know that? She and I haven't even talked about what happened. She won't talk to me."

Dr. Stern leans forward, placing her hand on my arm. "Marcus, you married someone else without breaking up with her first. She's not going to talk to you. It's over for her."

"How can it be over for her when we've never even talked about it?"

"It was over for her the minute you married someone else and let her hear that from other people."

"I didn't mean for any of that to happen."

"I understand that, but it *did* happen, and now you have to find a way to live with the consequences."

"I'll never be able to live with it if I don't get the chance to talk to her."

"Do you understand that by continuing to reach out to her, you're probably hurting her all over again?"

That didn't occur to me, not in those terms, anyway.

"How long ago did you marry Ana?"

"A year."

"Did Dee think she was probably going to be the one you married?"

"We'd talked about that happening after she moved back to Miami."

"So Dee has had a year to pick up the pieces, to put her life back together and move on, and every time she hears from you, it has to be a reminder of what she's overcome. You hurt her, Marcus. You maybe even devastated her, considering she expected to be your wife. By continuing to reach out to her, you're compounding that pain for her."

"I don't want to hurt her. I only want the chance to explain and apologize."

"Then write her a letter, but stop calling and texting her. That's simply not fair to her."

I don't want to hear what she's saying, even if I can see the truth in it.

"This latest incident is the second time alcohol has caused a disaster in your life. The first one resulted in broken hearts. This one nearly caused your death. You say that wasn't intentional—"

"It wasn't. I swear to God. I'm not suicidal. Even as bad as this last year has gotten, I've never once thought about ending my own life. What good would that do? It wouldn't fix anything with Dee, which is my only goal."

"I think it's time for a new goal, one that focuses on you regaining your health. Would you consider in-patient rehab for thirty days or possibly longer if needed?"

"I, uh, I have to work."

"What do you do for a living?"

"I'm a branch manager at a bank."

"I can help you complete the paperwork to take a medical leave of absence."

"I'm not sure that's a good idea. The chaos in my personal life has spilled over to my work, and I'm sort of on thin ice there." Those were the words my regional manager used the last time we met after I was late on reporting some vital weekly information for the third week in a row. It's hard to concentrate on anything when all you can think about is making things right with the one you love.

"You're protected by federal law in this situation. If you have documentation of a medical condition, then your employer is required to protect your job."

I didn't know that. "Would I have to tell them what my condition is?"

"Let me ask you this... You said you're on thin ice there. Do you think you've been hiding your reliance on alcohol from your colleagues? Would they be surprised to hear you were in rehab?"

"Probably not. They might even be relieved."

"So what does it matter? If you had cancer, they'd hold fundraisers for you. Addiction is an illness, just like cancer or diabetes."

I recoil from that term. "I'm not an *addict*."

"No? Did you or did you not get married to a woman you didn't love, breaking the heart of the woman you *do* love because of alcohol? Did you or did you not mix Xanax and alcohol and nearly end your life prematurely?"

"I did those things, but I'm not an addict."

"The behaviors you've described are the hallmarks of someone in the grips of alcoholism, which is a form of addiction. Did your doctor talk to you about your liver numbers?"

"He said they were high."

"They're sky-high. Are you familiar with what liver failure is like?"

"Not really," I say, forcing myself to sit still when I want out of there.

"I wouldn't wish that death on my worst enemy."

Her stark words strike a note of fear in me. It's the first thing I've felt other than agony over Dee in more than a year.

"You're twenty-eight years old, Marcus, with the liver of a seventy-five-year-old alcoholic. You're headed for an agonizing early death if you don't make some changes soon." She puts her business card on my table. "Please consider getting some help. I can work with the hospital's team to get you into treatment and would be happy to continue to work with you while you're in rehab and after."

I eye the card with trepidation. Nothing says I have to do anything with it.

"In the meantime, I'll pray for you to find some peace. If I can help, don't hesitate to reach out. My cell number is on my card. Call me anytime."

"Thank you. Are you going to allow me to be released?"

"Not until after you complete withdrawal."

"What's that?"

"You're about to find out what happens when the body suffers from alcohol withdrawal. It's not pleasant, and you're going to be quite ill for a few days. The doctors will want to keep a close eye on your vital signs during that time."

I can't believe it's possible to feel worse than I already do.

"Thanks for coming by."

"No problem. Be well."

Long after she's gone, I think about the things she said, mostly about how I've been hurting Dee every time I reach out to her. I didn't think of what it would be like for her to hear from me after what I did to her. I've been so focused on trying to make things right with her. That's been the only thought in my head since things with Ana blew up and she left. I was glad she was gone so I could turn my attention to trying to get back the life I lost on that fateful night in Vegas.

Dr. Stern has made me realize that in the year since then, Dee has moved on without me. Maybe she's even seeing someone else. I'm filled with panic at the thought of her with another guy, even if I understand I have only myself to blame for this disaster.

I eye the card Dr. Stern left for a long time, thinking about what she said about my liver and the agony of liver failure. I don't want to put another thirty days between me and making good with Dee. I feel an urgent need to take care of that before I do anything else, but I don't want to hurt her any more than I already have.

The idea of writing her a letter is a good one. I'll give that some thought.

I reach for the business card the shrink left on the table and study the list of initials after her name. She's probably seen hundreds of patients just like me, which means she knows what she's talking about.

Before I can talk myself out of doing what I know I have to do, I dial her number on my cell.

"Dr. Stern."

"This is Marcus."

"Hi, Marcus. What can I do for you?"

"What you said about my job, how they're required to hold it for me. That's legit?"

"It is."

My eyes flood with tears when I think about Dee, what I've done to her, to us. If I hadn't gotten hammered in Vegas, there's no way I would've ended up married to a woman I have no feelings for beyond friendship. I love Dee. I'll always love Dee.

"Marcus?"

I wipe away tears. "I think I need help."

CHAPTER 5

CARMEN

*A*fter Dee and Wyatt leave, we end up back outside on the patio discussing the possibility of them as a couple. "Tell us everything about him," I say to my husband. "Leave nothing out."

"He's a good dude," Jason says.

If I didn't know him so well, he might've gotten away with that, but I can tell just by looking at him that something is troubling him.

"You don't like them together?"

"I never said that."

His sharp reply takes me by surprise. He never talks to me like that, which only furthers my suspicion that he's not sold on them dating.

"Do you think something happened between them at the wedding?" Maria asks.

"They danced a lot that night," I recall. "The photographer got a bunch of pictures of them together."

"I mean afterward. Dee never did say what she did that

night. The rest of us went out, but she said she had other plans. Do you think those plans were with him?"

"Holy crap! That's why he's here! Because of *her.*"

"He's here for an interview at Miami-Dade," Jason reminds me.

"Did he express any interest in moving here before the wedding?"

"No, but—"

"It *is* because of her!"

"This is awesome!" Maria claps her hands in glee. "He's *just* what she needs after the nightmare with Marcus. A super nice guy, a talented doctor, hotter than the sun…"

"Hello, honey," Austin says dryly. "I'm in the room."

Maria dissolves into giggles. "Sorry, but he *is* smoking hot."

"He is," I agree. "He's got that whole McDreamy thing going on with the hair and the eyes."

"We're going to head out," Jason says, standing.

I give him a perplexed look but keep my curiosity—and concern—to myself while we say good night and thank you to Maria and Austin. That lasts until we're in the car when I turn toward him. "What was that about?"

"What was what about?"

"You abruptly wanting to leave? You aren't mad about me agreeing with Maria that Wyatt's hot, are you?"

"Of course not. It was just time to go."

"So you're just not going to tell me why you're unhappy at the thought of Wyatt and Dee together—and don't try to tell me you're not unhappy about it. I know you too well."

"It's not that."

"Then what?"

"There are things… about him… Things she should know."

"And you don't think he'll tell her those things?"

"He won't."

"Why not?"

"Because it's something he never talks about with anyone in his personal life."

"What is it?"

He shakes his head. "Please don't ask me. It's not my story to tell."

"You know what she means to us, Jason, and what she went through with Marcus. If you know something that she should know, you have to tell me."

"No, I don't. But I *will* talk to Wyatt. The first chance I get. That, I can promise you."

My stomach starts to hurt at the thought of our friend hurting my sweet cousin, who's already had enough hurt. "Is she…" I swallow hard as the words get stuck in my throat. "Is she unsafe with him?"

"Not physically, no. I never would've let Dee leave with him if that was a concern, Carmen. Tell me you know that."

"I do, but you're being so mysterious. Surely whatever it is, you can tell me. I won't tell anyone."

"You'd tell her this. You'd feel obligated to tell her."

"You're scaring me, Jason. You know how much I love her and what Marcus put her through. I can't let a friend of ours hurt her."

"I know, and all I can tell you is I'll do what I can to make sure that doesn't happen. I'd tell you in a second if I could. But I can't. Wyatt has to tell her, and then she can tell you if she chooses to."

"And you'll make sure he tells her soon?"

"I will." He takes hold of my hand but keeps his eyes on the road. He's learned to be extra careful driving in South Florida. "It's possible that whatever's going on with them is only a passing flirtation. If that's the case, he won't tell her because it won't matter."

My brain is on fire as I try to read between the lines of what he's not saying. "How do you know about it?"

"He told me when we were first in med school. He told only me and emphasized how important it is to him that no one else knows about it."

"Why did he tell you?"

"That's something I can't get into unless he decides to talk to Dee about it. I'm sorry to be secretive, Carmen. I'd never keep anything from you unless I had to. You know that, right?"

"I think so."

"It's true. I'm not intentionally trying to be evasive. I'll talk to Wyatt the first chance I get. Try not to worry. I don't want to see Dee hurt any more than you do, especially by my friend."

"He seems like such a nice guy."

"He is."

"So, we're not talking about some sort of massive personality defect, then?"

"No." His jaw is tight, as is his grip on the steering wheel. This situation is stressing him out, and I hate that for all of us.

When we get home, he goes in to shower, and I reach for my phone to text Maria. *Something's up with Wyatt. Jason won't tell me, says it's Wyatt's thing to share or not share with Dee, but whatever it is, it's upsetting Jason. He said he's going to talk to Wyatt about it as soon as he can.*

She writes back a few minutes later. *Oh jeez. WTH?*

Whatever it is, he's stressed. He said it's not something Wyatt would tell her on his own.

Why all the secrecy?

No idea, but I don't like this, especially with everything with Marcus.

Agreed. Let's keep an eye on this and intervene if need be.

I don't want to have to do that.

I don't, either. The last time was bad enough.

When Jason gets in bed a few minutes later, I'm already there, staring up at the ceiling, thinking about my sweet cousin and wishing with all my heart that she could find her forever love. It's all she's ever really wanted—to fall in love and have a family. While Maria and I chased careers, Dee dreamed about being a mom. At one time, she told us how she and Marcus were going to have six kids. That dream, and all the others she had wrapped up in him, ended when he married someone else. Even when they were apart, we always knew she had her heart set on him.

"Are you mad?" Jason asks.

"No."

"Disappointed?"

"No."

He turns on his side to face me. "What're you thinking?"

"I'm thinking about Dee, who thought she was going to marry Marcus and have six kids with him before he suddenly married someone else and broke her heart."

"I hate how that happened to her."

I look over at him. "You can't let Wyatt hurt her. Please tell me you'll throw yourself in front of that."

"I promise I will. I won't let him hurt her."

I tell myself I need to be satisfied with his assurances, but my stomach hurts at the possibility of more heartache for Dee.

DEE

I lead the way up the stairs to my apartment over the garage. Thankfully, my aunt and uncle don't live here, or I never would. Maria felt the same way when she lived in the apartment before me. Our family is up in our business enough without living right next door to "parents." In our family, they're *all* parents, whether they gave birth to us or not.

"What a cute place," Wyatt says when we're inside the big room that makes up my kitchen, living room and dining area.

"It's not much, but it's home. For now, anyway." The best part is that the rent and my other expenses are manageable with what I make working five nights a week at the restaurant. I didn't think I'd still be waitressing at my age, but nothing has gone according to my plan.

I can't think about that or allow bitterness to invade this evening with a guy I like and who seems to like me just as much.

Wyatt follows me into the kitchen.

"You want a drink?"

He shakes his head and takes another step toward me until he's right in front of me. "This is what I want," he says, giving me a soft, sweet, undemanding kiss. "That's what I would've done if we'd been alone when I saw you again." His hands are on my hips as mine end up on his chest. "I would've said, hi there. I've missed you since the night we met."

"It's kind of odd to miss someone you hardly know."

"I know you." Raising a hand to move my hair out of his way, he kisses the spot on my neck that makes me sigh. "See? I know what happens when I kiss you right there. I know that if I do *this*," he says, cupping my breasts and running his thumbs over my nipples, "that your knees will buckle."

Sure enough, my knees give in, making him smile.

"I know you, Dee. I know you're gorgeous and fun and funny and so devoted to your family that you gave up your life in New York to be here for your mom while she's ill. I know how much you love your sister and your cousin, how close the three of you are and how much you love your Nona and Carmen's grandmother. Abuela, right?"

"Yes." I'm breathless from the kisses he leaves on my neck and the sweep of his thumbs over my nipples. I'm impressed that he remembers me telling him how vital Nona and Abuela have been to all of us cousins, how Carmen's Abuela isn't technically my grandmother, but don't say that to her—or me.

"I know you have two brothers, Nico and Milo, and that your extended family gets together every Sunday for brunch at the restaurant. I know your cousins are like extra siblings to you. And after tonight, I know your tender heart has been badly hurt by the man you loved, which is why you shouldn't be allowing me to kiss you and touch you."

That statement hits me like a blast of ice water to the face. I pull back so I can see him and the regret in his expression. "I don't understand."

"There are things... about me... Things you don't know, and you should, before we do this again..." He emphasizes his point by pressing his erection against my core, setting off fireworks throughout my oversensitized body.

All at once, I don't want to know why this is a bad idea or why he isn't good for me or anything that'll ruin this dream state I've slipped into after only a few minutes in his arms. Just like the first time we were together this way, his touch does something to me that's never happened before, and all I want is more of that incredible feeling.

"It doesn't matter," I tell him. "Whatever it is, unless you're telling me you're married or have an STD or something that could harm me, I don't need to know."

He brightens when I tell him that. "There is one thing you absolutely must know, and after I tell you that one thing, I promise I'll shut up so we can enjoy this."

"What's that?" I tip my head to give him better access to my neck. I had no idea how much I loved having my neck kissed until Wyatt did it after the wedding.

"This, you and me... It can't ever be anything more. Even if I get the job here, I can't commit to anything other than casual."

I want to ask him why that is, but I presume it's something I don't want to know. So I don't ask.

"I need you to tell me you understand, Dee. We can't have feelings for each other."

It's too late to warn me about feelings. I realized tonight, at Austin and Maria's, when my heart rate nearly went through the roof at the mere sight of him, that I already have feelings for him. But he doesn't need to know that. "I understand."

"You're sure? I can leave now and grab an Uber back to Jay's place. No hard feelings. Well," he says, smiling as he rubs his cock against me, "a *few* hard feelings."

I laugh, which breaks the tension that's been building over the last few minutes. "I don't want you to go, and I understand this can't be anything more than casual fun."

"And you know that no matter what happens between us, that's not going to change, right?"

The sadness and resignation I see in his eyes make me hurt for him. What could cause such a kind, handsome, sexy, successful man to draw such a firm line in the sand? Does he mean he won't get involved with anyone or me specifically? I tell myself that doesn't matter, either, but it does.

"I get it, but I have a question."

"Okay…"

"Do you mean it can never be more with me or with anyone?"

"Anyone. It's certainly not about you. If things were different, you'd be what I'd want for myself."

"What things would need to be different?"

"Stuff I don't talk about. It's just one of those 'it is what it is' kind of things, you know?"

I don't know, but what does it matter? I'm in no place to start something new with anyone. My mom is sick. Most of what I own is still in New York. I'm working at the family restaurant like I did when I was a teenager, and my ex may or may not have tried to kill himself because I refused to talk to him. The last thing I need is romantic entanglements or any more drama than I've already got.

He pulls back to look down at me. "I'd understand if any of this is a deal-breaker, Dee. You're such a great person. I don't want to lead you on."

"You've been very honest, and I appreciate that more than you know." Especially after what Marcus did.

"Do you want me to go?"

I shake my head. What I want, more than anything, is more of the way he made me feel the night of the wedding, as if I'm special and sexy and perfect. After a year of feeling like shit, that was a priceless gift.

"I want you to stay." I lead him into my bedroom and turn to face him so I can unbutton his shirt to reveal the amazing tattoo that spans his entire chest that I admired the first time we were together. It's a sphinx with the body of a lion and the wings of an eagle. The artwork is detailed and colorful and makes me wish I had all the time in the world to study it. Like the last time I saw it, I want to ask why he chose that particular image, what it means and how badly it hurt to have it done.

But like the last time, he kisses me, and I forget everything else.

Wyatt lifts my top, and I break the kiss long enough to let him take it over my head. His eyes go hot when he sees my breasts testing the confines of the sexy bra I wore in case we ended up just like this. "Damn," he whispers. "You're so fucking hot. I've thought about you so much after our night together."

See why I like him so much? Wyatt isn't going to be my future, but I'm thrilled he's my right now, and I plan to enjoy every second of this encore performance.

He continues to undress me, and since he seems to enjoy it, I let him have his fun. With every new part of me he uncovers, he's more appreciative. I remember that from our first time together, the way his attention did wonders for my wounded pride. When your boyfriend up and marries a blonde bomb-shell, the wounds run deep. Wyatt's commentary and obvious pleasure in how I look made me feel better about myself than I had since disaster struck.

Wyatt guides me to the bed and arranges me the way he

wants me before he kneels before me and dives right in, giving me lips and tongue and fingers in one coordinated effort that has me wailing in about two seconds flat. I've never even heard some of the sounds that come out of me before he had his wicked way with me.

I heard him when he said this couldn't be anything more than what it already is, but as he gives me the fastest orgasm of my life, I'm full of regret for what might've been. He's fun, funny, crazy intelligent, sexy as hell, and he's shown me desire unlike anything I've ever experienced, but for whatever reason, he doesn't want to be tied down. Why should he, when he looks like he does and is a freaking heart surgeon, for crying out loud?

He can have all the women. What would he want with only one?

"Hey." His lips are on my inner thigh as his fingers continue to slide in and out of me. "Where'd you go?"

"Nowhere. I'm here."

"You checked out on me."

And he *sees* me. Doesn't that just figure? I finally find the unicorn, and he doesn't want to be pinned down.

He kisses his way up the front of me, teasing my nipples with his tongue as he kisses a path to my lips. "What's wrong?"

"Nothing."

"Tell me."

I decide to be honest with him. What have I got to lose? "I'm trying to stay unattached, but then you swoop in and do... *that*..." I gesture down below with my hand. "And it's hard to remember I'm not allowed to keep you."

He drops his head to my chest. "I'm sorry, Dee."

"Dear God, don't be sorry for giving me the best orgasm I've ever had. It's just that a girl could become addicted to that kind of action."

"Don't do that."

"Yes, I heard you. Which led me to wonder why you'd want only one woman when you can have *all* the women."

Looking up at me, he seems stricken. "That's not it at all."

I shrug. "It's none of my business."

"I swear that's not it, Dee. If I were in a place to be with someone, I'd want that someone to be you. You're all I've thought about for months."

I need to stop this before he ruins me. With my hand on his chest, I give a gentle push. "Up."

He withdraws from me and sits on the bed.

I reach for the throw blanket from the foot of the bed and wrap it around myself. "I don't think I can do this. Wait, that's not true. I don't think I *should* do this."

Wyatt looks down at the floor, making it impossible for me to know what he's thinking or feeling.

"I'm not a fling kind of girl," I add softly. "Despite how I behaved after the wedding, that's just not me. I don't have casual sex, or I never did before I did it with you, and even that didn't feel casual. It felt important, and I've thought about you a lot since then, too." I swallow the huge lump that's taken up residence in my throat. "And when you tell me you've been thinking of me and... I can't."

"I understand."

I'm glad one of us does. "I'm sorry."

"Please don't be." He leans in to kiss me. "I enjoyed every second I spent with you."

"Same."

Realizing I might not see him again makes me feel desperate for something more. "I'll still show you Miami if you'd like to. I don't work again until Tuesday." I can do that much, or so I tell myself.

"I'd love to see Miami with you." He buttons the shirt he never took off and kisses me again. "I'm going to head back to Jay's."

"I'll pick you up there in the morning? Around ten?"

"Sounds good."

"Sleep well."

"You, too."

I watch him go, wishing for things that'll never be, and wait until the door closes before I go to lock up. My legs feel wobbly after the rather exceptional orgasm he gave me as a parting gift.

CHAPTER 6

WYATT

I feel sick. Leaving Dee is the hardest thing I've had to do in a long time, especially since all I want is to be with her, even if we only talk. I love talking to her. I've been lucky these last seventeen years. I've never met a woman who made me want more, so I was able to skate through life relatively unscathed, protecting my fragile heart from anything even close to heartbreak.

Until now.

I want to rage at the sheer injustice of having finally met a woman who checks all my boxes, only to have to walk away from her to spare us both from eventual disaster. I simply cannot subject her to the reality that is my life—and I can't do it to myself, either.

But God, I want to, and oh, how I ache from knowing I just can't.

In the Uber, I text Jay to let him know I'm on the way back to his place.

Hit me up when you get here, and I'll buzz you in.

Will do.

I didn't want to leave Dee. I would've given anything to spend another night with her, even if nothing else happened between us. Just being in the same room with her gives me a feeling of joy I've never experienced before. It's the highest of highs—and it's the best sort of high, the all-natural kind.

I've watched my brother and friends fall in love, settle down, give up their freedom for the chance to spend forever with one person, and I'll admit I just didn't get why they'd do that. Since meeting Dee, spending time with her, sleeping with her and then thinking about her obsessively for months, I'm starting to understand.

If they feel for their partners the way I do when she's nearby, then I see why they'd take the plunge if it means holding on to that amazing feeling for as long as they can.

The traffic is light, and I'm back at Jay's place fifteen minutes after I left Dee's. I shoot him a text to let him know I've arrived.

He replies with instructions on using the keypad next to the door and then buzzes me in.

I take the elevator to their floor and step off. The first thing I notice is Jay standing in the doorway, holding the door open for me. He's wearing only a pair of basketball shorts, which has me wondering if I got him out of bed.

"Sorry to be a pain," I tell him when I walk past him into the apartment.

"You're not, but we need to talk." He nods to the deck. "Outside."

What's this about?

"You want some seltzer or something else?"

"Seltzer is fine."

"I'll meet you out there."

I leave the sliding door open for him, and he joins me a minute later with the seltzer for me and a beer for himself. He slides the door closed behind him.

"What's up?"

"I guess that's what I want to know. What's going on with you and Dee?"

"Nothing." Even as I say that single word, the ache intensifies. "Now."

"What does that mean?"

"We spent time together after the wedding." I tell him the truth because he's one of my closest friends, and I refuse to be the source of trouble between him and his new wife. "But that's all it was."

"You seemed pretty damned into her tonight if that's all it was."

"I was into her. I *am* into her, but reality has reared its ugly head to remind me of why that's not possible. I was honest with her."

Jason's eyes widen with surprise because he knows I don't tell anyone the whole truth about myself. "You told her—"

"No, I said it couldn't be anything more than fun."

"What'd she say to that?"

"She was okay with it until she wasn't. Things were getting a bit... intense... between us when she called a halt to it. After everything that happened with her ex, she doesn't want to set herself up to be hurt again." I take a sip of my seltzer, hoping it'll wash down the massive lump in my throat. "I guess she's not really into the casual thing with guys."

"She was with her ex for years."

"There you have it."

I move to the rail and look out over Biscayne Bay, where the faintest hint of moon silvers the water. After living most of my life in the desert, the lush beauty of South Florida amazes me. I'd never been here before Jay's wedding, but the place has touched me in more ways than one.

"Are you bummed?"

I shrug because that's what he expects me to do. "No biggie."

He joins me at the rail. "I'm calling bullshit on that."

"How come?"

"I've known you a long time, seen you with a lot of women, and I've never once seen you act around one the way you did with her earlier."

His observation makes me feel a little too *seen*. "How was it different?" I ask, even though I already know. I want to hear it from him.

"You never took your eyes off her. You hung on her every word. You laughed like I've never seen you laugh with anyone."

Every one of his observations makes me sadder than I already was for what can never be. "It wouldn't be fair, Jay. To either of us." I lean my elbows on the rail and sag against the concrete, letting it hold me up. "One thing I've never been is unrealistic, and we both know I'm living on borrowed time and have been for a while now."

"What if you're the one who defies the odds?"

"I already have, and you know that. The average life expectancy after transplant is eleven years. I'm at seventeen. I should've had issues long before now."

"But you haven't because you take such immaculate care of yourself."

"Yes, I do, but eventually, reality will catch up to me, and then what? A sudden death that'll traumatize everyone who loves me or another agonizing wait for a donor that may or may not materialize, followed by months of recovery and the roller coaster of possible rejection. I can't bear the idea of that for myself. How do I drag someone else into that?"

"I'm sorry, Wyatt. It fucking sucks."

"Yep, but it sure does beat the alternative."

He laughs as I recite the refrain that sums up my life rather perfectly. I'm thankful for every second I've gotten since someone else had to die to give me the chance to live. I never forget how close I came to dying or how lucky I am to still be healthy. But I also never forget that the odds are stacked heavily against my good health lasting indefinitely.

"Anyway, I'm sure you've got better things to be doing than hanging with me. Go to bed with your wife."

"She's out cold by now. I'm glad to get the chance to hang with you, just the two of us. It's been a while since we've done that."

"Yeah, too long."

We had all the fun in med school. Jason is the first friend I made after regaining full health, and I appreciate that he's never treated me like an invalid, even after I told him the truth. My parents and doctors insisted that someone at Duke know the whole story in case I ran into trouble. Shortly after I met Jay and bonded with him, I decided he was the one I'd trust. I've never regretted that decision.

"I'm sorry you're bummed."

"It's okay. I'll survive. Well, until I die, anyway."

"Don't say that. I believe you're going to be the exception to all the rules. You already have been."

In all the years since my transplant, I've only thrived. From the first minute I woke up after the twelve-hour surgery, I felt reborn. I've never once come close to rejecting my donor heart or had any sort of scare. My case has been covered in numerous medical journals as a true success story.

Anytime another longtime transplant patient passes away, the media calls to interview me. Somehow, I've become the "poster child" for successful heart transplants. But even the poster child will one day have his day of reckoning, and I'm determined not to take anyone else down with me, even if I'm more tempted to break my own rules with Dee than I ever have been before.

"Enough about me," I say. "Let's talk about you. How are things?"

"Never been better. The best thing I ever did was take a job in 'Siberia,' aka Miami, where I met my beautiful wife and her incredible family. I love it here."

"I can see that. Marriage looks good on you."

"We're enjoying it. Carmen… She's the best person I've ever known."

"I'm happy for you both."

"We are, too," he says with a dirty grin. "It's funny how I had no interest in marriage for so long, but after I met Carmen, it was all I wanted, to be bound to her forever so she could never get away."

"She's not going anywhere. For some reason, she's crazy about you."

"I'm a very lucky man." He leans on the concrete wall, facing the water. "I wish you could have the same thing, Wy. Even if it's only for a few years."

His softly spoken words spark a fierce yearning in me, to know what it's like to be in love, truly in love, for the first time in my life. That could happen with Dee. I have no doubt about it. A big part of me wants to reach out and go for it, to hell with the consequences. But how can I do that to her? How can I ask her to take that kind of risk? I can't, and that's the end of it. Better to quit thinking about what can never be than to torture myself with what-ifs.

"I should hit the sack," I tell Jason, eager to end this conversation and to be by myself after this emotionally draining day. As I follow Jason inside, I realize I never should've come back here. That was the biggest mistake I could've made, and on Monday, I'll call Miami-Dade and cancel my appointment to meet with their chief of surgery and other management. I can't move here and live in the same city as Dee and not see her or want her. That's just not possible.

"Do you have everything you need?" Jay asks.

"I do. Thanks again for having me."

"Anytime. You know that. I'll see you in the morning."

"Night, Jay."

For a long time after Jason's bedroom door closes, I'm awake, staring up at the condo's high ceiling. Through the huge windows that make up one entire wall, I see stars twinkling above. Carmen warned me earlier that it would be bright after the sunrise, but I told her I don't mind that. I can sleep through just about anything, except heartache, it seems.

I have an extraordinary life, a career I busted my ass for and a calling to care for patients that comes from a place of understanding and compassion other physicians can't possibly have the way I do.

My incredible parents moved heaven and earth to save my life, mortgaging everything they owned to pay substantial medical bills that insurance didn't cover. Our community raised a lot of money for us that helped with the added expenses that come with serious illness. What was left over, my parents put into an account for me that my grandfather has managed and grown. It's not a fortune, but it's a nice little nest egg in addition to what I've managed to put away myself.

My parents saved my life as much as the doctors who operated on me. I'm blessed to have the love and support of my entire extended family and friends like Jason, who've become like family over the years. I've always known I'd never get married or have a family, and I made peace with that a long time ago. Or so I thought. Dee has made me wish for things I've never wanted before.

But I can't do that. I won't do it—to myself or her.

I turn on my side and stare out at the vast darkness of the bay, waiting for sleep to catch up to me.

My racing mind circles back to an earlier thought about how the media contacts me anytime a longtime heart transplant patient dies. Those interviews are online if Dee were to do a deeper search on me.

God, I hope she doesn't do that.

DEE

Dr. Wyatt Blake, a board-certified cardiothoracic surgeon at Valley of the Sun Health in Phoenix, Arizona, nationally recognized expert on aortic dissection and replacement and an international expert on the doctor-patient relationship stemming from his personal experiences as a patient.

I dig deeper into journal articles and media stories attached to his name. It takes about forty minutes before I hit pay dirt with a quote from him as a long-surviving heart transplant patient.

I gasp as I read that.

Oh my God.

He had a heart transplant when he was... I do fast math in my head... seventeen. Why doesn't he have a scar? I no sooner have that thought than I recall the massive, intricate tattoo on his chest that hides the scar.

I spend the next hour at the bottom of a deep rabbit hole of heart transplant websites, reading statistics about life expectancy after transplant and quickly realizing that Wyatt has defied the odds, having lived for years longer than most transplant patients do.

I'm at once thrilled and terrified. Wyatt defied the odds. But how long can that last?

Of those who survive the first year, only half survive to year thirteen. The numbers go down from there. Repeat transplants have an even shorter life expectancy, and most die from rejection issues as well as graft failure and something called relapsing graft vasculopathy.

I read about a man named John McCafferty, who received a transplant in the UK at thirty-nine and lived into his seventies. And then I read about how rare stories like McCafferty's are, and I begin to get a better understanding of why Wyatt doesn't do relationships.

Suddenly, I need to talk to him. Before I can take even one second to question the wisdom of continuing down this path with him, I fire off a text to him. *Are you awake?*

I'm thrilled to see the bubbles that indicate he's typing and wait for him to respond. *Yes, but why are you?*

I couldn't sleep after you left. Can you talk?

Sure. Hang on. Let me go outside, so I don't bother Jason and Carmen.

While I wait for him to call, I run my fingers through my hair as if I'm going to see him and need to make myself ready. My heart is beating hard in anticipation of hearing his voice. Am I going to tell him what I found out? Will he think it's a terrible invasion of his privacy?

When the phone rings and I nearly stroke out with excitement, I realize something else. I'm already falling for this guy, which could be very dangerous for my own battered heart. "Hi."

"Hey. Why are you awake at one-thirty?"

"I was, um, wound up after you left and… Wyatt?"

"Yeah?"

"I googled you again and dug a little deeper this time."

He groans. "I was afraid you'd do that."

"Are you mad?"

"No, sweetheart. I'm not mad. It's what people do in this day and age when we want to know the lowdown on someone who's being mysterious."

"Why didn't you tell me?"

I can hear his sigh loud and clear. "Because. I don't talk about it, except when another longtime survivor dies and the media calls for a quote. Otherwise, I try not to think about it and just do my thing. It dominated *everything* for the first half of my life, you know? I've been determined not to let it dominate the second half, too."

"This is why you don't do relationships, right?"

"Yeah. Wouldn't be fair to let someone have feelings for me when I might not be around to make it worthwhile for them."

"What about John McCafferty?"

"What about him?"

"He lived for forty-something years after transplant."

"That's extraordinarily rare."

"But that could be you, couldn't it?"

"Sure, but it's not likely, and it's why I made my peace a long time ago with going it alone. It wouldn't be fair to drag someone else into this situation. I'm like a ticking time bomb at this point. It could all go south anytime."

"What if it doesn't?"

"What do you mean?"

"What if it doesn't go south, and you just live a regular life?"

"That'd be awesome, but I don't expect that to happen."

"If it does, you'd spend your entire life alone because some-thing *might* happen?"

"I'm not alone, Dee. I have a wonderful family, terrific friends and colleagues—"

"Have you ever been in love?"

"No."

I wonder if he hears how sad he sounds. "You can't miss out on knowing what it's like to be in love, Wyatt. It's one of the greatest things in life." I still feel that way, even after how things ended with Marcus.

"You make me want to say fuck it to all my rules and fall the rest of the way in love with you."

"Do I?"

"You do. And no one else I've ever met has made me want to say fuck it to my rules, Dee."

Am I swooning? I'm definitely swooning. "Is that right?"

"It is."

"So, what're you going to do about this desire to say fuck the rules?"

"Nothing," he says softly.

"I reject that answer."

His laughter makes me smile. "Hear me out on this, okay?"

"I'm listening."

"Say I toss my rules aside, move here and go all-in with you."

"That sounds pretty good to me so far."

"It does to me, too. But then say we let things get totally out of hand and get married, and then I start to have problems. It may start as pain in my chest or an infection that refuses to clear up. Or maybe I have a stroke, or one day you wake up, and I'm gone."

"Th-that could happen?"

"Any of it could happen, among many other things. I don't want to do that to you, Dee. I don't want to do that to anyone, so it's just easier not to go there, you know?"

"I hear what you're saying. I do. However…"

"What, honey?"

More swooning. "I want you to know what it feels like to be in love, Wyatt. I want you to have that experience."

"I'd want that more than anything if things were different, but I keep going back to the matter of fairness and how it wouldn't be fair to let someone fall in love with me, knowing how the odds are stacked against me."

"What if…"

"You're making me crazy," he says with a low laugh.

"Should we stop talking about this?"

"Crazy in a good way."

"Oh."

"What did you want to ask me?"

"What if the person you fell in love with was willing to risk herself to give you that experience for however long it lasted?"

He groans. "Dee… You're lovely and sweet and so sexy. You make me want you just by walking into the room. But I could never do that to you."

I'm trying hard not to cry. "What if I wanted you to?"

"Sweetheart... If it were going to be anyone, I'd want it to be you."

"Let it be me."

His low moan travels through my body like a live wire. *"Dee..."*

"Wyatt. Let it be me."

"You don't know what you're saying. You've already been through an awful breakup and—"

"Can I tell you a secret?"

"Sure."

"He never made me feel the way you do."

"You don't mean that."

"I do mean it. I was with him for six years, and after the first night I spent with you, I knew I'd wasted all that time with the wrong guy."

"Stop."

"I'm telling you the truth. I thought about you constantly after that night."

"I thought about you, too."

"Did you come back for me?"

"Of course not. I came back for the job."

"Are you lying?"

His laughter makes my heart flutter with excitement and anticipation of seeing him again as soon as possible.

"Fall in love with me, Wyatt." I have no idea where the courage to say these things out loud is coming from. All I know is that nothing has ever felt so right.

"You don't know what you're saying. You're upset about Marcus."

"I'm not thinking about him. I'm thinking about you and how I feel when you look at me the way you do and when you kiss me and touch me. I want more of that, more of you, more of us, for as long as it lasts."

"Dee..."

"Yes, Wyatt?"

"How're you so calm when I feel like I'm having a heart attack over here?"

That has me sitting up straighter. "Do you? Really?"

"The best kind of heart attack."

"I wish you were still here with me."

"So do I. You have no idea how much I wish that."

"Could I come to get you?"

"I should say no. We should never see each other again."

"Let me come get you. Let's spend every minute we can together."

"I can't do that."

"Why?"

"Because I'll fall the rest of the way in love with you."

"I've never wanted anything the way I want that. I want you. After everything you went through to have that heart, I want you to know how it feels to lose it to someone else."

"I don't want to hurt you."

"You'll hurt me if you say no. Can I come to get you?"

After a long pause, he says, "Yes. Come get me."

"I'll be there in half an hour. And, Wyatt?"

"Yes, Dee?"

"You won't regret this."

"I know I won't. I'm just worried that you will."

"No chance of that. See you soon."

CHAPTER 7

DEE

I end the call and let out a shout of excitement. I can't believe what I said to Wyatt or the brazen way I told him to fall in love with me. I've lost my freaking mind, and I don't even care if it means I get to have this crazy adventure with him. Ever since he left earlier, I've regretted letting him go. As I jump out of bed, take a quick shower and get dressed in leggings and a shirt that shows off all my curves, I have a moment of panic about what I'm getting into.

I'm setting myself up for even bigger heartache than I had with Marcus. I've seen Wyatt on two occasions, and I already know he could be more important to me than Marcus ever was. I almost feel guilty acknowledging that, but it's true. I spent the night of Carmen's wedding with Wyatt because I was so afraid of never again feeling the way I did with him. It happened that fast, during one magical day and night.

Since then, I've tried to convince myself it wasn't as big of a deal as it seemed, mostly because he doesn't live here, so what was the point in hoping to see him again? But now he's back, the feeling is even more significant the second time, and he's interviewing for a job in my town.

Finding out about his health challenges changes nothing for me, except for one big thing. It makes me more determined to show him one of the best things in life. I want him to experience what it's like to love and be loved. The early years with Marcus were terrific. That feeling of being in love for the first time is the best feeling there is. Wyatt deserves to have that.

I hate that he could die young, but I'm not going to let fear run my life or his. Since my mom got sick earlier this year, I have a new appreciation for life and good health. Wyatt is robustly healthy, and I have to believe he's going to stay that way. I refuse to accept any other alternative. And no, I'm not delusional or being unrealistic about the odds he spelled out so starkly.

I get it, and *I don't care*. I love being with him and how he makes me feel sexy and desired, and *happy*. I want every minute I can get with him for as long as it lasts. I'm ready to move on from the nightmare with Marcus. Feeling like shit every minute of every day gets old after a while.

Before I leave the house, I pack a bag with a bathing suit, a cover-up, sunscreen, flip-flops and anything else I might need to go wherever this adventure may take us. On the way to Carmen's, I drive faster than I should, singing along to the radio the whole way. Between the meltdown with Marcus, the miscarriage and the horrors of my mother's illness, I honestly can't recall the last time I felt this good. Maybe it was that last weekend I spent in New York with Marcus, back when I was under the illusion that I was destined to spend the rest of my life with him.

Funny how life kicks you in the teeth, and you never see it coming.

I had no idea Marcus was in any way unhappy with me or our arrangement, as challenging as it could sometimes be to live

apart. Neither of us was ever needy or clingy in our relationship, so the long-distance situation this time around, when we
were older and wiser, wasn't insurmountable. We made it work
and had so many good times when he visited me or when I
came home to Miami. We always picked right up where we left
off, and it felt effortless. My relationship with him reminded me
of how my parents are with each other—easy, comfortable,
content.

Little did I know there's a whole lot of difference between
content and true satisfaction. If I hadn't indulged in that first
night with Wyatt, I might never have known what was missing
with Marcus. I might've let him convince me that his "marriage"
was a big misunderstanding. He might've been able to talk his
way back into my life as if nothing ever happened.

I shudder to think about how I might've settled for less than
what I deserve.

The night with Wyatt was a revelation in more ways
than one.

First and foremost, I realized how incredible it is to be the
source of someone's undivided attention, to know he wanted
me so fiercely that I was willing to make a massive detour from
my usual routine to take a walk on the wild side with him. And
what a walk it was. I can't think about that night with him
unless I want to end up driving off the road.

All I know is I can't wait for a repeat performance.

By the time I pull up outside Carmen's building, I'm buzzing
as if I've had a couple of glasses of champagne, high off knowing
I'm going to see him again any minute. I send him a text. *I'm
here.*

Coming down.

It's all I can do not to bounce in my seat from excitement.
Grabbing my purse, I find a mint to make sure my breath is nice
and fresh because I'm going to kiss him the second he gets in

this car. I hope he's ready for all-in Dee because she's ready for him.

When he comes through the door, I open my window and toss the rest of the mint outside. I'm so excited that I forget to unlock the door for him and then fumble with the button while he stands outside, waiting for me to let him in.

Then he's in the car and turning to reach for me in the exact second I reach for him. This kiss puts every other kiss with him to shame. We cling to each other, tongues dueling in a fierce battle that I'm happy to lose. Losing to him feels like the best kind of win. When he pulls back, I whimper.

"Easy, sweetheart." With his hand on my face, he caresses my cheek. "We should talk about this some more.

"No more talking. You told me what to expect. I understand and accept what I'm getting into. We need to get busy living and not worrying about what might or might not happen. My Abuela says the future is right now. This is it, the only guarantee we have. And I don't know about you, but I don't want to waste any more time."

"You're amazing," he whispers before he kisses me again, softer this time.

I have no idea how long we're there, kissing like teenagers who have no fear of getting caught before his stomach growls loudly.

I pull back from him, laughing.

"Sorry," he says with a sheepish grin.

"Are you hungry?"

"Always. There's never a time when I can't eat, even after I just ate."

"It's extremely unfair that you can eat like that and look like you do."

"I spend a lot of time at the gym."

"That's time very well spent. Want to find an all-night diner or something?"

His growling stomach answers for him, making us laugh.

"All righty, then." I put my seat belt back on and pull away from the curb, trying to think of where we can go. "We might be stuck with Denny's. I can't think of anywhere else that's open all night."

"That works for me."

"There's one on Biscayne Boulevard, I think."

"Want me to check my phone?"

"Nah, I know where I'm going."

He reaches for my hand and holds on during the short ride to the restaurant.

Just that small gesture has my heart racing. I can't believe the way he affects me, and it's been that way from the first second Jason introduced him to me at their rehearsal dinner. My first thought was, *whoa*. And then he smiled. Holy shit, that smile… Since we were matched up in the wedding party, I got to sit with him at dinner.

"What're you thinking about over there?" he asks.

"The night we met."

"That was an amazing night. I was a little worried about spending an entire weekend with people I don't know since I figured Jay would be with Carmen and doing wedding stuff. But you put me immediately at ease and made it so fun."

"I was in a horrible place that weekend. I'd just heard that Marcus was telling people he wanted me back." I barely remember anything from the night of Carmen's bachelorette party after hearing that news.

"That must've been hard to hear."

"It was surreal. For more than a year, I didn't hear a word from him. Not one word after he married *her*."

"Did you know her? Before?"

"I knew of her. She's the sister of one of his friends. She and a group of her friends tagged along on their trip to Vegas for one of the guys' bachelor parties, and Marcus woke up married to her."

"Seriously? That's how it happened?"

"Yep."

"And how did you hear about it?" He quickly adds, "We don't have to talk about this if you don't want to."

"It's okay. It was a long time ago." That's true, but the pain of it still feels fresh in many ways. "My cousin Domenic told me he heard from a friend at home that Marcus had gotten married."

"That had to be so shocking."

"It was, especially since, as far as I knew, he was still my boyfriend. He'd just been to New York for a weekend a month before, and we'd had a great time."

"I'm sorry that happened to you, Dee."

I shrug as if it wasn't one of the most painful experiences of my life to hear—through the grapevine—that my boyfriend married someone else and let me hear about it from others. Not to mention what happened after that.

"Did you ever talk to him again?"

"Nope. What's there to say? 'I hope you and your wife will be very happy together'?"

Wyatt blows out a deep breath. "What an awful thing to do to someone you love."

"Of course, now I'm left to wonder if he ever actually loved me. He's been texting me lately, apologizing, telling me there're things I need to know about what happened, it wasn't me, it was him, et cetera."

"Why haven't you blocked him, sweetheart?" he asks gently.

"I know I should have, but I just never did. I never expected to hear from him again. In some ways, it's vindicating to hear he has regrets. And the evil, nasty side of me was happy to hear the marriage didn't work out."

"You don't have an evil, nasty side."

"If the thoughts I was having about her and them together are any indication, yes, I do."

"Anyone would feel that way after what he put you through."

And he didn't know the half of what I went through. "One of his friends called me a couple of weeks later. He told me it happened during a drunken night out in Vegas, that it didn't mean anything and that he was sure Marcus would tell me that himself before too much longer."

"But he never did."

"Nope. It was like he and I had never happened. It was just… over."

All at once, I snap out of it and realize I'm doing a terrible job of convincing Wyatt he needs to experience love. That thought makes me laugh.

"What's so funny?"

"It just occurred to me that I'm not exactly selling you on how great it is to be in love."

Since we're stopped at a light, I get to see the smile that stretches across his sinfully handsome face. "Marcus is an idiot for letting you go." He brings my hand to his lips and kisses the back of it. "And I, for one, am extremely thankful he got drunk and married the skank."

I start laughing and worry I might never stop. Hearing Wyatt call her that… I was already on my way to loving this guy, but that just about seals the deal for me. "She's probably a perfectly nice person," I say when I finally quit laughing. "We don't know her at all. She may not deserve that nickname."

"She married someone else's boyfriend and then stayed married to him after he sobered up and probably told her he'd made a mistake. That's the definition of skank, in my opinion."

"No kidding, right? I mean, she *had* to know about me. We'd been together on and off for years. It was hardly a secret. And what did he say the next day when he came to and found himself married? Was he freaking out? Was he worried about me finding out? Did he even *think* of me?"

I stop myself because there's no better way to ruin a new thing than by dwelling on an old thing that's better off left in the past. "Sorry. I didn't mean to go on about it. I was well on my way to being totally over it when I came home for Car and Jason's wedding and heard about his regrets. I was doing much better, so I don't want you to think I'm still messed up over him. I'm not."

"I don't think that. I think you loved the guy, he disappointed you profoundly, and then just when you were getting back on your feet, he ends up in the hospital, possibly because you wouldn't take his calls. I understand how that brings it all back up again."

"It did." His understanding touches me, and I appreciate that he isn't acting like a threatened fool, the way some guys would while hearing about a painful breakup with another man. "Anyway, thanks for listening."

"Of course." He glances at me, which I can see out of the corner of my eye. I'm so tuned in to him that I feel like every breath he takes registers with me. "Could I ask you something?"

"Sure."

"That night after the wedding, was that like a rebound?"

"No!"

"Not even kinda?"

"The one-night stand part of it maybe, but not the rest. That was about you and how much I liked you after hanging out at the rehearsal dinner and wedding. We had fun, and you were so..."

"What?"

"Attentive."

"I was hot for you from the second I met you."

My laughter sounds like a girly giggle. "That was extremely flattering, especially after feeling so discarded."

"Anyone who had you and let you go is the biggest kind of idiot, and you know, it's kind of satisfying that he's eating his heart out over it. He should be."

"It's very sexy when you take my side like that."

"Is it?"

"Uh-huh."

"Well, I'm very much on your side."

We pull into Denny's parking lot. Before he lets go of my hand, Wyatt kisses me again. When we get out of the car, he puts his arm around me to walk inside. I love the way he doles out affection so naturally.

I lean into him like a needy puppy. Did I just compare myself to a puppy? If the analogy fits...

The hostess shows us to a booth.

Wyatt sits across from me, and the loss of his body heat leaves me chilled. Or it's just that the air-conditioning on deep freeze mode.

"It's like a meat locker in here," he says as he scans the menu.

"I'm freezing."

"Come over here. I'll keep you warm."

He doesn't have to ask twice. I bring my menu with me when I move to his side and snuggle up to him.

"I have to be honest with you," he says.

"I thought you'd already told me your deepest, darkest secret."

"This one is about couples who sit on the same side of a booth."

"What about them?"

"I've always thought that was so stupid like can't they get through one meal without being all over each other?"

"And now?"

"I get it." He kisses the top of my head. "The time it would take to eat is too long not to touch you."

"So far, you're doing an excellent job of being in a relationship."

"Am I?"

"Uh-huh. Step one, make the woman feel special, listen to her when she goes on and on about her ex, say all the right things while making her feel sexy and desired. Are you sure you haven't done this before?"

He's making me crazy with kisses to my neck that have me leaning in even closer. "I'm very sure. I've never met anyone who made me want to turn my life upside down so I could be with her all the time."

"Is that how you feel about me?"

"Hell yes. I'm ready to give notice at my job in Phoenix, and I haven't even had the interview here yet."

I turn toward him. "Don't do that." I love his smile so much, the way it makes his dark blue eyes sparkle and leaves deep grooves in his cheeks. "You have the most beautiful face." I run my thumb over one of the grooves.

"So do you." He kisses my cheek, nose and lips. "The first time I saw you, I said to Jay, '*Who* is that?' He said you were Carmen's cousin, and I said, 'Introduce me. Right now.'"

"Safe to say, I immediately noticed you, too. I'd been dreading the need to put on a happy face for three days, and then there you were to make me smile. You'll never know what that meant to me at that moment."

"You made me smile, too. It was the most fun I've had in a very long time, and as I was getting on the plane to go home on Monday, it felt wrong to leave without you."

It's all I can do to remember we're in public.

The waitress appears by our table, forcing me to snap out of the thrall. "What can I get y'all?"

"I'll have coffee and an English muffin, please," I tell her.

"I'll do an egg-white veggie omelet with wheat toast, please."

"Coffee for you, love?" she asks with a flirtatious smile that makes me want to claw her eyes out.

Wyatt hands her his menu. "Just ice water with lemon. Thanks."

"Coming right up."

"Don't tell me you don't drink coffee."

"I won't tell you that caffeine isn't good for my heart, so I avoid it."

"I have a question."

"You can ask me anything you want." He links his fingers with mine. "It's such a relief that you know the truth. I wanted to tell you that first night, and I don't tell anyone. For some reason, though, I wanted you to know."

"Why don't you tell people?"

"I developed that habit the first time I left home and went to North Carolina for med school. It was like this fresh start, away from everyone who'd known me as the sick kid. I loved that no one knew, so it became my routine when I met new people. Plus, I don't want to be defined by that, you know?"

"I can understand that. But that wasn't the question I was going to ask."

"You're allowed to ask as many as you want."

"When I read about life after a heart transplant, one of the things they talked about was avoiding sick people and germs."

"That's right."

"But you work in a hospital."

"That's an excellent question. Most of the patients I see aren't sick with the kinds of things that would endanger me. They have cardiac or pulmonary concerns that aren't contagious. And I'm super careful. If I think there's any chance of being exposed to something, I wear a mask and keep my distance."

"It's kind of scary that a random germ could put your life at risk."

"That's why I didn't go into pediatrics," he says, grinning. "I don't overthink it. I just do everything I can to avoid germs and crowds."

"It's admirable how hard you work to stay healthy."

"I know what it's like to be sick—really, *really* sick—and I never want to be there again if I can avoid it. I hope that when my donor heart quits, it's sudden. I don't want ever again to spend months on end in the hospital."

The thought of him dying suddenly makes me ache for him and myself.

He seems to pick up on that. "I'd understand if you're second-guessing—"

"I'm not."

"You should, Dee. The idea of you signing on for almost guaranteed heartbreak because of me is unbearable."

"I don't want you to worry about that. You told me what I was risking, and I understand it. I'm choosing to spend time with you and to feel *things* for you. It's what I want. *You* are what I want."

"That makes me feel so fucking lucky." He stares at me for the longest time as if trying to memorize every detail of my face. "So, you feel *things*, huh?"

"Yeah. Lots of *things*."

"Me, too. All the *things*." He's about to kiss me when the waitress returns with my coffee and his water. "To be continued later."

I shiver from the promise in his words. I can't wait until later.

CHAPTER 8

WYATT

She's got me so wound up, I can barely eat—and anyone who knows me would tell you that's a rare thing. Now that I've permitted myself to take this leap with her, all I want is as much of her as I can get. I can't believe this is happening or the way I said fuck it the minute she told me she didn't care about my rules. I still have significant reservations, but damned if I can be bothered to think about them with her sitting right next to me, the heat of her body pressed against mine making me crazy for her.

And not just physically. Sure, that's a big part of it, but it's so much more than that. Dee makes me yearn for the intense connection I've never shared with anyone before. Yes, I've dated a lot, had a few women who might've been considered "girl-friends" by other people's standards, but I've never once gone all-in with anyone, knowing that just wasn't possible for me. I didn't want to star in one of those real-life, movie-of-the-week stories where the hero dies and leaves the heroine devastated to pick up the pieces in the aftermath of my tragic and premature death.

No, thanks. Why would I do that to someone I love?

But Dee... Wow, well, all bets are off when it comes to her. I want to soak up every second we can have together. I want to move to her city and spend the rest of what remains of my life with her. And who knows? Maybe I will get lucky and have a long and healthy life. Yes, the odds are stacked against me right now, but who knows what'll change as medical research marches forward with dizzying speed?

With her warm and soft and fragrant next to me in the vinyl booth, I'm not thinking about dying. Nope. I'm incredibly focused on *living.*

After I pay our check, we walk back to the car, arms around each other. While she ran to the restroom, I took the morning meds I brought with me in case I stayed out all night. She doesn't need to see me popping the pills that keep me alive.

"What do you feel like doing?" she asks.

If I could do anything I wanted, I'd suggest we go back to her place and pick up where we left off earlier. "You tell me. This is your city."

"You need to get some sleep, and then we'll go play tourist."

"I'm so wired, I don't think I'd sleep anyway." Feeling all the things is such a high that sleep is the last thing on my mind. But if we go back to her place, we'll spend the rest of the weekend in her bed, and I don't want her to think that's the only thing I want. Even if I want that. Badly.

"Hmmm, well, let's take a ride out to the beach, then."

"That sounds good."

We end up in a parking lot in Miami Beach that Dee assures me will provide a spectacular view of the sunrise in a few hours.

"Is this safe?"

"Probably not, but I don't think anyone will hassle us here."

I double-check to make sure the doors are locked, just in case.

We listen to music, sing along—her so badly, it's cute—and we talk.

I cradle her hand between both of mine because I need to be touching her.

"You know all about my family, but what about yours?" she asks. "Do you have siblings?"

"One of each, both younger. My illness put my whole family through hell while we were growing up."

"What're their names?"

"Audrey and Liam. She's a retail manager in Phoenix, and he's a firefighter in Scottsdale."

"Are they married?"

"Liam is, with his first child on the way."

"That's exciting."

"It is. I'm looking forward to being an uncle." I stroke the back of her hand, fascinated by how soft and silky her skin is. "I was almost an uncle a long time ago. My sister got pregnant in high school, but she had an abortion. My parents don't know that. And my brother had drug issues for a while, but he's been clean for more than ten years. Everything was about me back then, and they paid the price, too."

"How old were you when you started having problems?"

"Eight. At first, the doctors thought I had the flu, but it quickly escalated from there. I went from being a perfectly normal kid on Friday to having a life-threatening condition by Tuesday. Nothing was ever the same for any of us after that."

"Jeez, it's kind of scary to think something like that can even happen."

"It was a nightmare. My parents have never recovered. When I came here, my mother texted to make sure I'd brought my meds. I'm *thirty-four* and a *doctor.*"

Her smile does amazing things to her gorgeous face. "That's sweet."

"It's annoying! She's going to lose her shit when I tell her I'm moving to Miami. If I get the job, that is. She'll be calling me every day to remind me to take my meds. I wouldn't be surprised if they moved here to live near me."

"Aw, that's adorable."

"No, it isn't. It's smothering."

"They love you."

"They do," I say on a sigh. "The only reason I'm alive today is because of everything my parents did for me. They sacrificed *everything*. So I can't exactly tell my mom to F off and let me live my life."

"You'd never do that anyway."

"No, I wouldn't, but sometimes I want to."

"They must be so proud of what you've accomplished."

"They are, although at first, my dad couldn't understand why I'd want to work in the cardiac field after what I went through, but it was the only specialty I considered. It's what I know. While I was in the hospital, tied to machines and hoping for a transplant, I started studying everything I could get my hands on about my condition. I wanted to know what was happening to me, you know?"

"That makes sense."

"My deep dive led to an obsession of sorts that led to me finishing college in three years so I could go to medical school somewhere far from home. Three years after the transplant, I had to get out of there, away from the concern of my poor parents, who were so traumatized by it all. I needed to be with people who didn't know my story. That's when I started the pattern of not telling people. If no one knew, they wouldn't treat me like a special snowflake. I was so sick of that by then. I just wanted to be normal."

"So no one knew about the transplant?"

"My parents and the doctors insisted that one person in North Carolina needed to know in case I ever had a problem. After I was there a few weeks and got to know Jason, I decided to tell him, but no one else knew about it. It was such a freaking relief after years of everyone hovering over me."

"You must've loved that."

"I did. Med school was the first real freedom I ever had. Other than the constant studying, it was fantastic. Made some great friends, had all the fun."

"Slept with all the girls."

I sputter with laughter. "I didn't say that!"

"I'm sure they were like flies on honey when the handsome med student came to town."

"Are you jealous?"

"Of every single one of them."

"You don't need to be. I never felt *all the things* for any of them."

"Not one of them?"

"Nope. Not until I was in my buddy's wedding and met the cousin of the bride, sexiest bridesmaid ever." I lean in to kiss her neck. "I almost swallowed my tongue when Jay told me you were my bridesmaid."

"When Carmen said, 'That's Jason's friend Wyatt from medical school,' I was like, oh, tell me more, please. And PS, please don't swallow your tongue. That'd be a crying shame."

She makes me laugh. She makes me want. She makes me *feel*.

"When did you get the tattoo?"

"Before med school."

"Did your doctors freak?"

"I cleared it with them first. They said it wasn't a good idea because of the risk of infection. Still, I was determined to hide the scar, so they put me on preventive antibiotics beforehand, which is something they probably wouldn't do now that doctors don't give out antibiotics like candy anymore. It worked out fine, but it's the riskiest thing I've done since the transplant."

"And it helped to keep your secrets."

"Exactly."

"Do you know where your heart came from?"

"A nineteen-year-old woman named Emma, who was killed in an accident. I still hear from her mother every year on her birthday."

"That's amazing. I'm sure it's a big comfort for her to know her daughter's heart lives on."

"It is. She listened to it through a stethoscope once, about ten years ago. Cried her eyes out."

"Wow. That's so cool."

"It was. You know what else is cool?"

"What?"

"That I can talk freely about this with you, and it's not making you treat me differently."

"If I do that, will you tell me?"

"Sure." She's turned in her seat, making it easier for me to stare at her gorgeous face. Thick lashes that other women pay for frame her dark eyes. Her skin is golden brown, her lips full and lush, and her smile dazzling. Being with her is the single greatest thing I've ever experienced, and the thought of leaving here on Monday without her, even if it's temporary, is unbearable. That gives me an idea. "If I get the job, do you want to come to Phoenix with me to pack up my place and drive my car back to Miami?"

"I'd love to do that, but I might not be able to. I help take care of my mom. My brothers are on duty this weekend, but I'm usually there every day."

"Ah, right. Well, it was just a thought."

"If I have a little notice, I might be able to work it out."

"I'd love that." I tuck a strand of silky dark hair behind her ear. Her hair was straight the first time we met, but the humidity has it curling tonight, and I love the curls. "I can't believe we're making plans and diving into all this."

"It's fun."

"Yes, it is, but what about..."

"What?"

"Marcus. He wants you back. Maybe you should at least talk to him." Part of me still wants to talk her out of getting involved with me, but that part is getting smaller with every second I spend with her.

"I'm never going back to him. I don't care what he says or does. That's over. It was over the minute he married someone else." Her brows furrow with displeasure that makes me sorry I mentioned his name.

"I'm very sorry he hurt you."

"I am, too. He texted me earlier to say he didn't try to take his life and that he's sorry his sister made me feel guilty. None of this is my fault. Yada, yada. It's all too little, too late for me." Her eyes fill with tears, and she looks down, her hair forming a curtain that hides her face from me. "Right before I heard he got married... I found out I was pregnant."

"Oh my God, Dee. Oh, God." I reach for her and hold her as closely as I can with the center console between us. "I can't imagine what that was like for you."

"It was horrible, and I couldn't share it with him or tell him or anything."

"He never knew?"

"No," she whispers. "I had a miscarriage at four weeks, right after I found out Marcus had gotten married. I tell myself it was for the best but at the time..."

"It was hell."

"Yeah."

"I'm so, so sorry, sweetheart. I hate him for breaking your heart that way." And it makes me more concerned about doing the same thing—albeit for different reasons.

"No one knows that. I only told Maria earlier today—or I guess it was yesterday now."

"Why didn't you tell her when it happened?"

"I couldn't bear to talk about any of it. I was so humiliated by what he'd done, and then when that happened, I just kind of shut down. I was a mess for a long time. My cousin Dom, my roommate in New York, threatened to tell my parents I wasn't eating or working, using that to get me out of my room. It was bad."

Hearing that, picturing her flattened by heartbreak, gives me pause. I'd never want to be the cause of that. "Dee, honey, I want you to think some more about this with me. If I ever did to you what he did, even if the circumstances were different... I just can't bear the thought of you hurting like that over me."

"It'd be different with you. It wouldn't be because you betrayed me the way he did or disregarded me, or disrespected the love I had for you. If I lost you, it would be because of something you couldn't help. At least I hope that's the only way I'd lose you."

"It is." I'm so sure of this, of her, of how I feel about her, that I don't hesitate to offer that assurance. "If I were lucky enough to be loved by you, I'd never let you go for any reason other than something I couldn't help. And even then, I'd still love you."

"See? Totally different."

"Heartbreak is heartbreak, though. I don't want that for you."

"When someone you loved for years does what he did to me, that's a kind of heartbreak that comes from a place of betrayal and disappointment. Losing someone you love to a death they couldn't prevent would be brutal, but there'd be love to go with the grief. I'm not sure if that makes sense, but it wouldn't be the same kind of pain. At least, I don't think it would be. And besides, I don't want to talk about you dying. I want to talk about you living a long and healthy life and continuing to defy

97

the odds for decades to come. Just because it's rarely happened doesn't mean it can't happen to you."

I can't help but smile at her conviction. "My heart is feeling very healthy since you texted me earlier. It feels better than it ever has."

"Is that so?" she asks with a sexy little grin that has the organ in question beating faster.

"Mmm-hmmm." I lean in to kiss her, and the second my lips connect with hers, every worry I have disappears under a tsunami of desire for this amazing woman who's determined to make me fall in love with her. Falling for her is the easiest thing I've ever done.

CHAPTER 9

JASON

J wake to a text from Wyatt that he's gone out with Dee. *I told her everything, so don't worry. It's all good.* His words are hardly comforting. Dee knows about his health situation and came to pick him up in the middle of the night, which means they're only more involved than they were before he and I talked last night. As I make coffee, I feel unsettled and deeply concerned about this development.

I was relieved after hearing he'd decided to take a step back from Dee, and finding out they're back on this morning isn't great news. I love Wyatt like a brother. I have for years, and Dee is terrific. She's been such a great friend to me since Carmen made me part of their family. The possibility of my close friend with her would be fantastic if it weren't for the cloud of uncertainty that hangs over Wyatt's life. I hate that uncertainty for him, but he likes to say it beats the alternative. It sure does, except for when my wife's adored cousin gets caught in the storm.

By the time Carmen joins me on the deck with her coffee,

I'm picturing all sorts of hideous scenarios, each of them leading to my wife blaming me for her cousin getting her heart broken—again.

"What's wrong? And don't say it's nothing. You tossed and turned all night."

Since Wyatt told Dee about the transplant, I feel like it's okay to tell Carmen. I have to tell her because it's killing me to keep it from her. "Wyatt took off with Dee in the middle of the night."

"Wait, I thought he was with her before that."

"He was, but he came back here after you were asleep because they'd decided to take a chill. Apparently, that's off now."

"Why'd they decide to chill?"

"He told her he doesn't do relationships, and she decided it was too risky for her to spend time with someone who'd drawn that line in the sand."

Carmen drinks the Cuban coffee that Abuela says will put hair on her chest. "So what changed?"

"He was honest with her about why he doesn't get involved."

"And why is that?"

"If I tell you, you have to swear it stays between us. It's important to Wyatt that this not be something everyone knows."

"Okay…"

"Promise me, Carmen."

"I promise."

"No one—not even Maria or your grandmothers."

"I get what 'no one' means, Jason."

She already sounds pissed, and that's the last thing I need. "When Wyatt was seventeen, he had a heart transplant."

"Oh. Wow. He's okay, though, right?"

"He's done great for seventeen years."

"Why do I hear a 'but' in there?"

I put my coffee cup on the table and lean forward, elbows

resting on my knees. "Because he's six years past the average life expectancy for heart transplant patients."

Her little whimper says it all. "Jason..."

"I know."

"This is why you're worried about him spending time with Dee."

"Yeah."

"Does she know?"

"I guess he told her at some point after I went to bed, and now they're off somewhere together. It's just that after what she went through with Marcus..."

"Is he... Is he going to die?"

"There's no reason to think he's in any imminent danger. He takes excellent care of himself."

"This is why he doesn't drink."

"Right, and he's very, very careful in all aspects of his life. Protecting his health is vital to him. He's never had so much as a scare in all these years."

"So it's possible he could keep beating the odds, then, right?"

"Anything is possible, but the odds are stacked rather heavily against him."

Her eyes fill with tears that tug at my own heart. I hate to see her upset. "Dee knows about this, and she's with him anyway?"

"I guess so."

"I need to talk to her."

"That might be a good idea."

Carmen reaches for her phone and dashes off a text to her cousin. "I told her to call me." She stares at the phone as if she's willing it to ring. It chimes with a text that she reads to me. "'Can't right now. Wyatt and I are going fishing. Talk later?' Ugh, not good. The more time she spends with him, the harder it'll be for her to take a step back."

"It doesn't sound like she's stepping back. It seems like it's the opposite."

"I don't want her to get hurt."

"I'm sorry about this."

"It's not your fault. Wyatt is a great guy, and I hate to hear this about him. I'm sorry for him and you and everyone who loves him that this is such a big worry. But Dee..."

"I know, babe. I get it."

"She's the softest one of us. She loves so hard, and when she breaks..." Carmen's deep sigh says it all. "I'm worried about her."

"Me, too."

DEE

The idea to go fishing is sparked by Wyatt sharing a childhood memory of fishing with his grandfather when he spent summer vacations with his extended family on Cape Cod before he got sick and everything changed. "Those were some of the best days of my life," he said.

As soon as the sun began to rise, we headed for Knaus Berry Farm to pick up their famous cinnamon rolls—Wyatt is hungry, *again*—before continuing to Black Point Marina. I've done a lot of fishing, too, with my dad and Uncle Vincent, so I know just where to go to rent a boat and the equipment we need.

"This is awesome," Wyatt says when he sees the marina.

It's tucked away off the beaten path, and you'd have to be a native even to know it exists. I love showing Wyatt places the tourists rarely find. The older guys who work in the marina store recognize me after I give them my name. "My favorite restaurant in the world," one of them says. "How's your uncle Vincent and aunt Viv doing?"

"They're great. Going strong."

"Do your grandmothers still think they're in charge?"

I don't correct him. Abuela is my grandmother in every way that matters. "They don't just think it."

Laughing, he says, "Love how nothing ever changes there. Is your fishing license still active?"

"Sure is. My dad renews it for my birthday every year."

"Excellent. Here's a one-day license for your friend, sweetheart." He hands me the keys to one of the center console boats they rent. "It's all set up with everything you need, and here's a coupon for fifty percent off at the restaurant. Pick up some lunch on your way out."

"Thank you so much, Mr. Gordan."

"My pleasure. Tell your family we said hello. Gotta take the missus in for dinner some night soon."

"You let us know when, and we'll get you a good table."

"Will do. Have fun today, and be careful."

"We will."

They give us two life jackets, and we head down the main dock to the slip with our assigned number. "Here we go."

"This is so awesome." Wyatt bought a swimsuit and tank in the marina store and changed in the men's room. "I can't believe you do this so much that you have a license."

"It's one of my favorite ways to spend a day."

"Mine, too," he says, smiling at me.

That smile makes me all fluttery on the inside. He's so handsome all the time, but when he smiles... *Yum.* I produce sunscreen that we both slather on before we head out. We stop at the restaurant to pick up sandwiches—grouper for me and a shrimp po'boy for him—as well as bottles of water and some other snacks before we head toward the open ocean. It's a gorgeous day with hardly any wind or seas, the perfect kind of day to fish.

Wyatt slips his arms around me from behind and rests his chin on my shoulder. "You're a very sexy captain."

His words send a thrill down my spine. Part of me wishes I'd taken him home to my bed when I had the chance earlier, but I'm glad we're doing other stuff and getting to know each other better before we jump back in bed. The night we spent talking in the car was the best time I've ever spent with anyone. I loved hearing his stories and his laughter and sharing in the pain of his memories from when he was ill. I want to hear everything he has to say.

Our connection is like a live wire that sizzles with awareness and desire. "I'm so glad we could do this. I used to love coming with my dad and uncle. It's been a while since I went with them because I was away."

"Did Maria and Carmen like to go, too?"

"Oh hell no. They both get seasick, and Carmen can't bear to watch them clean the fish. She once threw up on Uncle V's shoes when he was cleaning fish in their driveway."

"Aw, that's so cute."

"He didn't think so!" Speaking of Uncle V, I send him a quick text asking if he can get me a table for two around eight.

He writes right back. *For you, kid, anything. Save me a minute after brunch tomorrow, ok? I want to talk to you about an idea I had.*

For you, anything.

He sends back the laughing emoji. *Love ya, see you tonight.*

Love u 2.

Wyatt is watching over my shoulder. "Your family is adorable."

"They're pretty great."

"Do you ever fight?"

"Oh my God, I used to fight with my brothers like crazy. Especially Nico. He's always been so full of himself. Drove us all crazy, but he's a good guy. He and Milo have really stepped up for my parents since my mom got sick. It's good to know they have it in them."

"You didn't fight with Maria?"

"Hardly ever. We always got along, and the three of us, including Carmen, were together all the time."

"She's an only child?"

"She is. Her mom had nine miscarriages before she had her."

"Yikes. That's awful."

"I guess it was pretty bad. My aunt and uncle had all but given up on having a child when she came along. She was the most coddled child in the history of the world. When she needed to bust loose, she came to our house."

"You guys had so much fun."

"We still do."

"So what kind of fish are we looking for out here?"

"Anything from grouper to swordfish to sailfish. Tarpon is the most commonly found fish in this area, but they're out of season until about May, so it'd be rare to find one this time of year. We're heading out to the Bodenhamer wreck, one of the best spots in the area. We might see some snapper and amber-jack out there, too."

"It's very sexy that you know all this."

I waggle my brows at him. "Wait till you see me bait a hook."

"Hot as *fuck*."

He makes me laugh as easily as I breathe, and I love being with him. I don't care what we're doing or not doing. It's so easy with him. I realize that's the way it should be, and because we might be short on time, I want to share that with him. "Can I tell you something?"

"Anything."

"I've never felt an easier connection to anyone who wasn't my family than I do with you."

He draws me in closer to him with an arm around me and kisses the top of my head. "I feel it, too. Why do you think I came back here?"

"You had a job interview."

"If there were no Dee Giordino, there'd be no job interview."

"Ah-ha, I knew it! You *did* come back because of me."

"Of course I did. You were there in that hotel room after the wedding. You know exactly why I came back—for more of that and more of this—the talking, the laughing, the fishing."

I bump my hip against him. "You didn't know we were going fishing."

"I knew I'd have all the fun with you. And it turns out I was right."

"But you didn't plan to tell me about your situation."

"No, I didn't. I hope you know… It's just so ingrained in who I am after all this time that *not* telling people is my default."

"I get that. I wouldn't want to be defined by something like that, either, especially with everything you've accomplished since then."

"That's far more important to me. I've tried to make lemonade from the lemons, and I'd much rather focus on that."

"I've only known you a short time, but I'm so proud of how you've handled what had to be such a huge challenge."

"Aw, thanks. I wasn't always admirable. I was an awful patient. I drove everyone crazy with my impatience. I wanted out of that hospital in the worst possible way."

"That's kind of funny when you consider what you do for a living."

"I know, but there's a big difference between being there because I want to be and not being allowed to leave because of the machines keeping me alive."

"That had to suck."

"It was the worst." He gives me an affectionate squeeze. "Thanks for letting me talk to you about this stuff. Hiding such a big part of who I am can be exhausting sometimes."

"I always want you to feel like you can talk to me about anything, and you have to promise me that if you ever don't feel well, you'll tell me. You can't hide it from me."

"I won't."

I look up at him. "You promise?"

"I promise."

We seal the promise with a kiss that quickly turns into two kisses and then three.

I break apart from him, laughing, and glance behind us to see the zigzagging pattern of the boat's wake. "Look what you made me do."

"Um, ma'am, are you under the influence?"

"Yes, Officer, I'm under the influence of a sexy doctor who's very distracting."

His hand slides down my back to cup my ass, and it's all I can do to remain standing. I want him so much. "In that case, we'd better take you in and give you a full exam."

I swallow hard. "Is that necessary, Officer?"

"Very necessary."

And then we're kissing again, and I couldn't care less if the boat spins in circles. I have the presence of mind to pull the throttle back to idle before I curl my arms around his neck and open my mouth to his tongue. Dear God, the man can kiss like a dream, and I just want to gorge on him. I have no idea how long we stand there kissing each other's faces off, but it feels like it could've been an hour. Or maybe it was just ten minutes. Who knows? Who cares?

"We're supposed to be fishing," I remind him when we come up for air. "The fish won't catch themselves."

"Ah, right. Fish. I'd forgotten about that."

I love the way he makes me feel so desired. That's such a revelation to me. Being with Wyatt has shown me I love his kind of affection and the emotional connection that comes with it.

We spend the afternoon at one of my dad's favorite spots, made up of a reef created around the sunken O.L. Bodenhamer Liberty Ship. I know exactly where it is because I've been there so often. We're the only ones out here, and the fish are cooperative. Wyatt quickly catches a grouper and then a snapper. We put them in the Styrofoam cooler full of ice the marina provided.

He's so excited to be fishing that his joy has become mine. Just that quickly, if he's happy, so am I. I've stepped way outside my comfort zone over the last few remarkable hours with him. I was with Marcus for six months before I told him I loved him. To be all in with Wyatt this fast is a huge departure for me, but nothing has ever felt so good or so right.

I get another text from Carmen. *Jason told me about Wyatt. I need to talk to you. Call me.*

I know what she's going to say: *Are you out of your ever-loving mind?* Maybe I am, but I'm not going to let her or my sister or anyone talk me out of loving Wyatt for as long as I possibly can. I don't care what happens in the future, and I sure as hell don't want to hear all the reasons it's a bad idea.

While I ignore my phone, I troll for sailfish, impressing Wyatt with my technique. The lure skips across the surface of the water. I hit the jackpot with a twenty-pounder that fights me every step of the way. My arms are toast by the time Wyatt helps me land him.

"You're a total badass," he declares when we have my fish on ice with the others.

"I'm exhausted." I shake out my arms. "I'm glad I'm off this weekend."

"I'm glad you're off, too. How'd that happen, anyway? Aren't weekends prime time at the restaurant?"

"They are, but I alternate weekends with Sofia. She's a single mom, and her ex has her son every other weekend, so we take turns. Her son had a brain tumor, and Jason operated on him. He discovered it when he was volunteering at the free clinic where Maria works. He saved Mateo's life."

"That sounds like Jay. Speaking of badasses. Neuro is the rocket science of medicine."

"Cardiac is pretty impressive, too."

He shrugs. "It's not neuro. Jason is one of the most brilliant doctors I've ever met. He was a rock star from the start in med school. The rest of us had to scramble to keep up with him."

"That's interesting to hear. He seems so normal."

"He is, but he's also fucking brilliant. I'd love to work at the free clinic with him if I get the job here, but I couldn't do patient care. Too much exposure to germs. Maybe there's a board of directors I could sit on or something."

"I'm sure they could find a way for you to help out."

"Can we take a swim to cool off?"

"Sure." I toss the ladder down and execute what I deem to be a flawless dive off the boat. When I resurface, he's grinning down at me.

"That was hot."

"What was?"

"You just diving off the boat like that."

"Been doing it all my life."

"First time I've ever seen it."

"Are you going to join me?"

"Don't mind if I do."

He dives in and comes after me, making me scream with laughter as I try to get away. His arms come around my waist, and the next thing I know, we're kissing like fools in the water.

I only come to my senses to make sure we don't stray too far from the boat.

After the swim, he continues to cast while I stretch out on a bench seat as the sleepless night begins to catch up to me. Between the sun, the lull of the ocean and the view of shirtless Wyatt fishing, I'm as content as I've been in a very long time. This last year has completely sucked, and it's so great to feel good again. I want to hold on to that feeling with both hands, and I'm not going to let Carmen or Maria or anyone else talk me out of it.

The next thing I know, Wyatt is kissing me awake. "I think

we're almost to Cuba." He smiles down at me, and I reach for him as if we've been together forever, and we do this all the time. Wyatt responds enthusiastically and ends up on top of me with my arms and legs wrapped around him. I arch into the thick erection that presses against my most sensitive flesh, letting him know what I want.

"Dee…"

"Now, Wyatt. *Please.*"

He moves quickly to push down his swim trunks and to untie the bottoms to my bikini. And then he stops. "I don't have a condom."

I reach for him. "I'm on the pill. I haven't been with anyone but you in more than a year."

"I'm clean. I get tested regularly."

I smile at him and run my fingers through his thick dark hair. "Then I guess we're good to go." He's so beautiful. His skin is sun-kissed from the afternoon on the water, and his eyes are blazing with desire as he pushes into me.

"This is a first," he whispers against my lips.

"What is?"

"Two things—sex on a boat and sex without a condom."

"What do you think of it so far?"

He rolls his eyes back in his head. "Sublime."

It's been five months since Car and Jason's wedding, but I'm right back to the pleasure we found together during that unforgettable night. I emerged from that hotel room changed by him. "You taught me to set my expectations higher," I whisper to him as he fills me.

"Did I?"

"Oh yeah. I had no idea what I'd been missing."

"Me, either."

"Really?"

"Hell yes. It's never been like that—or this—for me." He pushes my cover-up out of the way and frees my breasts from the bikini top. "Hello, beauties. I thought of you gorgeous ladies so often after our last visit."

He makes me giggle while having sex, and that, too, is a first.

As he makes love to me, I feel free and sexy and happy—truly *happy* for the first time in longer than I can remember. Like the last time I was with him, I experience the highest of highs when he touches me and fills me so perfectly.

"I love this," I whisper in his ear.

"I love it, too. I love every single thing about being with you."

"Same." I place my hands on his face and kiss him. "Thanks for breaking your rules for me."

"I have a feeling that's going to turn out to be the best thing I ever did."

CHAPTER 10

WYATT

*T*he day on the water with Dee is the most fun I've had in years. Fishing was great, but being with her made my day spectacular—and it's not over yet. I carry our cooler of fish to the car while she turns in the keys to the boat. We're going to drop off the fish at the restaurant on our way back to her place to shower before dinner. I check my phone for the first time in hours and read a text from Jay.

I told Carmen. He doesn't have to specify what he told her. I know what he means. *She's wound up about Dee getting involved— and getting hurt.*

I hate that my friend's wife is upset about something to do with me, but Dee has all the info she needs to decide whether she wants to spend time with me. I type my reply. *Dee knows everything, and she's making her own choices with no pressure from me. I swear.*

He responds right away. *You don't do serious.*

I know.

So, this is different?

Everything about this is different.

Before Jason can reply to that, I stuff the phone in the back pocket of my swim trunks and reach out my hand to relieve Dee of the bags she's carrying. "Want me to drive?"

"I won't say no to that. I'm tired."

"Me, too. How about we pick up takeout from the restaurant rather than going back out later?"

"That's a brilliant idea. I'd be afraid of falling asleep in the soup."

"We can't have that."

"I'll text Uncle V. What do you feel like?"

"Let me look at the menu." My mouth waters as I read through the options. "I'll do Cuban chicken with the black bean quinoa bowl."

"I had that last weekend. It's so good." She texts her uncle. "I told him we're bringing him some fresh fish, too."

"What'd you order?"

"Pasta primavera and a house salad."

"Add another house salad if it's not too late."

She sends another text. "All set. He said it'd be ready when we get there."

"Have I mentioned that I love your family?"

"They do come in handy, except for when they're up in my business."

I look over at her. "Are they up in your business now?"

She shrugs and looks out the passenger-side window.

I reach for her hand. "What's up?"

"It's nothing."

I squeeze her hand. "We're being honest with each other, right?"

"Carmen wants me to call her. Jason filled her in, and now she wants to talk about it, except if I do that, she'll try to talk me out of this and you, and I don't want to hear it."

"Maybe you ought to listen to what she has to say."

"Are *you* trying to talk me out of this now?" she asks, smiling at me.

"Someone oughta."

"That ship has sailed," she says. "No turning back."

"Today was the best."

"Was it?"

"The very best day."

"We're going to keep topping the best day. We're going to do it so many times that all the best days will run together."

She makes me believe that's going to happen, and if anyone can make it so, she can. If this is what it feels like to be in a real relationship, to feel all the things for someone, I'm in. I'm *all* in, even if I'm well aware that none of the other reasons why it's a bad idea for her have changed. If I let myself think too much about those things, this day will lose its luster, and I don't want that to happen.

We arrive at the restaurant, and I carry the cooler inside. Dee holds the doors for me and leads me into the kitchen, which is alive with frenzied Saturday night activity. Her uncle Vincent is right in the middle of it. I recognize him from the wedding weekend, and he immediately zooms in on the fact that Dee is with a *man*.

He stops what he was doing to talk to us.

"We got a couple of groupers, a snapper and a sailfish," she tells him.

He kisses her cheek. "Looks like you got some sun, too."

"It was beautiful out there. You remember Wyatt from the wedding, right? Jason's friend."

"Of course." He shakes my hand. "Nice to see you again, Wyatt."

"You as well, sir."

"Call me Vincent—or V."

"Thank you."

"I've got your order all ready, sweetheart. You want a bottle of white to go with it?"

"Sure," Dee says. "What do you recommend?"

While they talk wine, I watch the goings-on in the kitchen. The team moves like a well-oiled machine that reminds me of an operating room.

"Can you hang out for a bit after brunch tomorrow?" Vincent asks Dee.

"Yep, that's the plan. You're being very mysterious."

"Nothing bad. Just an idea I want to run by you."

"Looking forward to hearing more."

"Wyatt, I hope you can join us for brunch tomorrow."

"He'd love to come," Dee says for me. "He's crazy about the food here."

"I thought about it for months after the wedding," I tell him.

"That's what we like to hear. Enjoy your dinner. I added some dessert for you, too."

Dee hands him her credit card, and he waves it away.

"It's an even trade—fish for food."

"You're the best, Uncle V." She goes up on tiptoes to kiss his cheek. "Love you."

"Love you, too, honey. Have a good night."

We're on our way to a clean getaway when we encounter Dee's Abuela and Nona in the parking lot. I can't hear what they're saying, but they're arguing about something.

"Ladies," Dee says. "What's going on?"

"Your grandmother is a menace behind the wheel." Abuela is tiny with perfectly coifed white hair next to Nona, who's a foot taller with salt-and-pepper hair. "She nearly got me killed."

Nona rolls her eyes. "It wasn't even close. If I wanted to kill you, I would've hit the brakes and let them T-bone you right out of my life."

Dee rolls her lips as if she's trying not to laugh.

"It's not funny," Abuela says indignantly.

"Not funny at all," Dee replies. "Where've you been?"

"We took dinner to your parents before the rush," Nona says. "I should've left *her* here."

"Oh, stuff it," Abuela retorts.

"How're they doing?" Dee asks.

"Your mom is having some trouble with her port, but Maria was there earlier to check it. She's keeping an eye on it."

And then, as if the argument never happened, Abuela seems to realize that Dee is there with a *man*, and suddenly, the fight ends, and all her attention is on me. Gulp.

"I know you." Abuela points at my chest. "How do I know you?"

"He's Jason's friend Wyatt from the wedding," Dee says.

"Ah, right. I remember now. You're a handsome devil."

"Um, thank you?"

"Don't embarrass him, Abuela," Dee says as she curls her hands around my arm.

The two women zero in on those hands on my arm. I can almost feel the heat of their laser beams as they sniff out a story.

We're interrupted, thankfully, when an older man approaches us.

"Hi there, Mr. Muñoz," Dee says. "How are you?"

"I'm very well and looking forward to my favorite dinner of the week." He speaks to all of us, but his focus is on Abuela. "Will you join me, Marlene?"

"No, I will not join you. As you know, I work on Saturday nights. And you know this because I tell you the same thing every Saturday night when you ask me to join you."

He smiles as if she didn't just cut him off at the knees. "Can't blame a man for wanting to share his dinner with a beautiful woman. I'll see you inside. Dee, I'll look forward to seeing you next weekend."

"See you then, Mr. Muñoz. Sofia will take good care of you tonight."

"Have a lovely evening."

After he walks away, Dee pounces. "What's that about, Abuela?"

"That is about nothing. He's a shameless flirt and old fool who can't take no for an answer."

"He *likes* you, Abuela."

"Pish." She waves her hand dismissively. "Who has the time for his nonsense? I'm going to work." She stomps off toward the back door and lets it slam shut behind her.

"Methinks she protesteth too much," Nona says.

"Shakespeare," I say before I think about whether I should.

"Mr. Muñoz is in love with her, and she knows it," Nona tells me. "He comes in every week just to see her. He sits in C32 on her side of the house and orders a different entrée every week, so he has something to talk to her about. He's delightful, but she doesn't give him the time of day."

"How have I never noticed this?" Dee asks.

"You usually work on my side of the house."

"That's true. How long has he been coming in?"

"About four years, since a year after his wife died," Nona says. "And he asks her every week to eat with him. Vincent tells her she ought to cut the guy a break, but she never does."

"Aww, that's so sad."

"I agree, but I've learned to avoid that topic with her. She gets madder than a wet hen over it. I think that means she likes him, too, but is scared to take a chance."

"We need to give her a push," Dee says.

"Just leave me out of that," Nona says. "I worry she's going to make good on her threat to stab me in my sleep one of these days."

Dee laughs and hugs her grandmother. "You two are hilarious. You'd take a bullet for each other, but all you do is fight."

"She's a pain in my ass, but I love her."

"And she loves you, too. I'll see you tomorrow?"

"You will. I hope you and your handsome young man have a very nice evening." She waggles her brows for emphasis.

"Hush," Dee says, her cheeks flaming with color that has me instantly aroused.

That's not a good idea with her sharp-eyed grandmother watching. I get busy stashing the bags containing our dinner in the back seat of Dee's car. When I turn back, her grandmother is hugging her and whispering something in her ear that adds to Dee's embarrassment.

"Go to work, Nona."

"Love you, honey. See you at brunch."

"Love you, too."

I hold the passenger door for her. "FYI, embarrassed Dee is sexy Dee. Actually, all Dees are sexy Dees."

She covers her face with her hands. "Stop."

"Never." I lean in, nudge her hands out of the way and kiss the peach hue of her cheek. "You're adorable."

"She is incorrigible."

"What'd she say?"

"I can't repeat it. It's scandalous."

Laughing, I close her door and go around to the driver's side. After I've put on my seat belt, I turn to find her watching me. "What'd she say?"

"That she hopes I'm taking you home to bed before someone else does."

I howl with laughter.

"My freaking *grandmother*."

"I love her."

"She's crazy. They're all crazy."

"Nah, they're funny."

She pulls her phone out of her bag. "I can't believe I haven't even checked on my parents today. Do you mind if I give them a quick call?"

"Of course not. Do your thing."

Dee puts through the call on the car's Bluetooth.

"Hi, honey," her dad says. "How're you doing?"

"I'm fine. I heard Mommy had some trouble with her port. Is she okay?"

"She seems fine, but she's got some redness around it that Maria said could be the start of an infection. She's watching it."

"I heard you got a special delivery from the restaurant."

"We did! That was a nice surprise."

"I thought Nico was bringing dinner tonight."

"He was, but Nona called him and told him they were doing it. Everyone has been so good to us."

Her dad sounds a little tearful, which is so sweet.

"What've you been up to?"

"I took a friend out fishing from Black Point. Everyone there says hello."

"Ah, that's lovely. I miss seeing them. We need to get back out there soon."

"We will. Are you guys coming to brunch?"

"That's the plan. We'll see how your mother feels in the morning. She's in the shower now, or I'd let you say hello."

"Tell her I called, and I love her."

"I will, honey. Thanks for checking in."

When Dee ends that call, she puts through another to her sister. "Hey, what's up with Mommy and the port?"

"It's a little red around the edges and causing her some discomfort. I treated it with antibiotic ointment and have a call into her doctor."

"Do we need to be worried?"

"Not at the moment."

"Okay, good. Thank God for you, sister. What would we do without you?"

"Aw, you're sweet. Where've you been all day?"

"I, uh, took Wyatt fishing."

"That sounds fun."

"It was. I have to run. He's waiting for me to tell him how to get to my place."

"Don't let me get in the way of that. Have a good time. I'll see you tomorrow?"

"Yes, you will."

After she ends the call, I tell her, "I hate to say it, but I need to run by Jay's and get my stuff. I need my meds."

"That's no problem." She directs me where to go, and I realize we're backtracking.

"Sorry, I should've said something before the restaurant. Blame it on not knowing the lay of the land."

"No worries." She yawns and puts her head back against the seat. "I'll be lucky to last until eight tonight."

"I'll make sure you get a good night's sleep."

"And I'll make sure you get one, too."

We hold hands on the way to Brickell. My mouth is watering from the smell of the food. "I'm not sure what Carmen and Jason are up to, but if you want, we can eat on their patio. The view is amazing."

"I'll text her to see if they mind." She taps away on her phone. "She says they already ate, so feel free to use their patio and table."

"Excellent. I'm starving."

"I'm starting to realize that's a common theme with you."

"There's never a time when I couldn't eat. The people I work with in Phoenix call me Tapeworm. They like to bring in food for me and then get pissed because I never gain a pound."

"That's irritating."

"I can't help that my metabolism is spectacular." I glance over at her. "You want to hear something crazy?"

"Uh, sure?"

"The being-hungry-all-the-time thing started after I got my new heart. I later found out that Emma, the girl it came from, was always hungry, too. She was known for that—and she, too, never gained a pound."

"Wow."

"Right? It does happen in some cases. I've heard of others who've reported similar things, such as a woman who never liked coffee until she got the heart of a coffee drinker."

"Wow. That's so cool. It must've strange to hear Emma was always hungry."

"I was! At first, we thought it was because I was healthy again, and my appetite was rebounding along with the rest of my health. But when I connected with her mother, and she told me that…"

"It's really amazing. Emma is alive in you."

"That's how it seems. There are other weird things besides that. Like I used to hate peanut butter, and now I love it. She did, too."

"My mind is truly blown by this."

"Mine was, too. It took a long time to wrap my head around the magnitude of someone else having to die so I could live. I had a lot of guilt—and therapy—about that."

"Did the therapy help?"

"It did. The therapist helped me accept that Emma was going to die whether I got her heart or not, and her death wasn't my fault."

"That's some heavy stuff for a seventeen-year-old to deal with."

"Yeah, I was messed up about it for a while. It helped to meet her family and to hear more about her."

"What happened to her?"

"She was in a skiing accident. She crashed into a tree and suffered a severe head injury."

"That's so sad."

"It was, but she saved the lives of five people with her

organs. Her family took great comfort in it. They said she would've loved that."

"I find myself feeling sad for someone I've never known."

"I felt that way for a long time after the transplant. All I knew at first was that it had come from a nineteen-year-old woman, so I had these visions at first of her trying to get used to living inside a seventeen-year-old boy."

"That'd make for a cool movie."

"My sister has always said the same thing."

I park outside of Jay's building and bring the food with me when we get out of the car. They buzz us into the building. In the elevator, I look over at Dee. Her face is radiant from the day in the sun, but her eyes are tired. We both need some sleep before too much longer. "Don't let Carmen talk you out of this." After spending today "all in" with her, I'm terrified of her changing her mind. I've had a taste of what it would be like to be in love, and I'm already addicted.

She looks me square in the eyes. "No chance of that."

Carmen is waiting in the doorway of their condo when we come off the elevator. I don't know her very well, but even I can see she looks worried and stressed. That's probably my fault. I hope Dee meant it when she said no one could talk her out of being with me. I have a feeling if anyone could, it's probably Carmen or Maria.

Dee kisses Carmen's cheek. "Cut it out. Everything is fine. Stop doing that thing with your eyebrows."

"What's wrong with my eyebrows?"

"They're all furrowy."

"That's not a word."

"And yet, you know what I mean."

"Where's Jay?" I ask her.

"Out for a run. He should be back soon."

"Come on, Wyatt. Let's eat." Dee grabs silverware and a

wineglass from Carmen's kitchen and leads me to the patio. "Come hang with us, Car, but no furrowing."

I love the way she's right at home in her cousin's place and that they speak so freely to each other. I've never achieved that easy closeness with my siblings—or anyone. Probably because I was absent for big chunks of our childhood, and when I was home, I sucked up all the parental attention. I don't know if either of them resents me for the chaos my illness caused for all of us, but how can they not? I probably would if I were them.

Carmen pours herself a glass of wine from a bottle she already had going and comes out to sit with us.

"Let's air it out," I say to her between bites of the best-tasting chicken I've ever had.

Dee's eyes widen as she looks at me as if I'm crazy. Maybe I am, but I can't bear for my friend's wife to think I'm going to hurt her precious cousin. She needs to know that's the last thing I'd ever want.

"I understand you're worried about Dee getting involved with me in light of what you now know about me."

Carmen wasn't expecting me to put it right out there, but I figure I have everything to gain and nothing to lose by confronting the elephant in the room. Dee wasn't expecting it, either, but that's okay. I want her to relax and enjoy what's happening between us and not be upset by her family's concerns.

"I, uh…" Carmen takes a sip of her wine. "I don't want Dee to get hurt again. The first time was more than enough."

"I'm fine." Dee spins pasta like a pro. "Nothing to see here."

Carmen's brow goes from furrowed to raised. "Really?"

"As Jason has told you, I had a heart transplant seventeen years ago. I'm six years past the average life expectancy, but you should know I'm perfectly healthy. I undergo regular checkups, and I take fanatically good care of myself. All that said, I tried to tell Dee I'm a bad bet, but she refuses to listen to reason." I glance her way and find her smiling like a fool. God, I already love her. How can I not?

"I want Wyatt to know what it's like to be in love. I want to spend the rest of his life with him, and there's nothing anyone can say to talk me out of that, so let's not waste our time going on about all the ways this can go wrong and focus on the many ways it's so, *so* right."

"But you only met at the wedding… How can you know this is what you want?"

"We slept together after the wedding," Dee says matter-of-factly. "It was the best night of my life."

Carmen chokes on her wine.

I pat her on the back until she catches her breath.

"What the hell, Delores? Why didn't you tell us?"

"Tell us what?" Jason asks when he joins us on the patio, sweaty from his run.

"They slept together after the wedding!" Carmen tells her husband.

"And it was the best night of my life," Dee says.

I lean in to kiss her. "And mine."

Jason seems as stunned by this news as Carmen was. "Wow, how'd you keep that secret in this family?"

Dee shrugs and continues to spin her pasta as if nothing special is happening. "I just didn't tell anyone."

"So you've been, like, talking all this time?"

"We've kept in touch," Dee says.

I can tell her nonchalance is driving Carmen crazy. She turns her laser beam focus on me. "That's why you're interviewing for a job at Miami-Dade. You came back for Dee."

"I wanted to see her again, but I didn't come here thinking any of this was going to happen."

"He told me he couldn't get involved, and when I found out why, I told him that's bullshit, and here we are. Involved."

"Dee…" The single word from Carmen drips with agonized concern.

I don't blame her. I really don't. Didn't I have the same concerns twenty-four hours ago, before Dee blew my mind with her courage and her determination? That seems like a lifetime ago after the day we've spent together, in which everything changed.

"I know what you're going to say, Car, and I fully understand what I'm getting into. I know Wyatt may not live to be an old man, and I'm choosing to care about him anyway." She pauses before she adds, "Wait. That's not exactly true."

"It's not?" I ask her, surprised.

"I'm choosing to *love* you, not just care about you."

Carmen gasps. "But you… you've seen him twice."

"How soon did you know that Jason was going to change your life?" Dee asks her cousin.

"I… uh…"

"You told me you knew the day you met him that he was different from everyone else. I knew at your rehearsal dinner that Wyatt was special, and I wanted to spend more time with him. We were together all day at your wedding. He never left my side except to get me another drink. We had the best time I've ever had with any man. And when he asked me to come back to his hotel room, I never hesitated. Did I suspect then that it was going to be more than one night? Nope, but then he texted me, and I texted him, and he came back, and here we are."

"Yesterday, you were crying over Marcus," Carmen says.

Oh, low blow.

"I was crying because I thought he tried to take his own life because of me, not because I still love him. Any love I felt for him died the day he married the skank."

"So, what's the plan?" Jason asks, drinking from a bottle of water.

"We're hoping I get the job at Miami-Dade." I reach for Dee's hand, and she links her fingers with mine. "And if I do, I'm going to move here and live happily ever after with Dee."

"Just like that?" Jason asks.

"Just like that," Dee says, her gaze never wavering from mine.

"What if you don't get the job?" Carmen asks.

"Then we'll figure out a plan B," Dee says. "Either way, we're going to be together from now on, and that's the end of it."

I can tell Carmen has a lot she wants to say to that, but she isn't sure where to start.

Before she can formulate a thought, Dee says, "Imagine it was Jason who'd been through what Wyatt has. Would you love him any less simply because his life might be shorter than ours?"

"No, but—"

"No buts, Carmen. This is happening, and I'm asking for your support."

"You have it. It's just that…"

"I know," Dee says softly. "But I promise that no matter what happens, I'll be okay." She reaches for Carmen and hugs her. "Be happy for me."

"I am. Of course, I am."

They hug for a long time, and both are teary-eyed when they pull back from each other.

"Can we go?" Dee asks me. "I'm so tired that I'm about to fall over."

"Let me just grab my stuff." I carry our takeout containers inside, rinse them out and put them in the trash. I'm pleased that Giordino's uses paper rather than plastic for takeout. Having that thought buys me a second to collect myself before I have to face off with Jason, who's followed me inside.

"What happened to your rules?"

"Dee happened. I'm going to make it so worthwhile for her, Jay. I promise. And afterward, she'll have all of you to lean on. You'll get her through it, right?"

He runs his fingers through sweaty hair. "Jesus, Wyatt, are we talking about us taking care of Dee after you die?"

"Yeah, I guess we are. I need to know you'll be there for her."

"Of course I would, but this is a lot to process. I'm just finding out about what happened after the wedding. I had no idea it was more than a bridesmaid hanging out with a groomsman."

"It was much more than that from the minute we met."

"So you said."

"I know it's a lot to wrap your head around, but I'm going to take excellent care of her in every possible way. We're going to live the hell out of whatever's left of my life."

"Sounds like a plan."

"You don't approve?"

"It's not about whether I approve. It's just that you had rules that you lived by for seventeen years, and now you've decided to say fuck the rules, and you're doing it with my wife's cousin."

"I'm sorry if this causes trouble for you, Jay. I really am, but I already love her. And I want this. I want her. I want a chance to have what you have with Carmen for however long it lasts. You can understand that, can't you?"

"I get it."

"Well, then, I guess I'll grab my stuff and get out of your hair. See you tomorrow at brunch?"

"We'll be there."

I decide to get out while the getting is good. In the living room, I grab my backpack and roll my suitcase to the door as Dee and Carmen come in from the patio carrying wineglasses and what's left of Dee's bottle of wine.

"Thanks for letting us borrow your patio," I say to Carmen.

"Anytime." She surprises me when she hugs me. "Take good care of my cousin. I love her very much."

"So do I, and I will. I promise to make her happy every day I get to spend with her."

When Carmen releases me, I notice tears in her eyes.

Dee hugs her. "See you tomorrow."

We walk to the elevator and wait for it to arrive.

"Are you okay?" I ask her.

She nods, but her chin is wobbling. I'm not sure if it's emotion or exhaustion or both that has her on the verge of a meltdown.

I put my arm around her. "Hold on to me. We've got this."

Inside the elevator, she wraps her arms around me and holds on for the ride to the ground floor.

Outside, I stash my suitcase and backpack in the trunk and get in the driver's side. "Did she say something to upset you?"

"No, just that she loves me and doesn't want anything ever to hurt me the way Marcus did."

"I'd never hurt you like that."

"No, you wouldn't." After a pause, she looks over at me, her expression full of trepidation. "She's probably already on the phone with my sister. The whole family will know by tomorrow. I'm sorry. I know you don't like for people to know."

"It's okay. It's not something we can keep secret in a family like yours. I don't care if they know."

"They're going to make a BFD out of it—at first—but that'll blow over. Eventually. I apologize in advance for that."

"They love you. They're worried. I get it." I can feel my phone vibrating nonstop in my pocket, which can mean only one thing. My mother is freaking out that she hasn't heard from me today. I pull it out of my pocket and hand it to Dee. "Can you check my texts?" She may as well find out now that when I tell her my mother hovers, I mean it.

"Your mom is worried that she hasn't heard from you today. Should I reply for you?"

"Yes, tell her I was out fishing all day and didn't have service. All is well."

She types in the message for me. "She wants to know if you're taking your meds."

I grit my teeth against the urge to scream. "Tell her of course I am because I want to stay alive."

"You want me to say that?"

"It's okay. I say that to her just about every day when she reminds me, a *doctor*, to take my meds the way she did when I was a teenager."

She sends the text. "Your mother says to quit being fresh."

"And she says that back to me just about every day. Welcome to my world."

"She sounds sweet."

"She's the best, and I love her, but sometimes I wish she loved me just a *tiny* bit less than she does."

"What will she say if you get the job here and move?"

"My parents will lose their shit," I say with a deep sigh. "But that won't stop me from moving, so don't worry about it."

"We'll have to assure them that I'll take outstanding care of you."

"You can't hover, sweetheart. That'll drive me crazy."

"Who said anything about hovering?"

CHAPTER 11

DEE

I'm *so* going to hover. How can I not? I'll want to know all the time that he's okay, that he's healthy, that he's taking his meds, that...

Oh my God, he'll hate that, and I need to get it under control quickly. I take a deep breath and blow it out as it occurs to me that anxiety over his health will be my constant companion, the way it's been since my mom's diagnosis.

"You don't need to do that," he says.

"What am I doing?"

"Realizing that worrying about me is going to be a full-time job. I don't need you to do that. I promise you I'm on it every single day. I don't want you to worry."

"That's easier said than done, but I'll do my best not to make you feel like you've gone all-in with your mother." Those words are no sooner out of my mouth when we're crippled with laughter. "That came out wrong."

"Ya think?"

"Blame it on exhaustion. I'm not firing on all cylinders."

"You're adorable when you're exhausted—and even when you're not. You're adorable all the time."

"I'm glad you think so."

"I do. I also think you're sexy, beautiful, funny, smart, and did I mention sexy?"

"I think you did, but a girl can never have too much sexy." Did I really say that, too? "I need to shut up until I sleep."

"Oh please, keep talking. I can't wait to hear what's next."

I direct him through the neighborhood to my apartment over the garage.

"If I get the job, we're going to need a bigger place."

"I'm going to require sleep before I have that conversation. Probably caffeine, too."

"Got it. We'll table that until tomorrow, then."

Inside, I head right for the shower. "Care to join me?" I ask him.

"Hell yes."

When we're standing face-to-face in the shower, I take the time to study the tattoo that spans his chest. Now that I know it's there, I see the faint scar that runs vertically between his pectorals. I trace it with my fingertip. "Was it painful?"

"Pretty brutal at first, but I healed quickly."

I kiss the faint scar from top to bottom. "I wish I could've been there to help nurse you back to health."

"Would you have worn a sexy-nurse costume?"

"No, because everyone knows it's not good to mess with the patient's blood pressure after major surgery."

His low laughter makes me smile. "Everyone knows that, do they?"

"Uh-huh. That's right, isn't it?"

"Yep, and having you around would've seriously tested my fragile cardiovascular system." He takes my hand and wraps it around his thick erection. "Case in point."

"This feels like a critical cardiovascular concern."

"It's very critical." He puts his arms around me and kisses me until I'm clinging to him, all thoughts of exhaustion and sleep forgotten in a wave of desire so intense, it requires my full attention.

He lifts me and presses my back against the cool tile. "Is this okay?"

"So okay."

All the air leaves my body in a long gasp when he slides into me in one deep thrust. God, nothing has ever been like it is with him. When I think about how close I came to never knowing *this* existed... He knows just where to touch me to make me scream from the release that rips through me almost without warning. It's too much and not enough at the same time. We're still panting in the aftermath, and I'm already wondering when we can do it again.

After our shower, Wyatt towels me off, giving special attention to my breasts.

"I'm becoming obsessed," he whispers, kissing each of them. "I can't get enough of you."

At least once in every lifetime, a girl should have a boy look at her the way he looks at me right then. In that single second, he proves to me that he's worth any risk I might be taking to have whatever I can with him. I place my hands on his chest and place a kiss on his breastbone. When I look up at him, his eyes are heated and glassy with unshed tears.

"You're beautiful, strong, sweet and sexy. And the only reason I had any interest in coming to Miami to interview for that job was so I'd have the chance to see you again." He kisses me, and I cling to him as our previously sizzling connection becomes positively incendiary in light of his confession.

With my arms around his neck, I cling to him as his tongue tangles with mine. We kiss for what feels like hours before he hooks an arm around my waist and lifts me right off my feet. I want to tell him not to do that, not to strain himself or take risks, but I'm already sure that wouldn't be something he'd want to hear.

Wyatt puts me on the bed and comes down on top of me, all without missing a beat in the kiss to end all kisses. He breaks the kiss only long enough to remove both our towels before recapturing my lips in another tongue-twisting duel for the ages. No one has ever kissed me this way, as if my life and his depend upon it. We hold each other so tightly that it's a wonder either of us can breathe. There's needy desperation to this kiss that hasn't been there before he told me his truth.

In the throes of life-changing desire, it occurs to me that shortly after finding out he could die young, I feel *more* than I ever have in my life. I want to give him everything I can for whatever time he has left, even if I'm well aware that road may lead to ruin for me. I can't find it in me to care about what might happen to me.

All I want is to give him everything I've got for as long as I possibly can.

CHAPTER 12

DEE

I'm nervous at brunch the next day. My uncle wants to talk to me. He says it's nothing big, but it's odd for him to ask for a minute alone with me. I'm also anxious because my parents didn't come to brunch. Mom has a 102-degree fever, and Maria is concerned the port might be infected. She's waiting for a call from the doctor, but my parents encouraged her, Austin and Everly to come to brunch.

In addition to all that, the word is out about me, Wyatt and his heart transplant. I can tell because everyone is acting weird, which I can't stand.

We're on Nona's side of the house today, and Wyatt raves about the eggplant. I'm sure it's great, but I can barely taste anything from being so wound up about everything.

"Why are you so tense?" he asks.

"Just everything."

"Do you want me to check on your mom after brunch?"

"Would you?"

"Of course I would. I'd be happy to."

"That'd be great. Thank you." I already feel better knowing a doctor will examine my mom today, rather than another doctor making educated guesses over the phone. "I just have the thing with my uncle, but that shouldn't take long."

"I'm with you, sweetheart. Whatever you need to do is fine with me."

On our second full day together, it already feels like we've been a couple much longer. Maybe that's because we skipped all the preliminary bullshit and went straight to fully committed within a few life-changing hours. I have to say that there's something to be said for cutting out the bullshit and getting right to the heart of the matter—no pun intended. After sleeping in his arms last night, I know where I want to be every night for as long as I possibly can.

Under the table, I squeeze his hand. "I'm so happy you're here with me."

"I'm thrilled to be here. I love your family."

"I do, too, even when they're staring at my new boyfriend and me and wanting me to stand and give a speech about all the details they're dying to know."

"Is that what they want? Well, that's easy enough." He releases my hand, stands and taps his knife against a wineglass full of water. When the room falls quiet, he says, "Hi, everyone. I'm Wyatt, and you probably remember me from Jason and Carmen's wedding, which is where I met the amazing, beautiful bridesmaid named Dee Giordino. She and I have kept in close touch since the wedding, and when I had a chance to apply for a job here in Miami, I jumped on it. My interview is tomorrow. Keep your fingers crossed I get the job because Dee and I have decided to take the plunge and be together from now on."

My family listens to him in stunned disbelief that they're getting the scoop on us without having to dig for details. That never happens. My siblings, cousins and I have made a blood sport out of making them wonder what we're doing.

"I know the word is out about my medical situation, but for those who haven't heard, the gist is I had a heart transplant seventeen years ago when I was seventeen. By that time, I'd spent nine years battling cardiomyopathy, which came on suddenly when I was eight. After the transplant, I was truly reborn, and my health has been excellent ever since. I'm hoping it'll stay that way for many years to come, but the fact of the matter is, I've already exceeded the average life expectancy for a heart transplant patient by six years. I've never had any kind of life-threatening issue or any sign of rejection."

He looks down at me with his heart in his eyes. "I also know how much you all love Dee, and I certainly understand why. I love her, too. She's convinced me to abandon all my rules about not getting romantically involved with anyone and go all-in with her. If you're concerned about what she may be getting into with me, I promise you I'll do everything I can to make her as happy as we both are today for as long as I possibly can. If the worst possible thing happens, I hope I can count on all of you to be there for her when I can't be. And, ah, that's all I wanted to say."

Through my tears, I see Maria, Carmen, my aunts Vivian and Francesca, as well as Abuela and Nona tending to their tears.

Nona leads a round of applause for Wyatt. "Welcome to our family, Wyatt. You're right—we love our Dee very much, and it's obvious to us that you two share something special. If there's one thing I've learned in my life, it's that today is all we have. I hope you and Dee will be very happy together, and you have our word that, should the time come, we'll take very good care of her if you're not able to."

"Thank you, Nona," I say softly. To Wyatt, I add, "I can't believe you did that. You're amazing."

"They needed to know how I feel and that I'm going to make you happy."

"That means everything to them." I notice my brother Nico watching me with an odd look on his face. "What's up, Nico?"

"Everyone's so happy for you," he says. "I want to be happy, but Jesus, Dee." His gaze shifts to Wyatt, who's talking to Nona and Abuela. "The guy is like a ticking time bomb."

Thankfully, the seats between us are empty at the moment, so we can have this fight in relative privacy. "No, he isn't. He's in better health than you are."

"Right now, maybe. Look, I know it's not what you want to hear, but I think you're crazy to take a chance like this."

"Thanks for your input."

"Dee, come on. What would you say to me if I was the one telling you I was getting involved with someone who had a looming expiration date?"

"I'd tell you to be thankful to have found someone to love and who loves you and to be grateful for every second you have with her. Look at what happened to Carmen when Tony went to work one day as a perfectly healthy twenty-four-year-old and never came home. Do you think she regrets the time she spent with him because of how it ended?"

"She doesn't, but still… It's different going into it, knowing it probably won't last."

"Let me tell you something, Nico. I spent *years* with the wrong man, and you know how I know that? Because I found the right one. I'll take whatever time I can get with him and be thankful for every second of it. I appreciate your concern, but frankly, I don't want to hear it."

Maria approaches us. "Um, what are you guys fighting about?"

"Nico doesn't approve of me being with Wyatt."

"I never said that. I said I'm worried about you taking on something like this." He softens his tone. "None of us want to see you hurt again, Dee."

"And I appreciate that. I really do. I know what I'm getting

137

myself into, and I feel very good about it. I just want you to be happy for me. Can you do that?"

"I'll work on it." He glances toward Wyatt, who's laughing at something Uncle V is telling him. "He seems like a nice enough guy."

"He's a great guy. If he weren't, I wouldn't care the way I do."

"You've said your piece," Maria tells our brother. "Let it go now."

Nico holds up his hands. "Don't hate on me for caring."

"No one is hating on you," I say. "But I don't want to talk about gloom and doom today. I'm happy. Oh, and Wyatt offered to take a look at Mommy's port after this."

"That'd be great," Maria says. "I could use another opinion."

"Uncle V wants to talk to me before I leave, and then we'll head over there."

"What's up with Uncle V?" Maria asks.

"No clue." We watch as Nico goes to talk to Sofia, who smiles like I've never seen her smile when he says something to her. "What's up there?"

"I have no idea, but he'd better not be messing with her."

We've all become protective of Sofia and her son. It was Nona's idea to hire her to work at the restaurant, and she and Abuela have taken the young single mother under their formidable wings ever since.

"Let's keep an eye on that," I say to Maria. We love our brother, but because of the trail of broken hearts he's left in his wake, we don't always have faith in him to do the right thing when it comes to women. There's no way we'll let Sofia end up on that ignoble list.

When I see Uncle V heading toward the bar, I decide to follow him, hoping we can talk about whatever's on his mind so I can get on with my day with Wyatt. "I'll be back in a few," I tell Wyatt.

"Take your time."

While the rest of the family starts to leave, I take a seat at the bar.

Uncle V pours me ice water and tops it with a lemon. "Thanks for sticking around."

"Sure. What's up?"

"I've been thinking. Well, Viv and I have been thinking, I should say."

"What about?"

"Retirement."

"Seriously?" If you'd asked me to bet on what he might want to tell me, that wouldn't have made the top one hundred.

"Ever since your mom got sick, it's been a big wake-up call to us that we've become all work and no play. We've got stuff we want to do, places to see... Carmen has no interest in the business. We've known that for quite some time, and it's fine. She needs to follow her path, but we've decided we want to hire someone to be our general manager so we can take some time off and leave the business with someone we trust. That way, we can enjoy ourselves."

"That sounds like a great idea." I can't imagine why he's telling me this. Does he want my advice on who to hire?

"When we got to seriously talking about who we might hire, we kept coming back to you."

"*Me?*" I must be looking at him like I think he's crazy. "Why me?"

"You have a business degree and worked for years as an office manager—"

"That's not the same thing as running a restaurant of this magnitude."

"It's management experience. It's supervisory experience. We can teach you the rest of what you need to know. We plan to hire someone now and start taking a step back in six months or so. If you want the job, it's yours." He recites a six-figure salary that has my mouth hanging open in shock and then sweetens the deal with three weeks of paid vacation, a 401(k) and health insurance. "I'm not joking, Dee. We need someone we can trust, and we're offering it to you."

My aunt Vivian joins him behind the bar. "Judging by the shell-shocked look on Dee's face, I take it you've shared our idea with her."

Vincent puts his arm around his wife. "I have, and she's indeed shell-shocked."

I'm also on the verge of tears. That they'd think of me for something like this is beyond overwhelming. "You guys... I have no idea what to say. I'm so honored that you think I'd be capable of this."

"It's not just us, honey," Viv says. "Nona and Abuela also think it's a brilliant idea. You've worked here on and off since you were fifteen. You know the customers, the routine, the menu, the culture of the place. You're perfect."

"I'm speechless. When you said you wanted to talk to me, I never imagined this." As I swipe at a stray tear, I can't find the words to tell my aunt and uncle what this means to me.

"If you need some time to think about it, we'd certainly understand," Uncle Vincent says.

"No, I don't need time to think about it," I say, laughing. "I'd be so honored to be your general manager, to run your business for you so you can take some time to enjoy yourselves." I get up from the stool and go around the bar to hug them both. "You have no idea how badly I needed this. Thank you, and I promise you'll never be sorry you asked me."

"We know we won't, honey," Vincent says as he pulls back from me. "You were the only one we considered. We're relieved you said yes because we didn't have a plan B."

"What did she say?" Nona asks as she, Abuela, Carmen, Jason, Maria, Austin, Everly and Wyatt come into the bar area.

"She said yes!" Vincent says with a fist pump.

Excited family members hug and congratulate me.

"What am I missing?" Wyatt asks when he's finally able to break through the group and get to me.

"My aunt and uncle offered me a fabulous opportunity to be the restaurant's general manager."

"Wow!" His face lights up with pleasure. "That's fantastic. Congratulations, honey." He hugs me tightly. "I'm so happy for you."

"Thank you. I'll be happy for me when the shock wears off."

Carmen hugs me. "You'll be great. When Mom and Dad told me what they were thinking, I couldn't have been more excited for them or you."

"Thank you so much for trusting me with this." I'm well aware that this place is her legacy, even if we all feel like it belongs to us.

She's been after her parents for a while now to work less and play more.

Vincent pours flutes of champagne for everyone. "You know what this means, ladies," he says to Nona and Abuela. "We made a deal."

"What deal?" Carmen asks.

"When we told Abuela and Nona our plan to ask Dee to be the general manager, we got them to agree that if Dee said yes to our offer, they'd also take more time off to do the things they've been too busy to do."

"I have no idea what to do with myself if I'm not working," Abuela says, frowning.

"It's high time you figured that out, don't you think?" Carmen asks her.

Abuela shrugs, seeming sad. We'll rally around her and try to help her figure out some things she can do outside of work.

"Maybe it's time to say yes to poor Mr. Muñoz in C32," I suggest.

"Bite your tongue," Abuela snaps as the rest of us crack up. "The last thing I need is an old man to take care of."

"Maybe he would take care of you," Carmen says.

Abuela dismisses the topic with a fierce scowl. "Pish."

"What about you, Nona?" Maria asks.

"I'm signing up for flying lessons."

Vincent stares at his mother. "What did you just say?"

"You heard me. I've always wanted to learn to fly, and if I'm going to have more time off, that's what I want to do."

"Now, wait just a minute," Vincent sputters.

We laugh at his reaction.

Nona gives her son a defiant look. "You're not the boss of me, but you *are* the one saying we need to live more and work less. I've already looked into it, and there's a great flight school at MIA. I've got a call into them."

"I hate to ask this," Jason says tentatively, "but is it possible you might be past the age where you can be licensed?"

Nona gives him her most withering look. "Are you saying I'm old, young man?"

He swallows hard. "Not at all, ma'am."

Laughing, she says, "There's no age limit on private pilots, as long as my vision checks out and I have all my faculties, which I certainly do. My father was a pilot, and we'd always planned for him to teach me, but he died before he could. I'm closing that circle. I'm doing it for him."

"That's amazing, Nona," Carmen says. "I'm so excited for you. Isn't it awesome, Dad?"

Vincent frowns but gives a subtle nod. "I'd feel better knowing you won't be up there by yourself, Mama."

"Don't worry about me. I'll be *just* fine."

She seems so delighted with her plan that I can't help but be happy for her.

"I may even give sky-diving a try while I'm at the airport."

"*Nona!*"

She bursts into laughter, thrilled to have gotten a rise out of us.

Carmen, Maria and I end up off to the side of the others by ourselves.

"What do you guys hear about Marcus?" I keep my voice down so no one can overhear me.

"I heard he checked himself into rehab for thirty days," Maria whispers.

I'm shocked to hear that. "What kind of rehab?"

"Alcohol."

"Seriously? Since when?"

"From what I heard from two other people, for a while now. He was blackout drunk when he married *her* and has no memory of any of it."

"Come on," Carmen says. "Is that the truth or what he wants people to believe?"

"I did a little more digging around and heard from two of his close friends that he's been a mess with booze for quite some time."

I'm shocked. "How did I not know this?"

"You'd been living apart for a long time," Maria reminds me.

"Still, he came to New York and spent days with me, and I never saw him drink like that."

"He probably made an effort to keep it under control in front of you, and it's not like his friends were going to report to you about what was going on down here while you were in New York."

"Me staying in New York when he moved home screwed up everything."

"Don't go there," Carmen says fiercely. "Maybe it put some added stress on him, but it's not your fault he's an alcoholic."

That may be true, but I feel sick hearing this. I notice Nico talking to Sofia at one of the waitress stations. He's smiling, and her face is flushed as if she's overheated or embarrassed. Knowing Nico, it's probably the latter. I nudge Maria and use my chin to point her attention toward them. "What's he up to?"

"I don't know, but I don't like it."

"I don't, either," Carmen says when she tunes in to what we're discussing. "Sofia is a sweetheart. I'd hate to see him play his games with her, of all people."

"I'll talk to him," Carmen says. "It'll go better coming from me. I'm not his sister."

"Let us know what he says."

"What if..." Maria's unfinished question hangs in the air.

"What if what?" I ask her.

"What if she's really into him and is encouraging his attention?"

"If she's into him, she doesn't know him well enough to make that decision." I feel immediately guilty for the harsh words about my brother, but his track record with women is awful. "And yes, I feel terrible saying that out loud."

"It's the truth," Maria says bluntly. "I wouldn't fix him up with my worst enemy."

"Maybe we can fix him up with the skank to get him away from Sofia," Carmen says, and the three of us lose it laughing. We laugh so hard that we have to hold each other up.

When we finally calm down, I find Wyatt watching me with the sweetest look on his face, as if it makes him happy to see me having a good time.

We leave the restaurant a short time later and head to my parents' home to share our news with them and, if my mom is amenable, have him take a look at the chemo port that's giving her trouble. I'm nervous about them hearing his story, although, knowing my family, they probably already know all about him. I'm sure one of my aunts called them after brunch to fill them in on the goings-on.

"My parents might already know everything." We're at a red light on Calle Ocho. "News travels fast in our family."

He squeezes my hand. "I'm ready for them. Don't worry."

I love how he always wants to be touching me, even if we're just driving somewhere together.

"Any thoughts on the possibility of coming to Phoenix and driving back with me?"

"I'd love to. My uncle and I agreed I'd start next month. He said they need some time to get a few things figured out on their end, but we're going to start training this week."

"That works since I'd have to give a couple of weeks' notice to my current job. Can you get coverage for your shifts at the restaurant so you can come with me?"

"I won't be able to leave the same day you do, but I'll make it so I can come there later so I can help you pack and drive back with you."

"That means a couple of weeks with no Dee. How am I supposed to deal with that?"

"We can FaceTime every day."

"I guess. See what you've done to me in three days? The thought of being without you for even two weeks sends me into a deep, dark depression."

"Stop being dramatic," I say, laughing even as he sets my heart to racing with his sweet words.

"I'm not dramatic. I mean it. I'll miss you."

"I'll miss you, too. Hopefully, it won't be for long."

"I'm probably jinxing myself by making plans as if I've already got the job."

"You'll get it. They'd be crazy not to hire you."

"They may have the same concerns you do about my expiration date. I'm under no illusions that they haven't already discovered I'm a transplant recipient."

"I have no concerns whatsoever about your expiration date. I happen to believe you're going to live to be a cranky old man who drives me crazy chasing me around the house trying to get lucky."

"Will you still want to be caught when I'm old and crotchety?"

"Hell yes."

"You give me hope it might happen."

"We just have to believe. My mom has been reading a lot of self-help stuff since she got sick, and the one thing she's always telling us is that we have to stay positive, that an optimistic mindset is as critical as the medical treatment she's receiving."

"She's right. I see that a lot in my practice. Patients who stay positive and keep fighting tend to be the ones who live the longest. It makes a big difference." He pauses before he adds, "I appreciate that you have such a strong belief that everything will be okay as long as we stay positive."

I take my eyes off the road to glance over at him. "But?"

"The odds are what they are, no matter how much faith we have in miracles. We need to stay positive, but keep it real at the same time."

"We can do that, can't we?"

"We can certainly try."

"I refuse to obsess over what *might* happen sometime far off in the future."

"That makes you a unique woman, love."

"I am rather unique, and did you hear I'm going to be the general manager of one of the most popular restaurants in Miami?"

"I did get that memo, and I couldn't be prouder of you."

"I have no idea what I'm doing, but Vincent and Viv told me they'd teach me everything I need to know, and of course, they'll always be available if I need them. It's just so crazy that they asked me."

"No, it isn't. They see something in you they need, and not just family loyalty, but a practical, no-nonsense, get-things-done professional woman who already knows their business and can pick up the reins from them and run with it."

"Wow, you make me sound so amazing."

He kisses the back of my hand. "You *are* amazing, and everyone knows it, especially me."

"This weekend started awful and turned into one of the best of my life."

"For me, too, only it didn't start awful like yours did."

"I heard some stuff about him today." I don't even stop to wonder if I should be sharing things about my ex with him. It's so easy to talk to Wyatt about anything and everything, and it was like that from the start. We talked about so many things at the wedding, which was why I didn't hesitate to take him up on the invitation to hang out afterward.

"What kind of stuff?"

I tell him what Maria found out. "How can he be an alcoholic, and I had no idea?"

"I've heard of instances where spouses didn't know that their significant other was a secret alcoholic."

"Really? That can happen?"

"Sure it can. People go to great lengths to keep addictions hidden from their loved ones."

"I hate that he was suffering like that, and I was oblivious."

"He chose to hide it from you, Dee. There's probably nothing you could've done differently."

"I could've moved home from New York."

"Why didn't you?"

"Maria would tell you there's nowhere better than right here, and I agree with that, but I had this... I don't know how to describe it except as a burning need to get out of here and be somewhere else for a while before I settled down and got married and raised a family here. That's why I only applied to colleges in New York and Boston. Marcus and I had started dating by then, and he applied in the same places, so we could still see each other. Everyone here thought I was crazy to go so far from home, but I needed it."

"You wanted an adventure."

"Yes," I say on a sigh, relieved that he gets it. "My cousin Dom, who'd been there a year by then, made it sound like so much fun, and for him, it is because he makes bank as a sales rep for a medical supply company."

"It wasn't for you?"

"Not so much after college. Living in New York City is hard. It's insanely expensive and crowded, and even the simplest thing, like grocery shopping, is complicated. I barely made enough for my half of the rent, so I didn't get to go to all the shows I thought I'd see or the concerts or the museums. But hey, at least I can say I did it."

"That's a big accomplishment for someone so close to her family."

"I was so homesick at first. It was awful. I missed everyone so much."

"It's interesting to me that you missed them, but you didn't say you missed Marcus."

"I did. Of course, I did." Sighing, I add, "But not like I missed them."

"Interesting."

It is. I vividly remember yearning for my family, especially on Sundays when everyone would be together at brunch. While I missed Marcus after he went back to Miami, it wasn't the same way that I missed everyone else. And I never really thought about it that way until right now. I already know I'd never be content living away from Wyatt. Now that I know he exists in the world, all I want is to spend every second I can with him.

Very interesting, indeed. Maybe Marcus did us both a favor by blowing up our relationship and giving us a chance to find something better than what we had together.

When we get to my parents' house, I park behind my brother Milo's silver Toyota Highlander. "Milo's here, so you'll get to see him, too."

"Great."

He follows me inside to the kitchen. My dad and brother are at the table playing dominoes while they drink coffee. "Uncle Vin sent some leftovers." I put the boxes from the restaurant in the fridge.

"Thank you, honey," my dad says when I kiss his cheek.

"Wyatt, you remember my dad, Lorenzo, and my brother Milo from the wedding."

He shakes hands with both of them. "Good to see you again."

"You, too." My dad takes a closer look at Wyatt. "Heard you two made quite a stir at brunch."

"I told you they'd already know."

Wyatt's smile tells me he doesn't care.

"You had a heart transplant," Milo says. "That's sick."

"Not so much if you're the one getting your chest cracked open."

"Ouch," Milo says.

"Not the most fun I've ever had."

"They said…" Dad looks up at me and then at Wyatt. "That it only lasts for so long."

"That's right, but so far so good for me seventeen years in."

"Where's Mommy?" I don't wish to dissect Wyatt's situation again. We've already had enough of that for one day.

"She's in the living room watching the news."

"How's she feeling?"

"So-so," Dad says.

He looks exhausted and pale. My mother's illness is taking its toll on him, too.

"Wyatt said he'd take a look at the port for her if she wants him to. He's a doctor."

"Let's go see what she has to say."

I take one look at my mom and can tell she's got a fever. Her eyes are glassy, and her cheeks are rosy. "Mom, my friend Wyatt from Car's wedding is here. He's a doctor and said he'd be happy to take a look at the port if you want him to. Wyatt, you met my mom, Elena, at the wedding."

My mom smiles at the way I come in hot. "Hello to you, too, my sweet."

I lean in to kiss her cheek and come away alarmed by how warm she is. "Hello, Mommy."

"If your handsome doctor wants to take a look, I won't say no to that." She unbuttons her blouse and tugs it to the side so he can see her port.

"How long has it been red and puffy?" I ask her.

"Since Friday. The doctor gave me antibiotics, but they don't seem to be working."

Wyatt takes a close look at the site and then sits back to speak to her. "I think you should probably go to the ER, Elena. The port is infected, and you may need IV antibiotics."

She moans at the thought of being back in the hospital.

"Sorry to be the bearer of bad news, but you don't want to let that get out of control. Infections can be risky."

My mom's deep sigh says it all. "If you think it's that serious, then I guess that's what we'll do."

She wants to shower before she goes, so I help her through that, blinking back tears as I always do when I see the scars from her surgery as well as the weight loss, bruises and other ravages of her illness. I engage in cheerful conversation as I help her get dressed in loose-fitting sweats, always focused on keeping her spirits up, regardless of the latest setback.

"Your Wyatt is gorgeous," she whispers, even though there's no one around to hear her.

"I think so, too."

"We need to talk."

"I know, but not now, okay? Let's get you to the ER so we can figure out what's going on and get you home as soon as possible."

My dad insists on taking his car, so Wyatt and I follow them to Miami-Dade in my car. On the way there, I call Jason to ask if he knows anyone in the Emergency Department who can pull some strings, so my mom won't have to wait in a room with sick people for hours.

"I'll make a call and get right back to you," he says.

"Thank you so much."

"Good idea to call in favors," Wyatt says. "Her immune system is compromised from the treatment."

"I feel so bad that she's dealing with this when she's already had so many setbacks."

"Cancer treatment is like that. Hell, a lot of treatment is like that. It was for me. One step forward, three steps backward until there was nowhere left to go but on the transplant list."

"What do you think will happen for my mom?"

"They'll start her on broad-spectrum antibiotics."

"What if that doesn't work?"

"They may have to remove the port and put in a new one after she recovers from the removal."

My heart sinks. That'd be two more surgeries.

"But port removal is rare. Try not to worry about that until you have to."

Thankfully, he offered to drive because I can't see through my tears.

His hand covers mine, infusing me with comfort.

"I hate to drag you to a hospital on a day off," I say. "If you don't want to come—"

"I'm with you, kid. It's all good."

"It's all good because you're here with me."

"Nowhere else I'd rather be."

"It was so heartbreaking just now… helping her in the shower." I wipe away the tears that slide down my cheeks. "She's so embarrassed to need the help."

"I remember what that was like, too. I was twelve or thirteen, and my dad was helping me in the hospital, and I was just *dying* from embarrassment. You know what he said?"

"What?"

"That he and I have all the same parts and that I shouldn't be embarrassed about him seeing me. I needed to pretend we were just a couple of guys in a locker room doing what guys do."

"That's so sweet. Your dad knew just what you needed to hear."

"He did. After that, it wasn't as weird to let him help me. Better than my mom, anyway."

I laugh at the grimace he adds to the end of that sentence. "I'm sure."

"Bottom line—as someone who's been where your mom is, you appreciate the help even if you wish you didn't need it. Having you guys around while she's going through this makes all the difference, even when it's hard."

"I'm so thankful I can be here to help them both through it. My dad is so heartbroken she's sick that all he does is weep when she suffers. Part of what we're doing is keeping him busy, too. Nico and Milo take him golfing at least once a week, and I'm hoping to get him out on the water again soon. He doesn't want to be unreachable, so that's why we haven't done it before now. And Uncle Vin is planning to take him to some of Austin's games this summer. We're all doing what we can."

"They're fortunate to have so many people looking out for them. Believe it or not, someday when your mom is back to full health, you'll look back at this very intense time as a blip in the grand scheme of things."

"I look forward to that day. Do you think she'll fully recover?"

"There's no way to know for sure, but someone very wise once told me we have to stay positive and hope for the best."

I smile at him, which is miraculous when you consider how low I was feeling only a minute ago. "She must be *very* wise."

"One of the wisest people I've ever met."

"Surely that's not true."

"Yes, it is. She makes me believe anything is possible—even things I used to think were *im*possible."

"And you make me feel much calmer than I would if you weren't here to tell me my mom is going to be okay."

"It's hard to stay calm when the setbacks happen, but my therapist used to tell me that each setback was a step forward on the overall journey. It took me a while to wrap my head around that, but with hindsight, I could see she was right."

"That perspective must mean so much to your patients."

"I think it helps. Knowing I've been there, done that makes them feel like I get what they're going through. I want to write a book about going from a transplant patient to a cardiothoracic surgeon."

"You totally should. That would be an amazing story."

"It's on my bucket list."

As we're driving into the hospital parking lot, Jason calls me back. "Hey, ask for Dr. Simmons, and he'll get you right in. He also reached out to your mom's oncologist to let him know you're on your way in."

"Thank you so much, Jason."

"Keep us posted on how she's doing."

"I will."

Dr. Simmons takes Mom straight back to a room, examines the port area and orders the IV antibiotics. We send Dad to the cafeteria to get coffees for everyone to give him something to do besides fret over Mom. Milo tags along with him.

"Thanks for sending him on an errand," Mom says when she, Wyatt and I are alone. "He makes me so nervous with how upset he gets over everything."

"It's hard for him to watch you suffer," Wyatt says. "I remember what that was like for my parents when I was sick. Sometimes I felt like it was harder on them than it was on me."

Mom eyes him with new appreciation. "So, a heart transplant, huh? Way to one-up breast cancer."

Wyatt tips his head back to laugh. "It's not a competition. It all sucks equally."

She pats the side of the bed. "Come sit with me."

He glances briefly at me before he accepts her invitation.

She takes hold of his hand. "You seem like a lovely young man."

"Oh, thank you. That's nice of you to say."

"My Dee is an extraordinary person."

"I agree. I think she's amazing." He leans in to add, "And *super* pretty."

Mom smiles as big as I've seen her smile since this nightmare began. "I know I'm biased, but I think my girls are the prettiest girls in the whole world."

"You won't hear me arguing about that," he says, winking at me.

Could he be any cuter?

"I want you to know something," she says, continuing to hold his hand. "Before I got sick, I probably would've told Dee not to take this chance with you. They say the odds aren't too good for you, right?"

"That's right. I'm about six years past the average survival rate."

"But you feel good?"

"I feel great, especially since I met Dee."

"Being sick like this… It changes how you look at things. Did that happen to you, too?"

"It did. You have a new appreciation for every good day."

"That's what I was going to say. And I want you to enjoy every good day you have left with my Dee."

"That's our plan."

When he extends his free hand to me, I grab hold of it while trying not to lose my composure once again.

"Dee's convinced me that I need to know what it's like to be in love."

"What do you think so far?" Mom asks him.

He looks right at me when he says, "It's the best feeling I've ever had."

CHAPTER 13

DEE

My dad encourages us to go home since it will be a while before we know if the antibiotics are working. Maria, Nico and Milo are with us, and we can't talk Dad into going, too, so we leave him with orders to check in later and let us know how she's doing.

We walk out into late afternoon sunshine so bright it makes my eyes hurt after the manufactured light in the hospital.

My siblings and I are like the walking wounded as we absorb the shock of yet another crisis in our mother's cancer journey.

"She's going to be fine, guys," Wyatt tells us. "Port infections are far more common than you might think. The antibiotics work most of the time. Try not to worry too much."

I can see his words make a difference to the others, even Maria, who's a nurse. It can be difficult for her to rely on her professional know-how when her emotions are all out of whack.

"Do you guys want to get some pizza or something?" Milo asks.

The others quickly agree with his idea, and they settle on Crust, which is close to home. I don't want to go, but I defer to Wyatt.

"You know me, babe. I can always eat."

"So it's already 'babe,' huh?" Nico asks.

Wyatt never blinks when he says, "Yep."

"MYOB, Nico." I use Nona's favorite acronym from when we were kids and constantly minding each other's business. Some things never change.

"I'm just askin'," Nico says with indignance.

"No worries, man." Wyatt puts his arm around me. "I love your sister. We're together. It's kinda simple."

It's not easy to shut down Nico, but Wyatt succeeds beautifully.

Maria sends me a smug look that tells me she's thinking the same thing I am.

We head for our cars, and Wyatt holds the passenger door for me.

As I get in, I notice that Nico is watching us, and I wonder what his problem is. Not that I plan to let him bother me. I've got enough on my mind without him adding to the load.

"Well done with Nico," I tell Wyatt when we're on our way to Little Havana.

"I was hoping you'd think so. What's his deal, anyway?"

"Who knows? He's always poking at someone or something. That's how he rolls. Mostly we ignore him."

"Siblings can be annoying that way."

"Yep. He's a button pusher. That's why Nona calls him Button."

"That's cute."

"He doesn't think so, but he'd never tell her that. She's the one person he never messes with because she could destroy him with a few sharp words. And he knows it."

"I love that. Your grandmothers are awesome."

157

"I have a third one who lives in Palm Springs—my mom's mother. We aren't as close to her as we are to Nona and Abuela. My mom thinks her mother is jealous because we're close to Abuela, which is so dumb. Abuela was at every sporting event, concert and play we did as kids. We hardly saw my other grandmother, and she's jealous? People are ridiculous."

"They can be. That's for sure. My grandparents were a big part of our lives growing up. My mom's parents moved to live near us in Phoenix to take care of my brother and sister when I was in the hospital. My dad's parents were already there."

"They must've been a huge help to your parents."

"They were for sure. But it was four more people to hover over me. Not that I don't love them, but by the time I busted loose and moved to North Carolina, I was ready to be out from under all that *parenting*."

The way he says that makes me laugh. "I can only imagine how confining that had to be."

"It was. They were all so thankful for my return to good health, but they wanted to roll me in Bubble Wrap and keep me safe from anything and everything. I had to have a sit-down with the six of them and beg them to let me enjoy the second chance I was so lucky to get. And then I sprang it on them that I intended to go to med school in North Carolina."

"What'd they say to that?"

"They started talking about moving there, and I threatened to ghost them."

"They were really going to move?"

"I think they might've until I told them I'd never speak to them again if they did. Not to mention my siblings wouldn't have, either. They were in high school by then, and their lives had been disrupted enough by me. Thankfully, they reconsidered that idea, but they're still far more involved in my life than they would be if I hadn't nearly died about six times before I was seventeen."

"Jeez, Wyatt. Six times?"

"Yeah, that's how many times I coded, and that was so trau-matizing for them. I try to be mindful of what they went through, too. Which is my roundabout way of saying they're going to be super pissed that I'm planning to move, and they might take that out on you."

"Yikes."

"I don't want you to worry about them. They'll come around. They always do."

"We never even talked about me moving to Phoenix."

"You can't do that right now with your mom battling cancer. Not to mention this amazing job offer from your aunt and uncle."

"I appreciate how you never even hesitated on that."

"I understand where you need to be, and since I need to be with you, we'll do it here. Provided I get the job, but I'll look elsewhere in South Florida if I don't. Something will come up."

"Does it still seem weird to you that two days ago, you were determined to keep your distance from me, and now we're making life plans?"

"Nope, it's not weird at all because it's you. Being with you feels so good, no matter what we're doing, and now that you've convinced me, I need to know what it's like to be in love. I want to feel like that for every day that I have left."

His sweet words move me to tears. "I can't believe every-thing that's happened in one weekend. My head is spinning."

"In a good way, I hope."

"In the best possible way."

"We're going to need to find a place to live. I love Carmen and Jason's place. What about something like that?"

"I love their place, too, but I'd rather live in a house with a yard and maybe a pool."

"We can do that. Do you know any Realtors?"

"I'll ask Car and Mari who they used."

"Get whatever you want."

"You have to give me some parameters of what you want."

"I want to live with you. That's my parameter."

"It's amazing to me that I'll be able to buy a house with you because of my new job. On any other weekend, that'd be the lead story."

"I'll buy the house and put it in both our names."

"*We* will buy the house."

"Let me do this, Dee. I want to make sure you're set up, you know, just in case."

I ache when I think of the "just in case" scenarios, but I'm determined to take my own advice about remaining optimistic until there's cause not to be. "It's important to me that we do it together. I want to contribute."

"And I want to take care of you for as long as I can and set things up, so you're always protected and safe. You have to let me do that."

"Since you broke all your rules for me, I suppose I can break one of mine for you."

"Look at us compromising and everything. We're going to be couple goals for other people."

Laughing at that, I direct him to the parking lot for Crust. We're the last ones to arrive, and the others already have a table. Wyatt sits between Nico and me at a circular table.

"We ordered our usual pizzas," Milo tells us, "but we weren't sure what Wyatt wanted."

"I'll just do a salad," he says, perusing the menu.

He misses the lip curl Nico directs his way. "You're just gonna eat salad?"

"Yeah," Wyatt says. "Is that a problem?"

"Leave him alone, Nico. He has to watch what he eats because of his condition."

"Oh, right. The condition that could kill him at any point."

"Why are you being a bigger dick than usual?" Maria takes the words right out of my mouth.

"I swear to God I'm not being a dick," Nico says. "But am I the only one who's worried about Dee getting involved so quickly with someone who has... You know..." He rolled his hand for us to fill in the blank.

"An early expiration date?" Wyatt says.

"Wyatt, don't." He doesn't have to do this again. The only opinion that matters is mine, and he already knows how I feel.

"It's fine, hon. Your brother has concerns. I get it."

"That's all it is," Nico says, softening his tone. "After what happened with Marcus, I can't bear to see you hurt again."

I'm appalled when my eyes fill with tears. He's never sweet like that.

"Aw, Jesus, do *not* cry," Nico says, sounding more like himself again.

"I'm not crying."

"Liar."

"It's just so shocking when you're nice to me."

Maria and Milo crack up laughing.

"Shut up," Nico says. "All of you."

I dab at my eyes with a paper napkin and glance at Wyatt, who's taking in the Giordino family shenanigans with an amused expression.

Austin arrives with Everly, and we shift the seating to make room for them.

"What'd I miss?" Austin asks after he kisses Maria and expertly buckles Everly into a wooden high chair. He pulls crayons out of Everly's backpack and has her working on a drawing on the restaurant's paper placemat in a matter of seconds.

I'm always impressed by what a wonderful father he is. He tends to Everly with a natural, practiced ease that's so sweet.

"Nico was being a D-I-C-K, but then he was nice to Dee and

made her cry," Maria tells him. They have to watch everything they say around Everly. "Pretty much business as usual."

"Sounds like it," Austin says, smiling. "You'll get used to them, Wyatt. After a while."

"Good to know."

"Why was Nico being a D this time?" Austin asks, earning a scowl from his future brother-in-law.

"I'm worried about Dee. So shoot me."

The waitress returns with a pitcher of beer and glasses.

"Could I please get a water with lemon?" Wyatt asks.

"Make it a double," Austin adds. "I'm driving my baby."

"Anything in addition to the pizza?" the waitress asks.

"I'll do the kale salad with salmon, please," Wyatt says.

"And a kid's cheese pizza," Austin says.

"Coming right up."

"Back to talking about Nico behind his back in front of his face," Austin says, grinning at Nico.

"Here's a big idea," Nico says. "Let's move on."

"As much as I'm all for that," Wyatt says, "we should talk about this so you can get it off your chest."

"I'm more worried about your chest than mine," Nico says, making us all laugh.

The laughter helps to relieve the tension.

"My chest is totally fine," Wyatt assures him. "I get checked monthly, and I'm super vigilant between checkups. I eat healthily, work out religiously—except for this weekend when I've been distracted in the best possible way—and I take excellent care of myself. I think that's why I've never had any issues with my new heart."

Nico, Milo and Maria hang on his every word, and I appreciate their concern and interest in his situation.

"That doesn't mean you're in the clear, though, right?" Milo asks tentatively.

He'd never want anyone to think he's a dick like Nico can be.

Nico isn't a bad guy. He just shoots from the hip sometimes, and that can be irritating to whomever he's shooting at.

"No, it doesn't mean that. I have no idea what to expect going forward. The life expectancy for transplant recipients is about eleven years. I'm well past that but have no reason to be concerned at the moment."

"At the moment," Nico says. "That's the part that worries me."

I glance at Wyatt. "Allow me."

He gestures for me to have at it.

"This moment, right here, right now, is all we have, Nico. There is nothing else. Being with Wyatt makes me happier than I've ever been, and I already know that after just a few days, even if that might seem crazy or impulsive to you. We got to know each other really well the weekend of the wedding, and we've kept in touch ever since, so it's not as fast as you think. I want more of the feeling I get when I'm with him. I want as much of that feeling as I can possibly have, and since we might be short on time, there's none to waste. We're grabbing this moment, the only one we have, and soaking it for as much as we can get out of it. If the worst possible thing happens, we'll deal with that when we have to, but I refuse to waste any of the precious time we have together dreading the future. My eyes are wide open to what might happen. I'm not reckless or foolish or stupid. I'm making an informed decision with full appreciation for the possible risks. And I've decided Wyatt is worth any potential risk or future heartbreak."

For a long time after my word vomit ends, no one says anything until Milo clears his throat and breaks the silence.

"That's beautiful, Dee," he says.

"I agree," Austin says. "And for what it's worth, as someone who's dealt with a potentially fatal illness in the person I love the most, I'll just say bravo to living to the fullest right here and now. You just never know what's lurking around the next bend,

waiting to disrupt your entire life. You guys certainly know that since your mom got sick."

"That's true," Milo says, glancing at Nico.

My younger brother is a love. Whereas Nico is all sharp edges, Milo is a softie. As the youngest of the four of us, he's always played the role of peacemaker. He can't stand conflict and wants everyone to get along.

"I can see where you're coming from," Nico says tentatively as if he's not sure he should fully speak his mind after everyone calling him a dick earlier.

"Whatever you want to say, just say it," I tell him. "Get it out there so we can move on."

It's unusual for my older brother and me to talk this way, so I want to run with it while I have him.

"When everything happened with Marcus," he says, peeling a straw and bending it around his fingers, "I wanted to kill him for doing that to you."

I had no idea. "I'm glad you didn't. You'd look washed-out in prison orange."

His lips quirk with the start of a smile. "I'm serious. For him to marry someone else and not even tell you, I wanted to kill him."

I reach over Wyatt to put my hand on Nico's. "Thank you for caring. It means a lot."

"Of course I care. Maybe I don't act like it all the time—"

"*Any* of the time," Maria says with a cough as the rest of us crack up.

"I care," Nico says, his face flushing. "I never want to see any of you guys hurt the way Marcus hurt you."

"Thank you, Nico," I say. "I appreciate that."

"While we're having this come-to-Jesus conversation," Maria says, "what're you up to with Sofia at the restaurant?"

He recoils from the question. "I'm not up to anything. What does that even mean?"

"You know what I'm talking about, so don't play dumb with me."

I've never in my life seen Nico squirm the way he does under the heat of Maria's intense glare.

"I'm honestly not 'up to' anything," Nico says after a long pause. "We're friends. That's all it is."

"She means a lot to everyone," Maria tells him. "Abuela and Nona would castrate you if you ever did anything to hurt her."

"For Christ's sake, Maria. Why would I want to hurt her?"

"Oh, I don't know." My sister can be ruthless when she wants to be, and I love that about her. "Maybe you're just looking to get lucky and move on, and if that's the case, find someone else to mess around with."

"Ease up, will you? We're just friends. Don't make it into anything more than that."

"As long as you don't, we're all good," Maria says.

Nico is saved from further inquisition when the food arrives, but I'm glad Maria put him on notice.

"We need a toast to Dee," Maria says, smiling. "The new general manager at Giordino's!"

"*Shut up*," Milo says, grinning. "Is that what V and V were talking to you about after brunch?"

"How do you know that when you weren't even there?"

Milo gives me a withering look. "We got a full report from Aunt Francesca."

"I still can't believe they asked me. They said Mommy's illness has been a wake-up call for them, and they want to take some time for fun before they're too old to enjoy all their hard work."

"That's great for them and you," Nico says. "Congrats."

"Thanks. I'm excited about it—and nervous. But Uncle V promised he'd teach me everything I need to know, and as he said, he's not going anywhere that I can't reach him if I need him."

"You'll be great," Austin says. "Congratulations."

Their excitement and encouragement mean everything to me. "Thanks, everyone."

"So this situation with Mommy," Milo says tentatively. "How worried do we need to be?" He addresses the question to Maria and Wyatt.

"It looks like just an infection," Maria says.

"And that can happen with chemo ports," Wyatt adds. "It's not uncommon. How long ago did she have scans?"

"A month," I tell him, "and they were clear."

"That's the most important thing," he says. "Try not to panic. There'll be setbacks and a few steps forward, followed by a few steps backward. It's always like that with these sorts of illnesses."

"Was it like that for you?" Maria asks.

"Hell yes. One month I'd be feeling good and thinking I turned a corner, and the next month, I'd be back in the hospital fighting for my life again. It was a total roller coaster until I had the transplant."

"And you immediately felt better?" Milo asks.

"I felt reborn. Your mom is doing great. This is a setback, but she's heading in the right direction with clear scans. That's the most important thing."

Nico insists on picking up the check, probably to prove he's not a dick, and we say our goodbyes in the parking lot. Maria promises to check in with my dad and then update us on our mother's condition to keep from overwhelming him with texts.

She gives me an extra-tight hug. "I love Wyatt," she whispers in my ear.

"I do, too."

"I'm so happy for you."

That means everything to me, and she knows it.

As Wyatt drives us back to my place, I feel content in a way that I haven't in a very long time. I'm worried about my mom but comforted by what Wyatt said about setbacks being common when fighting major illness.

I look over at him, drinking in the sight of him while I still can. I hate that he's leaving tomorrow. "Thanks for being so great with them. It helped them to hear that setbacks are common. It helped me to hear that."

"I'm glad it helped. The setbacks can be scary for the families. I get that."

When we get back to my place, he asks if he can borrow my iron. I find one that some previous tenant left under the kitchen sink and set it up for him. While he irons his shirt for the interview tomorrow, I check my texts and find one from my cousin Domenic.

Hey, cuz, I hope things are good there, and Aunt Elena is doing ok. I found a new permanent roommate and wondered if it's okay for me to pack up your stuff and ship it home. I figured with everything you've got going on, that would save you a trip to NYC. Let me know —and I'll ask Tori to pack your underwear drawer. Ewwww.

I laugh as I respond to him. He's been dating Tori for a while but refuses to call her an actual girlfriend. *That'd be AWESOME. Just let me know what I owe you for boxes and shipping. I'll Venmo you. My mom is doing ok. She had a minor setback with an infection in her port, so she's in the hospital. We're told it's nothing to worry about, but that's easier said than done. Also, LOL about the underwear drawer. Tell Tori thanks for me. How's it going with her, anyway?*

It's good. We're having fun. Not sure she's THE ONE, but I guess we'll see. I'll get your stuff packed up this week. Sorry to hear about Aunt Elena—keep me posted on that. I heard some interesting stuff about you. What gives with the doctor with the bad heart?

I look over at Wyatt, who's concentrating on what he's doing. How is he adorable even when ironing? *His heart is just fine—it's just not the one he was born with. He's my ONE.*

Shut up! Seriously?

Very.

That's awesome, D. I'm so happy for you. Can't wait to meet him.

I can't wait, either. When are you coming home again?

Maybe next month. We'll see. What else is new in Miami?

You won't believe it. Uncle V and Aunt V asked me to be the GM of the restaurant. They're ready to start working less and wanted someone they trust to run the business.

That's AMAZING, D. You'll be great at it.

I hope so. It's super exciting. Thanks again for packing me up. That's a massive load off my mind.

Happy to help you out. I'll let you know when it's on the way.

Thanks, Dom.

"Well, that's a huge relief," I say to Wyatt.

"What is?"

"My cousin Domenic, who was my roommate in New York, is going to pack up my stuff and ship it for me. That saves me a trip to the city."

"That's great. How's he related to you?"

"He's my dad's sister Francesca's son. She and her husband, Domenic Senior, own this place."

"I'm going to need a map of your family."

"I can draw you a picture."

He comes to me and slips his arms around me. "That'd help." He gazes down at me for a long moment before he kisses me softly. "Today was great. I loved every minute with you and your incredible family."

I smile up at him. "Even when we were telling Nico what a dick he is?"

"That was particularly entertaining. I admire the way you guys just put it out there."

"We don't usually do that, so it was interesting to see him on defense. Usually, he's on offense, as in being as offensive as possible. But he has a good heart. He's been amazing to our parents since my mom got sick. He's really stepped up. We all have, but I wouldn't have expected what we've gotten from him. It's good to know he's capable."

"For sure." He brushes aside my hair so he can kiss my neck. "And what you said about me and us…"

It's all I can do to remain standing because his kisses have made my knees weak. "You liked that, did you?"

"Mmm, I loved it. I can't begin to tell you what these last few days have meant to me and how humbled I am that a beautiful woman like you would go all-in with me, even knowing what might be ahead."

"I've never felt this way before, and it's freeing to know we might have a time limit because it cuts out all the usual nonsense that people go through before they get to the heart of the matter."

"And what is the heart of this matter?"

"I love you. I love being with you. I want to be with you as much as I can for as long as I can."

"That makes me feel like the luckiest guy who ever lived because I love you, too. I love everything about you. I love the way your hair is so shiny and has red highlights in the sun. I love the way your gorgeous brown eyes give away everything you feel and how easily you tear up."

I laugh as my eyes flood with tears brought on by his sweet words.

"I love watching you with your family, the way you fit in with them so perfectly, the way you love them and how they love you. You make me want to be part of them." He tucks a strand of hair behind my ear. "I love how you are with Maria and Carmen. The bond between the three of you is so adorable. And more than anything, I love the way you make me feel truly optimistic about the future in a way I've never been before."

With my arms wrapped around his neck, I draw him into a deep, sensual kiss that's somehow more than anything I've experienced so far with him. Sharing our feelings has turned up the intensity, and I can tell how he responds that he feels it as much as I do. And then he's walking me backward toward my room, without missing a beat in the kiss of all kisses.

I'm not sure which one of us is more eager to get the other naked, but the competition is fierce and funny when his shirt gets stuck on his head. Laughing, he pulls it off and then goes to work on my bra, which he removes with breathtaking speed.

"You're very good at that."

He cradles my bare breasts in his hands as he looks at me with fire in his gorgeous eyes. "I did a lot of practicing for the main event." Easing me onto the bed, he follows, hovering over me, propped on one arm while he caresses my breast with his free hand. "It was all leading to you."

I want him so badly. I want everything I can have with him, and I want it right now. When I reach for him, he comes down on top of me, kissing me again with the same desperation as before. I wrap my arms and legs around him, wanting him more than I knew it was possible to want anyone. After so many years in a relationship, I thought I understood love and sex and desire, but I knew nothing until I loved Wyatt.

He fills me so completely, so perfectly, that I'm on the verge of release before he's begun to move. Every part of me tingles with awareness and a desperate kind of need that's all new to me.

This is love. This is what I want and need, and there's nothing I won't do to hold on to him for as long as I possibly can.

CHAPTER 14

MARCUS

*D*r. Stern's unblinking stare puts me on notice that
she's not here for my bullshit. "How're you feeling?"

"Much better." Detox was a bitch. I've never been sicker in
my life.

"And you're settling in well here?"

"So far, so good." The rehab facility is better than expected,
not that I had any idea of what to expect.

"And you're going to the group sessions every day?"

"That's a requirement."

"Are you participating?"

"I haven't said much yet, but I'm listening."

"That's a good place to start. Are you hearing stories that
sound familiar to yours?"

"Yeah, for sure."

"People in recovery find comfort in knowing they're not
alone. My patients often tell me that the fellowship element of
AA is one of the best parts for them. They find people who get

it, who understand the struggles and how difficult it can be to stay sober."

"I can see how that would be helpful."

"What've you been thinking about since you've been here?" Dr. Stern asks.

"I've been thinking about Dee. I can't wait to see her and have the chance to apologize and explain to her about what happened."

"What would you say to her if she were here?"

"I'd tell her how sorry I am for everything that happened, that I wasn't thinking clearly when I was drinking, and I never stopped loving her."

"Let's play out that conversation, shall we? I'll pretend to be her."

I'm not at all sure how I feel about that, but if it kills the time I'm required to spend with the good doctor, then so be it. "Sure."

"If I were Dee, I'd say this apology was a long time coming, like more than a year after you married another woman while we were in a relationship. I'd ask where you were for all that time you were married while supposedly feeling bad about what you did to me. How would you respond?"

I swallow the huge lump in my throat that forms anytime I think about the pain I inflicted on the person I love the most. "I'd say again how sorry I am for everything that happened, that I never intended to hurt her or to go so long without trying to make things right with her. I'd tell her I was sick over what I did, so sick I could barely function."

"But you managed to function well enough to stay married for most of a year to a woman you say you married by mistake."

"It *was* a mistake! The whole thing was a gigantic fucking mistake! The only one I ever wanted to be married to was Dee." I'm appalled when tears flood my eyes. I brush them away with the back of my hand, mortified to break down in front of the doctor. But she's probably used to it.

"Why did you stay married for so long if it was a mistake, Marcus? Why not immediately request an annulment or a divorce or whatever it would take to end a marriage you never intended to have?"

"I was so, *so* messed up. Ana tried to help me, and I was afraid to face Dee after she found out what I did. I know it was cowardly, but I couldn't bear to face her knowing I hurt her that way."

"So instead, you let it fester for a whole year, during which time Dee presumably picked up the pieces of the life she thought she was going to have with you and figured out a new plan for herself. Is that right?"

I have no idea what to say to that.

"A year is a long time to let something like that go without a single word from you. If I'm Dee, I'm thinking, well, if he didn't care enough even to try to make things right with me for the entire year after he married someone else—and stayed married to her—I guess it's safe to assume it's over with him, and I need to move on."

Is she trying to piss me off, or does it just seem that way? "It's not safe to assume that."

"Marcus, I want you to listen to me. Really listen. Can you do that?"

"Isn't that what I'm doing here?"

"I need you to hear me when I tell you Dee isn't coming back. There's nothing you can say or do at this point to fix what you broke with her. Do you understand that?"

"You don't know how we were together for years."

"No, I don't, but as a woman myself, I can tell you that if the man I'd been with for years up and married someone else without so much as a word to me before or after, I wouldn't have much to say to him more than a year later. I think it's also pretty safe to assume that all the people who love me would put up a wall so big and so tall that that man would never be able to get near me again. I assume Dee has friends and family who love her."

Her family is fantastic, and I miss them almost as much as I miss her. I give a quick nod to answer the doctor's question. She's right about Dee's family and friends. Carmen and Maria alone must want to stab me through the heart, not to mention what Abuela, Nona, Nico, Milo and Dee's parents, aunts, uncles and cousins must think of me.

"They won't let you get anywhere near her. You have to know that."

"If I don't have the possibility of reconciling with Dee to look forward to, then why am I even here? Why am I bothering with rehab? What does it matter?"

"Don't do that. Don't tell yourself there's no point to all this unless Dee is part of the equation."

"Well, there isn't. She's the only reason I'm here."

"That can't be the reason. You have to do this for *yourself*, first and foremost. You have to want to get better, restore your health and fight your addiction. That has to be the primary reason, or all this will be for nothing."

"It's for nothing if I have no chance to reconcile with Dee when it's over."

"Marcus, you have no chance of reconciling with Dee."

"How can you know that for sure? Have you talked to her or something?"

"No, I haven't talked to her, but I don't need to talk to her to know for certain there's almost zero chance she's going to suddenly decide to forgive you for marrying another woman and take you back as if nothing ever happened."

I honestly can't bear to hear that. The doctor's words extinguish the tiny flame of hope burning inside me that's been keeping me going over the last few horrific days.

"Imagine she'd been the one to marry someone in New York. Imagine you'd been with her just a few weeks earlier when suddenly word starts to reach you, through other people, that Dee had gotten married. What do you suppose that would've been like for you to hear it that way?"

"It would've sucked."

"And then imagine you didn't hear anything from her at all for a year after she married this other guy you had no idea she even knew. Imagine having to picture her living with him and sleeping with him when you still hadn't heard a word from her directly."

While she takes a breath, I try to tamp down the rage I feel at this scenario she's painting for me.

"And then, after a full year with no contact whatsoever with her, you hear—again through the grapevine—that she's left that guy, and all she wants is another shot with you. What do you think you'd say to her at that point?"

I hate to admit the situation looks different to me when she spins it that way.

Dr. Stern leans toward me, her expression earnest. "There are some things that can never be fixed, no matter how much we might wish otherwise. Some hurts can never be undone or overcome, no matter what we say or do to make amends. The cuts are too deep ever to heal properly."

This isn't at all what I want to hear. Knowing I don't stand a chance to fix things with Dee makes me feel hopeless about the future. "So what do I do now if you're telling me there's no chance I can ever make things right with her?"

"You have to make things right with *yourself*. You can't do it for Dee or anyone other than *you*."

Despite the doctor's dire commentary, I refuse to believe I have no chance to put things back together with Dee. I cling to that possibility. It might be the only thing keeping me alive. But if I tell the doctor that, she'll flip the panic switch and declare me suicidal when I'm not. I'm determined. When I get out of here, I'll find Dee, and I'll tell her the truth about what happened. Hopefully, I'll make her see that I made a huge mistake because I was in the grips of an addiction I'd yet to realize or accept fully.

Until Dee looks me in the eye and tells me there's no chance for us, I won't give up on her.

"Do you understand what you need to do, Marcus? How you need to put yourself first in your recovery?"

"I understand."

CHAPTER 15

DEE

*W*yatt and I are ravenous for each other, like two people who've been separated for years and finally found our way back to each other. By the time daylight begins to filter into the room, I'm sore, tired and exhilarated after the most fantastic night of my life. It's even better than the first night we spent together because now I know he loves me, and he knows I love him.

Love makes all the difference.

I'm lying on my side, facing him, holding his hand as we stare at each other in a state of stunned disbelief. At least that's what it is from my end.

"Is this real?" I ask him, breaking a long silence.

"So real and so perfect it's not even funny."

Smiling, I raise my head to look over him at the clock on my bedside table. "Your interview is in two hours. Do you want to sleep for an hour?"

"I can sleep on the flight home."

The reminder that he's leaving this afternoon is like a

pinprick to my good-mood balloon. I feel deflated and sad, and he hasn't even left yet.

"Don't do that."

"What am I doing?"

"Thinking about me leaving and things getting messed up. That's not going to happen."

"How do you know?"

"Because neither of us will let that happen. You're the most important person in my life, and we're going to make this work. I promise."

His sweetness and certainty have me choked up, over-whelmed with all the emotions.

He slides closer to me, puts his arm around me and kisses me. "Don't worry about anything."

"What? Me worry?"

"You have to take your own badass warrior princess advice and stay optimistic. I'm going to get the job at Miami-Dade, I'm going to move here, we're going to live together, and we're going to be so fucking happy that people will be jealous of how happy we are. And that's how it's going to go. You got me?"

I release his hand and place mine on his face, feeling the subtle tickle of his whiskers against my palm. "I got you, and I'm not letting go."

"Don't you dare. I'd never forgive you after you talked me into falling in love with you."

"I won't. I promise."

We stay there for another half hour, whispering, kissing, making plans. I want to exist inside this bubble with him forever and never come out.

"Come help me in the shower," he says. "I need you to wash my back."

Laughing, I drag myself out of bed and immediately feel shy when the sheet falls away.

He's right there, wrapping his arms around me and holding

me close. "Don't ever, *ever* feel self-conscious around me. I think you're a fucking goddess come to life."

"You make me feel very good about myself."

"You ought to feel exceptionally good about yourself." Smiling, he adds, "I feel exceptionally good about you." He takes hold of my hands and walks backward toward the bathroom, bringing me with him as he feasts his eyes on every naked inch of me.

My entire body is on fire with embarrassment and arousal and desire, although I can't fathom any more of what we've already had repeatedly.

The warm water raining down on my sore muscles feels like heaven, as does the sweet massage he gives my back and shoulders.

When I turn to face him, I trace a finger down the center of his pectorals over the faint scar from his surgery. "Who designed the image?"

"I did. It was how I saw myself after the surgery, spreading my wings, ready for anything that might come my way."

"It's beautiful. Have you drawn other things?"

"Lots of stuff. It was how I stayed sane during the months in the hospital."

"I want to see it."

"I'll show you everything when you come to Phoenix." He runs his soapy hands over my breasts and belly, making my legs feel weak and rubbery beneath me. "I was thinking about Phoenix. I know you said you have to work next weekend, but could you fly out next Sunday? I'm going to give two weeks' notice at work, and we can drive back the following weekend. That way, you could meet my parents before we leave."

My head is spinning but in the best possible way. "As long as my mom is doing okay, I should be able to do that."

"If she needs you, don't sweat it. I can drive back by myself."

"I have no doubt Maria and Carmen would be happy to

cover for me with my parents so I could make the drive with you."

"That'd be very nice of them."

"They've been saying for a while now that they wanted me to find my Jason or Austin. They wanted me to have what they do. I know they'll do anything they can to support us."

"It makes me feel lucky to have their support. I know how much that matters to you."

"It does. They're my ride-or-die girls."

"I'm glad you have them."

"We both have them. If I love you, they will do anything for you, too."

"That's good to know."

I kiss him and leave him in the shower to shave while I get dressed in leggings and a T-shirt that leaves one shoulder bare. Before I dry my hair, I check my phone, looking for an update on my mom, which Maria has provided.

Checked in with the nurses this morning. Mommy had a good night, and the antibiotics are doing the trick. Her fever has broken, and she should be released later today with a new prescription for more potent antibiotics. It seems the current crisis has passed.

I respond to the group text that includes my brothers, Vincent, Vivian, Francesca, Nona and Abuela. *That's such a relief. Thanks for the update. I'll handle dinner for them tonight.* Taking care of my parents will give me something to do after Wyatt leaves.

And just that quickly, my chest aches from the thought of him leaving. I know it's temporary, but after this whirlwind weekend, all I want in the entire world—other than my mother's complete recovery, of course—is to be with him.

I decide to let my hair dry curly because I'm too tired and lazy to bother with the drying-and-straightening ritual. I put it up in a bun to keep it from making my shirt wet.

Wyatt emerges from my bedroom wearing a gray suit with a white dress shirt and a navy patterned tie.

I'm rendered utterly speechless at the sight of him in a suit.

"Earth to Dee? You okay?"

I lick my dry lips. "You… You're so handsome."

His smile lights up his eyes. "Thank you. You're looking rather *handsome* yourself." He comes toward me with intent that can't be mistaken after the time we've spent together.

I hold up a hand to stop him. "Slow your roll, pal. You've got somewhere to be."

"I hate having somewhere to be, but if it allows me to relocate to my girl's hometown, then I guess it's worth it."

Hearing him call me his girl makes me feel light-headed and happy. So damned *happy*. "Good news—my mom's fever has broken, and they're sending her home today."

"That's fantastic news." He checks the fancy watch on his wrist. "I guess I should call for an Uber."

"I'll take you. I can visit Carmen's office while I wait for you. She's been telling me to come by for months now."

"Are you sure? I don't want to mess up your day."

"You're going to mess up my day by leaving later. I don't mind driving you. We can stop for a cortadito at our favorite ventanita."

"Um, translation please?"

"Cuban coffee."

"Ah, sign me up for a decaf."

"Oh crap. Sorry. I forgot you don't do caffeine."

"It's no big deal, babe."

I roll my lip between my teeth. "I need you to give me a full list of what's off-limits for you so I don't tempt you with things you can't have."

"I like when you tempt me."

"You know what I mean. I don't want to cook something bad for you or take you for coffee you can't drink."

"I bet there's a decaf option. Let's go find out."

"And you'll make me a list of what we need to avoid?"

"I'll make sure you have all the info you need."

He grabs a leather portfolio, and we head out with me driving to Juanita's ventanita, which is a hole-in-the-wall at a gas station. On the way, I describe the four types of Cuban coffee—cafecito, colada, café con leche and cortadito.

"Which one do you think I should try?"

"Since you're not a regular coffee drinker—and honestly, I don't know how people function without it—I'd try a decaf café con leche. It's milder than the cortadito, which Abuela says puts hair on your chest."

"But I don't want hair on your beautiful chest." He pretends to make a note in his portfolio. "Note to self. She needs kick-ass coffee to start her day."

"She does, or she isn't responsible for her crankiness, especially after almost no sleep last night."

"Best night ever," he says, glancing over at me. "Even better than the first one, and I wouldn't have thought that was possible."

"I was so embarrassed about that night afterward."

"What? Why?"

"It was just so unlike me to, um, behave that way with a man I'd only just met. It was like I was outside myself or something. I don't know how to explain it."

"Whoever you were that night, I liked you a lot. So much that I constantly relived it over and over and over again until I thought I'd go mad if I didn't see you again as soon as possible."

"Really?"

"Really. And that's never happened. I've never been obsessed with seeing someone again the way I was with you. I think I was already well on my way to being in love with you before you made me fall the rest of the way."

"I didn't make you do anything."

"Yes, you did. You made me *believe*, and you have no idea what a big deal that is for me. Before this, before you, I thought I was a pretty optimistic kind of guy. I didn't dwell too much on the uncertainty that's such a big part of my life, but I can also see that I was missing out on some pretty incredible things by putting limits on what I allowed to happen. So yeah, you made me see some things just shouldn't be missed, and I'll always be thankful to you for pushing me on that."

I flash him my best saucy grin. "I made out pretty good, too."

"Don't remind me of that, or you'll send me into my interview with a boner that won't quit."

"I'm surprised it still works."

He takes my hand and places it on the rigid column of his erection. "Works just fine."

"Stop!" I sputter, trying to pull my hand away, but he isn't having it. "Wyatt…"

"Yes, Dee?"

"We're here."

He looks up at the gas station, his brows furrowing with confusion.

I give my hand another tug. "You'll see, but you have to let me go."

"I'll let you go. For now."

We get out of the car and join the line for Juanita's magical coffee and pastries. It moves slowly because Juanita makes everything herself and takes the time to talk to each of her customers. We're doing good for time to get Wyatt to the hospital for his nine-thirty appointment, but he keeps checking his watch.

"I'll get you there on time. Don't worry."

"What? Me worry?"

I love him. I love being with him and how easy it is. It's easy, like breathing. I take hold of his hand with both of mine.

He gives mine a little squeeze.

I look up from our joined hands to see Juanita watching us, a big smile lighting up her pretty face. "Hola, amiga ¿Cómo estás? ¿Dónde encuentran tu hermana, tu prima, y tú estos chicos tan atractivos y cómo puedo conseguir uno para mi hija?" *Hi, friend. How're you doing? Where do your sister, cousin and you find these hot men, and how can I get one for my daughter?*

Laughing, I glance at Wyatt and say, "Lo encontré en la boda de Car." *I found this one at Car's wedding.*

"Ah, sabía que no me hubiera ido a mis vacaciones para ir a esa boda." *Ah, I knew I should've skipped my vacation to be at that wedding.*

"Why do I feel like you ladies are talking about me behind my back?" Wyatt asks with a grin.

Juanita fans her face. "We're talking about you, all right, but we're doing it right in front of your very handsome face."

"Oh, um, thank you."

"Juanita, this is Wyatt. Wyatt, meet Juanita."

"*Very* nice to meet you," she says.

"Likewise."

"I'll have a cortadito, and Wyatt would like a decaf café con leche."

Juanita makes a face that lets me know what she thinks of the word *decaf* and gets busy making our drinks. She asks how my mother's doing, whether Carmen is pregnant yet and not telling her, and how Maria and the sexy baseball player are doing. "His little girl is *adorable*. She likes the decaf café con leche, too."

"She's *so* cute."

Juanita brings our drinks to the window. "A cortadito and a decaf café con leche for the chico sexy."

"Did she just say I'm sexy?" Wyatt asks.

I sputter with laughter. "Like you didn't already know that."

"Me gusta éste, cariño," Juanita says. "Es bueno verte sonreír de nuevo." *I like this one, honey. It's nice to see you smiling again.*

"Gracias, a mi me gusta él también." *Thank you. I like him, too.*

Wyatt pays for the coffees and accepts the bag with delicious pastelitos that come with every order of coffee. I'm not sure if he'll eat one, but I hope he'll at least taste the buttery goodness.

"What's in here?" he asks, holding up the bag as we walk back to the car.

"Heaven."

"Heaven in a bag, huh?"

"Yep."

In the car, he takes a tentative sip of his coffee. "Wow, that's good."

"I told you." I take the bag from him, retrieve one of the pastelitos and offer him a bite. "I feel like Eve in the Garden of Eden, offering Adam something bad for him."

"One little taste won't hurt anything." He takes a bite, and his eyes roll back in his head. "Yeah, that's fucking awesome. I can't believe she works out of a gas station and sells the best coffee in Miami."

"She does a huge business out of that little hole-in-the-wall. People come from all over the city every day and wait in line for what she's dishing up."

He takes another sip of his drink. "I can see why. I usually could take or leave coffee of any kind, but this could become a habit."

"I'm glad you like it." I feel proud to have introduced him to something that's been such a big part of my life. "You can't grow up in Miami with close Cuban relatives and not have some sort of history with coffee. It's a cornerstone of our social fabric."

"I'm intrigued by the cultural aspects of Miami, and by the way, it was super sexy listening to you speak fluent Spanish." He fans his face dramatically. "I didn't know you were bilingual."

"That comes with growing up here. Everyone speaks Spanish. You can live your whole life here and never speak English."

"Did you take Spanish in school?"

"I did, but I was fluent by the time I was in middle school. I have so many close friends and cousins who speak Spanish that I learned just by being immersed." I glance over at him. "If you want, after your interview, we can poke around in Little Havana a bit." His flight isn't until five-thirty, so we have all afternoon to spend together.

"That sounds great. I'd love to poke around with you."

"I'm talking about *walking*, just in case you're thinking about *other* things."

"When you're around, I'm always thinking about *other* things, but in this case, I knew what you meant."

When we arrive at Miami-Dade, Wyatt takes a critical look at the place and says the landscaping is beautiful. "I can't get over the difference between here and Phoenix. Everything there is so dry and barren, and here, it's so lush and green."

"We're all about the landscaping in South Florida. Everything is beautifully landscaped."

"I love it."

I'm so glad he loves my town and wants to be here, because I don't think I could bear to leave again, not after having done it once before. Now that I'm home, I've realized how painfully homesick I was in New York, even having my cousin there with me. It wasn't the same as being here, surrounded by most of the people I love and being with them anytime I want.

We park in the visitor lot and walk inside together, taking the elevator to the executive offices, where Carmen works across the hall from the hospital president, who, along with the medical director, chief of surgery and head of cardiology, will meet with Wyatt.

"Maybe you should go in before me, so it doesn't look like you brought a date to an interview."

Smiling, he says, "I don't care if they think I brought a date to an interview."

"You need to get this job, Wyatt. I can't move to Phoenix."

"I know you can't, but don't worry. If I don't get this one, I'll apply to others. I'll find something."

"I want you to find something that makes you happy."

"I want to be with you. You make me happy."

Before I can reply to that, we've arrived at the hospital president's suite. I'm delighted to see Carmen in the reception area, speaking to a woman seated at a desk. I recognize her from the wedding, but I can't recall her name.

Carmen lights up at the sight of us. "Mona, you remember my cousin Dee from the wedding, as well as Jason's good friend Dr. Wyatt Blake."

"Nice to see you both again," Mona says.

Car hugs Wyatt and me. "I was hoping to see you before your interview, Wyatt, so I could wish you good luck." To me, she adds, "This is a nice surprise."

"I figured this was a good time to take you up on the invite to see your office. If you're not busy, that is."

"I've got time," she says.

"You look fantastic, by the way." She's wearing a black suit with a red silk blouse and sky-high heels. "You're rocking that suit."

"Aw, thanks."

Mr. Augustino emerges from his office. I remember him from the wedding.

Carmen introduces us to him, and he shakes hands with both of us. "Good to see you again. Dr. Blake, we're ready for you in my office."

"Lead the way." Wyatt trails a hand over my back as he follows Mr. Augustino into his office.

I'm a nervous wreck watching him go, hoping and praying he can land this job, the first step in making our plans a reality.

"Come in." Car nudges me out of my stupor toward her office, closing the door. "Look at you."

I take a seat in one of her visitor chairs. "Huh?"

She sits next to me. "You're all dewy-eyed and besotted."

"Am I?"

"Oh yeah, and it's very nice to see. Tell me every single thing, and don't leave out anything."

"Don't you have to work?"

She waves her hand as if to say *forget work*. "This is far more important. Tell me, Dee."

"I love him. Like really, *really* love him."

Carmen lets out a squeal and claps her hands. "This is the most exciting thing since Maria landed herself a hot baseball player."

"What about your hot neurosurgeon?"

"That was *so* last year."

I laugh at the face she makes. "So you feel better about this since you slept on it?"

"I like to see you so happy, and I'd never do anything to take away from that for you."

"Thank you. That means everything to me."

"It doesn't mean I won't worry about you—and him—but I can see how in love you guys are, and it's so sweet."

"I can't believe this is happening, Car. I mean, the night of the wedding was crazy, but I never expected to see him again. Now I can't imagine life without him."

"I so hope he gets the job. I put in a good word for him, and so did Jason."

"You did? That's amazing!"

"Of course we did. He's great, and Jason says he's one of the best doctors he knows. They'd be crazy not to hire him."

"I'm all wound up in knots. I feel like everything I've ever wanted is right within my reach, but I'm so afraid of something messing it up."

"It's going to be great. I know it. And I couldn't be more thrilled that my parents offered you the GM job. I've been after them for years to slow down and smell the roses. It took your mom's illness to get their attention."

"I'm so excited and nervous and humbled that they asked me."

"You were the only one they wanted. We talked about it, and we all agreed it should be you."

"Thank you for the vote of confidence. I'm looking forward to starting and learning the business side of things."

"I'm looking forward to my parents having some time to themselves. They've worked so hard. They deserve it."

"They sure do."

"So you haven't told me *everything* yet."

"He wants to get a house and live together."

"I think it is so awesome that you're cutting straight to the good stuff."

"We have no time to waste."

"About that..." She seems to choose her words carefully. "I made Jason explain it all to me in terms I'd understand."

"And?"

"It's kind of frightening. I wish I hadn't asked. How are you coping?"

"By pretending it's not an issue and just moving forward with our plans. And before you ask, I'm not in denial. I understand the odds aren't in Wyatt's favor, which is why we're trying to live in the moment as much as we can. That's all we can do."

"You're so brave, Dee. I've always thought so, but never more so than I do now."

"You've always thought *I* was brave? Seriously?"

"Hell yes. You picked up and moved to the biggest city in the country. I was so envious of you for that. I couldn't imagine leaving my safety net here to do something like that."

"You could've done it."

She shakes her head. "I couldn't have, especially after I lost

Tony. I needed the support of my people to keep moving forward. I wouldn't have done well somewhere else."

"You're the brave one. You survived something that would've killed a lesser person."

"I survived because I had no choice, and you will, too, if the worst thing happens."

"I hope so." I refuse to let thoughts of that possibility into a day so full of promise.

"Enough about that. Where will you live?"

"I want a house with a yard and maybe a pool. Where should we look?"

"I saw something for sale on the way to Maria's the other day." She pulls out her phone, calls up Zillow and, in a matter of minutes, has me booked to tour a three-bedroom, three-bathroom house tomorrow afternoon.

I laugh at her quick work. "You don't mess around, woman."

"You're the one who said there's no time to waste, right?"

"That's right."

"Here's another one close to Maria's. You can look at both tomorrow before work."

I blow out a deep breath. "I can't believe this is happening."

"Believe it. You deserve it after, you know…"

She doesn't want to say Marcus's name. "Have you heard anything about how he's doing?"

"Just that he's in rehab, but you know that."

"I can't believe I had no idea he was an alcoholic. How did I miss that?"

"You didn't miss it. He just did an excellent job of hiding it from you." She pauses before she adds, "You might be blaming yourself for staying in New York and putting that strain on your relationship. But I was thinking about that last night, and it occurred to me if you hadn't done that, it probably would've blown up much sooner because you would've realized he had a problem with drinking. You would've been here to see it."

"Part of me feels like I should've been here with him."

"No, that's not true. You wanted that time for yourself before you made a permanent commitment to him. You have no reason to feel guilty about that. He also had a choice to continue or not continue your relationship after you decided to stay. He chose to come back to you after the time you spent apart, which makes what he did that much worse, in my opinion."

"It's all so hard to fathom. Even after all this time."

"Bianca told Maria he's still determined to fix things with you."

I'm shocked by that information. "What does he think there is to fix after he *married* someone else?"

"No idea, but apparently, that's his only goal in life."

"I really can't hear that. I'm not available to be his only goal in life."

"That's right. He had his chance and blew it epically."

"I don't want to talk about him. Let's talk about something else."

"Such as how I'm starting to think your brother has a thing for Sofia?"

"I've noticed that, too. Maria and I called him out on it last night, and he claims they're just friends. We let him know we're watching him, and he'd better not pull any of his Nico shit with her."

"I'm glad you guys said something. I've been kind of worried about that."

"He swears his intentions are good, and he understands we'll kill him if he pulls any crap with her. But here's the thing… I think he likes her."

"As in *really* likes her?"

"Yep, and he has no idea what to do about it because he's only ever been a player. He has no idea how to do a real relationship. He's never had one."

"Except for Tanya. Remember her?"

"That was, like, eleventh grade."

"But he liked her, and she blew him off. After that, he started acting kind of shitty when it came to girls and women. Like he wasn't willing to make an effort and have something like that happen again. He was going to be the one to do the leaving."

"Huh, I hadn't thought of it that way, but you may be right." I glance at the clock on the wall behind her desk. "How long do these interviews take, anyway? Do I have time to pop in on my mother?"

"She was released already. I went to see her this morning, and they were on their way out."

"Oh wow, that's earlier than she expected."

"Sorry, I figured you'd already heard that."

"No worries. How'd she seem?"

"Good. Eager to get out of here and get home."

"That sounds like her." I text the update to my siblings and the others, letting them know my mom should be home by now.

Everyone responds with relief to hear the news.

A new message arrives from my mom to our family group chat. *I'm home and feeling much better. Thank you for all the good wishes. After she heard I was in the hospital, Mrs. Lopez brought over a casserole, so we're set for dinner. Everyone take the night off. All is well here. Love you, Mommy*

I show the message to Car, relieved that yet another crisis seems to have passed.

"She sounds good."

"She does, and I'm off the hook for dinner tonight, which is kind of a bummer because Wyatt is leaving, and I was glad to have something to do."

"Come to dinner with us."

"That's okay. You guys don't need to babysit me."

"We don't mind at all. I'll get reservations somewhere fun, and I'll invite Maria, Austin and Everly, too. We'll keep your spirits up."

"That sounds good. Thanks, Car."

"Anything for you, kid. When do you plan to see him again?"

"I need to clear it with your dad, but provided he gets the job here, I'm hoping to fly out there next Sunday and spend the week in Phoenix to meet his parents and help him finish packing. Then we'll drive back together the following weekend."

"This is so exciting!"

"Is it normal to feel like you have bats flying around in your belly when something like this is happening?"

"Perfectly normal. I felt that way the whole time I was first with Jason until I knew for sure he was going to work here, and we could make a go of it."

"I remember that. It was a roller-coaster ride for you."

"But *so* worth it in the end."

Her desk phone rings, and she gets up to take the call. "Sure, Mona, tell him to come in." She puts down the phone and goes to open the door for Wyatt.

My heart does this crazy somersault thing at the sight of him. I need to ask him if I should be worried about that, but I'm too busy staring at him to put the thought into words.

"How'd it go?" Carmen asks.

"Great," he says. "I think they liked me. Because my schedule is so crazy at home, I've already done several meetings and toured the facilities remotely, so today was kind of a formality. But we'll see."

"When will you know anything?" Carmen asks.

"Mr. Augustino said he'd call me as soon as they make a decision."

"Fingers crossed that it's soon, so you aren't twisting in the wind."

"That'd be nice."

I appreciate Carmen doing the grilling for me.

Wyatt smiles at me and reaches for my hand. "What've you ladies been up to?"

"Just talking."

"And shopping for houses," Carmen adds. "We found two possibilities near Maria's that might work."

"Let me see." He leans over the back of my chair, surrounding me with his warmth and the subtle scent of his cologne.

I show him the two houses we found, and he loves them both.

"I like the one with the pool," he says. "We could have some good parties in that yard."

We visit with Carmen for a few more minutes, and then she walks us to the elevator. "Fingers and toes crossed for you, Wyatt. Let us know as soon as you hear anything."

"Will do. Thanks again for the good word."

"Hope it helps."

When the elevator chimes, I hug my cousin. "Thanks for keeping me company."

"Anytime. Call me about dinner."

"Will do."

"You guys are doing dinner?" Wyatt asks as we ride to the main floor.

"My mom is home, and their neighbor took care of dinner for tonight. I said I was sad about you leaving and wouldn't have something to keep me busy. She immediately organized dinner so I'd have something to do."

"I'm glad your mom is home, and I sure love your family."

"They're pretty great."

He puts an arm around me as we walk to the parking lot. "I have a good feeling I'll be back here very soon."

"I so hope you're right."

CHAPTER 16

WYATT

*A*s my flight lifts off from MIA at six p.m., I look out at the place that's come to mean so much to me in such a short time. Dee is down there somewhere, probably feeling as shitty as I do after saying goodbye at the drop-off area. Leaving her was painful, even if it's only for a week. Less than a week. Six days.

We had the best time wandering around Little Havana. We saw cigars being made, watched the old men playing dominoes in the park and shared a Cuban sandwich. She cried when I bought her flowers and again when we said goodbye—for now.

I love her so much. She's perfect for me in every way, from her boundless optimism to her sweetness, to the connection she shares with her family, to the way she cares so much about the people she loves. I'm fortunate to be one of them, and I know it.

Right before I boarded the plane, I received a text from my mom inviting me to a welcome-home dinner tomorrow night. *We're so glad you're coming home!*

The thought of sharing my plans with them fills me with

dread, knowing they won't be happy for me if it means I'm moving to the other side of the country. I hate that my news will upset them, but after having tasted paradise with Dee this past weekend, I'm sure that moving to be with her is the right thing for me to do, even if it upsets my parents.

At thirty-four, I should be long past the point where my parents factor into my life decisions. Still, it's impossible to explain to people who haven't experienced what a serious childhood illness does to the parent-child dynamics, even long after the "child" is a grown adult.

I'm exhausted from the sleepless night and nap almost the entire four-hour flight to Phoenix. When we land, I power up my phone and listen to the voice mail from Miami-Dade's medical director, offering me a position on their cardiothoracic team. I was worried my health situation might be a deal-breaker. In the interview, they asked about my status, and I told them the truth—that I'm fine and intend to stay that way. I'm relieved that didn't derail the process. He asks me to call him in the morning to discuss the details. It's all I can do not to let out a whoop of excitement right there in the crowded plane cabin.

I put through a call to Dee.

"Hey, did you get there okay?"

"Just landed and got a message from Miami-Dade along with an offer."

She lets loose with the shout I had to contain in a plane full of other passengers. "Congratulations, Wyatt. I'm so happy for you."

"I'm so happy for both of us. It's all coming together, baby."

"It sure feels like it."

"How was dinner?"

"It was great. We had Thai at a cool new place downtown."

"Will you take me there sometime? I love Thai."

"Anytime you want. I'm so excited, Wyatt."

"So am I. I loved the people I met today at the hospital, and the job sounds great. But that's the least of it."

"Don't be silly. You just got an awesome new job. You have every right to be excited."

"The job has nothing on you. You're the exciting part. I miss you so much already. I missed you the second you drove away."

"I cried all the way home."

"Aw, I hate to hear that."

"They were good tears. The best kind. I just want to blink my eyes and have this week be over so we can be together again."

"One more week and then together forever."

"I can't wait for together forever."

"Me, either." I talk to her all the way home and late into the night until we're both yawning so much, we have no choice but to say good night.

I'm at work by six with back-to-back surgeries scheduled. Between surgeries, I meet with my department head and give him my two weeks' notice. As a contract employee, I made sure I had an easy out if I needed it in light of my health situation. Most of the time, they'd expect at least ninety days' notice. My boss is completely shocked to hear I'm leaving, but I never waver in my determination to chase the dream with Dee. When he realizes he's not going to change my mind, he shakes my hand and wishes me well in my new position. But I can tell he's pissed I didn't give him more notice.

Time is one thing I can't afford to waste.

I finish with my last patient just after five and leave my residents in charge of monitoring my patients, with orders to call if they need me. A little after six, I drive out of the parking lot in my black Audi SUV and head for my parents' home. On the way, I call Dee, feeling cut off from her after not having spoken to her all day.

"Hi there, how was your day?"

"Long. But the highlight was giving my notice. How about you?"

"I'm still at work. Can I call you later?"

"I'm heading to my parents' for dinner, but I'll text you when I'm leaving there."

"Sounds good. I miss you."

"Same, babe. So bad."

"I'll talk to you in a bit. Enjoy dinner."

"Love you."

"Love you, too."

I can't believe I'm saying those words to a woman or hearing them back from her. Being in love with Dee is the highest high I've experienced since getting my second chance at life. She makes all the hell I went through to survive worth it. She's the pot of gold at the end of a very long rainbow. Such thoughts would've been unimaginable to me before I met her. But now that I know she's out there somewhere, the only thing in the world I want is to be with her.

I take that resolve with me into my parents' contemporary home, covered in the solar panels my dad sells. His success in the solar industry has more than made up for the enormous financial hit they took when I was sick.

My mom is so happy to see me that she nearly squeezes the life out of me. I get my dark hair from her and my height from my dad.

"I'm so glad you're home. Did you have fun?"

The best time of my entire life. "So much fun."

"How's Jason?"

"He's great. Loving married life."

"I'm so glad to hear that."

She's put out veggies and hummus for me and cheese and crackers for them.

"Something smells good. What'd you make?"

"Shrimp stir-fry. I got those snow peas you love."

"Thanks, Mom." She tends to me like a mother who's seen her child through a nearly fatal illness—with relentless attention to detail.

"What's new with you guys?"

"Dad landed a big new client that he's excited about, and my class scored in the top one percent of all fifth grades in the state for reading on the recent statewide testing."

"That's fantastic on both counts."

"It's been a good month."

And I'm going to kill their buzz with my news, which dampens my excitement somewhat. But then I think of Dee's sweet face and what it feels like to lose myself in her, and I have no doubt I'm doing the right thing for myself—and her. We belong together, and it's up to me to take the steps necessary to make that happen.

My dad comes in from work, pops open a beer and greets me with a one-armed hug. "Good to see you," he says as if he hasn't seen me in weeks.

I saw them the Sunday before last when we had brunch with my siblings. "You, too. I hear business is good."

"Very good. Better than ever."

"That's great, Dad. Glad to hear it."

"How's the heart-and-lung business?" Dad asks.

"Busy as always. I did three surgeries today and have three more scheduled for tomorrow."

"You're not pushing yourself too hard, are you?" Mom asks. "You look tired."

"I am tired. I had a busy weekend and a crazy day at work." The lack of sleep over the weekend was worth it. "I'm normal tired, Mom. Nothing to worry about."

Over dinner, I hear that my brother's wife has gestational diabetes, and my sister is looking for a shelter dog to adopt. One set of grandparents is enjoying a visit in Palm Springs with friends, and the others are in upstate New York visiting my grandmother's sister. Everyone is happy, healthy and doing well, which means my parents are in a good place, too, and my news will upset them. I hate that, but as I help them clear the table and clean up the kitchen, I force myself to get on with it.

"So, guys, I've got some news."

They stop what they're doing and turn to me. Their expressions are wary.

"Nothing bad. It's kind of the best thing ever."

"What is?" Mom asks.

"I've met someone amazing."

"Oh, well, who is she?" Dad asks.

"Jason's wife's cousin, Dee. We were matched up at the wedding and really connected." Oh, how we connected that day —and that night. "We've stayed in touch since, and, well, I've fallen for her."

"That's wonderful, honey." Mom's eyes sparkle with delight. "I'm so happy for you."

"Thanks. I'm pretty damned happy for me, too. She's... She's everything. You'll love her. She's sweet and beautiful and funny and so devoted to her family. She's one of four siblings, but they have a huge extended family. Her aunt and uncle run a famous Cuban-Italian restaurant in Little Havana, and they recently asked Dee to be their general manager. She's so excited about the new opportunity." I realize I'm gushing, but how can I not when talking about Dee?

"So, if she lives in Miami and you live here, how's that going to work?" Dad asks, cutting to the chase the way he always does.

"I'm moving there. I got a job at Miami-Dade General Hospital. Dee and I, we're going to make a life together."

My mom is so flabbergasted that she stares at me in disbelief.

"Before you can tell me all the reasons why this is a terrible idea, let me tell you why I think it's the best idea I've ever had. I'm truly in love for the first time in my life, and all I want is to be with her for as long as I possibly can. Yes, I only met her a couple of months ago. Yes, it happened fast. But we all know time isn't on my side, and we want to go for it while we can."

Dad clears his throat. "So she knows… everything?"

"She does, and she's the one who convinced me to go all-in with her and us, to experience what it's like to be in love, and it's…" Now words can adequately express what she means to me or how it feels to be in love with her. "I had the best weekend of my entire life with her, and I can't wait for more."

"Is it fair?" Mom asks, tending to tears with a tissue. "To her?"

"Probably not, but she's decided everything is going to be fine, and we're not going to worry about what might happen in the future. We're going to live like hell right now." I can't even talk about her without grinning like a fool. "I'm telling you— you're going to love her as much as I do."

They glance at each other but don't say anything more.

"I'm sorry if this is upsetting to you, but I'm really happy, and I want you to be happy for me."

"We're happy for you, Wyatt," Mom says. "It's just a lot to process. We thought you were going to Miami to visit Jason, not to apply for a new job and start a whole new life on the other side of the country."

"I'm sorry I didn't tell you about the interview, but I didn't think there was any point in talking about it until I got the job. And when I went there on Friday, I had no idea what to expect with Dee or whether it would be as great as it was the first time we met." I didn't think anything could top that first day and night with her. I was so, so wrong.

"You're a grown man, son," Dad says. "You can do whatever you want, and if this woman in Miami is what you want…" His voice breaks along with my heart.

I hate upsetting them any more than I already have. "I don't want to live away from you guys. I hope you know it's not about that. It's just that I have a chance to have something I thought was never going to happen for me, mostly because I refused to allow it to happen. And now that it has…"

"I get it," Dad says, "and it makes me happy to know you'll have that experience. It's just, you know, hard for us. We worry about you."

"I know you do, and I hate being the cause of that. But I'm feeling great, better than I ever have. There's no reason to worry about anything. I'll live with Dee in Miami. We'll be surrounded by her family, and Jason will be there, too. It's not like I'll be moving somewhere with no support like I did when I went to Duke. Dee even has doting grandmothers to help keep an eye on me. And I was thinking… Maybe you could spend part of the winter with us in Miami. We're getting a house with plenty of bedrooms, and Dad, you've been talking about taking more time off now that the business is doing so well. Mom, you should retire one of these years and enjoy life. You've both certainly earned the right to relax."

My mom is on her second tissue as she mops up the tears that keep coming. I go to her and hug her. "I'm sorry to upset you, but I promise this is a good thing. The very best thing."

"What are we supposed to do if you have some sort of problem, and you're in Miami?"

"You can be there in a few hours if it comes to that, which it won't."

"You can't possibly know that for sure, Wyatt," Mom says.

"No, I can't, but I've made up my mind to quit living like I'm dying."

"You haven't been doing that!" Mom's distress turns to anger in an instant. "Look at what you've done with yourself—you're a board-certified cardiothoracic surgeon. How does that equate to living like you're dying?"

"My career is incredible. I'm very proud of what I've accomplished there. It's the rest of my life that's been lacking. I had fly-by relationships with women, never allowing myself to get too involved out of fear of my loaner heart giving out and how unfair it would be to ask someone to care about me when that could happen.

"Dee reminded me we're all one bad decision away from certain death. We could step off the curb at the wrong moment, accelerate through an intersection when someone is running a red light or any number of dreadful things that happen. I've been so busy pursuing my career with a ruthless determination that, somewhere along the way, I forgot to *live*. Dee has shown me something else—something I want more than I've ever wanted anything, and I'm going for it. I want you guys to be part of it. But what I don't want is to add to your stress. I want you to just be happy for me and not worry about me."

"It's tough for us not to worry," Dad says softly.

"I know, and I appreciate why. I hate that I put you through such hell, but this is the payoff for what we all went through. Dee is the payoff. She's my golden ring."

"And you know this for sure so quickly?" Mom asks.

"I knew it right away. The day I met her was unlike any day I've ever spent with anyone, and all I've thought about since then was seeing her again. Please… Just be happy for me. Let's not dwell on all the ways it could go wrong. Let's just be happy in this moment, the only one we have." I use Dee's words to seal the deal with them, or so I hope.

Dad closes the distance between us and hugs me as fiercely as he has in years.

My eyes burn with tears.

"We're happy for you, Wy, and we can't wait to meet your Dee."

"Thanks, Dad. You'll love her. I know you will."

When he releases me, I turn to my mom. "Are you okay?"

"I suppose I will be. I just can't bear the thought of you living so far from us."

"You got through the four years I was in North Carolina," I remind her.

"That was hell, always waiting to get a phone call."

"That never came. I was fine. I *am* fine. I'm going to *be* fine. We just have to have faith in that, and if the day comes when I'm not fine, we'll deal with it then. In the meantime, I don't want you to be upset."

"I'm sorry." She wipes away more tears. "I don't want to take anything away from your happiness. I just… I need a minute to wrap my head around this."

"Take as long as you need. Dee is coming next Sunday for the week before we leave for Miami. I hope you guys can spend some time with her while she's here. I promise you'll feel a lot better about this after you meet her."

At least, I hope so.

CHAPTER 17

DEE

*T*he week after Wyatt leaves drags like nothing ever has. Every minute feels like a year, except for the hours I spend talking to him, usually late into the night after my waitressing shifts. I'm so tired, I'm practically delirious, but I wouldn't trade the hours on FaceTime with him for sleep. So far, I've toured six potential houses and have narrowed the choices to two I love. I want him to see them before I make any decisions, but the thought of living with him in either of them fills me with unreasonable joy.

I've spent time with my parents every day this week but still haven't talked to them about Wyatt and our plans. I haven't even told them I'm leaving for Phoenix on Sunday. I'm planning to see them before my waitressing shift later to let them know.

It's finally Friday, and I'm due to meet with my aunt and uncle this morning, so I drive out of my way to stop by Juanita's to get a much-needed kick of caffeine.

"¿Dónde está tu chico sexy?"

Smiling, I say, "My sexy man is in Phoenix, where he lives. For now, anyway. He's moving here next week."

"That is *awesome*. It's so nice to see you smiling again after what that jackass Marcus did."

"You know about that, huh?"

"*Everyone* knows about that. And PS, I know the puta he married, and she's no Dee Giordino."

"Aw, thanks, but that's all in the past now. I'm in love with Wyatt, and we're making plans. It's all good."

"You deserve it, cariño." She hands over my cortadito. "Heard about your big new job, too. Congrats."

"Thanks." As I give her a ten-dollar bill, I gesture to the coffee. "This will be critical to my success on the job."

"I'm here for you."

"Bless you, amiga."

I drive to the restaurant in rush-hour traffic, feeling elated and tired and so ready to see Wyatt again. The time apart has been pure torture, which only confirms my decision to go all-in with him. If I feel this way after a couple of days without him, then I know I'm doing the right thing. It does occur to me that if the worst possible thing happens, I'll have to feel this awful ache every day for the rest of my life.

"No, you're not going there," I say out loud as if that might make me listen to my advice. "Just stop that right now."

I refuse to let my mind go to that possible doomsday scenario, not after I promised Wyatt I'd be fine no matter what happens. That's a promise I intend to keep.

When I arrive at the restaurant, my aunt and uncle are waiting for me in the office with mimosas to celebrate my first day of training. They're too cute.

"Here's to our new general manager on her first day of what we hope will be a long and happy career," Vincent says.

"I'll drink to that," Vivian adds.

Smiling, I say, "Me, too."

We touch glasses and sip from our drinks.

"And here's to the two of you, who've built this incredible business. I'm honored and humbled you've chosen me to guide it into the future. I promise to do my very best to be worthy of the faith you've placed in me."

"We couldn't be happier to have you," Viv says.

We spend the next three hours reviewing the weekly routine —everything from ordering food and liquor to linens and other supplies.

"I started keeping detailed daily notes about three months ago when this idea first began to take shape." Vincent hands a notebook to me. "It's all in there, what I do every day along with some explanations of what I do and when I do it, and details about how much of everything we usually order along with caveats to account for banquets, weddings, et cetera."

"It's a lot," Viv says bluntly. "We don't expect you to fully grasp it right away, which is why we planned for you to shadow us for the next few months until you feel confident flying solo."

"Thank God for that." I'm already overwhelmed but determined. I'll figure it out. It just won't happen overnight.

Since I'm working tonight, they send me home with a takeout lunch to rest up before my shift.

I'm eating homemade minestrone and a Caesar salad and poring over Uncle V's notebook when Wyatt calls. His name on my caller ID is all it takes to get my heart racing.

"Hi there."

"Hey, babe. I just wanted to say hi between surgeries. How'd your training go?"

"It was great but daunting. I've got a lot to learn."

"You'll be running that place by yourself in no time. I have no doubt."

"I'm glad you don't."

"You already have so much experience there. That'll come in handy as you take on this new role."

"Yes, it will. How was your surgery?"

"It went well—routine angioplasty. The patient should make a full recovery. Next up is an implantable cardioverter-defibrillator."

"It's very sexy when you throw around words like angioplasty and implantable cardioverter-defibrillator."

His ringing laughter makes me smile. "I'll have to remember that the next time I see you."

"How much longer?"

"About forty-eight hours."

"That feels like forever."

"I'm counting the minutes. I'll probably be at the airport two hours early on Sunday."

"I can't wait to see you."

"I can't wait to kiss you and hold you and—"

"Stop."

"Don't want to stop. In fact, after work tonight, why don't I tell you exactly what's going to happen when you get to Phoenix on Sunday?"

I swallow hard. "I'm not sure talking about it will make it better."

"Let's try it and find out." He groans. "I gotta go. Call me when you get home?"

"I will. Good luck with your surgery."

"Thanks. Have a good night at the restaurant. Don't talk to any strange boys who think you're hot."

Amused, I say, "I'll try not to."

"Love you."

"Love you, too."

"Mmm, I can't wait until Sunday."

The phone goes dead before I can reply that I can't, either. But he knows that. I feel like a teenager in the throes of first love. I can barely function from wanting to be with him all the time. The feelings are so big and overwhelming that I can't believe I ever thought I was actually in love with Marcus. I loved him. I truly did. But that was nothing like this.

The realization has me texting my sister, asking her to call me when she gets a break at the clinic.

She calls me five minutes later. "You caught me grabbing a quick bite between patients. What's up?"

"I wanted to ask you something kind of personal."

"Okay... Since when are we ever shy around each other?"

"This is about Scott."

"Uh, okay... What about him?"

"When you were first with Austin, did it seem weird to you that you ever thought you were in love with Scott?"

"It was different with Austin from the beginning, but I was definitely in love with Scott. Until he cheated, and I wasn't anymore."

"When you say 'totally different,' what do you mean by that?"

"My connection with Austin is deeper than what I had with Scott. It's hard to explain. It's just *more*."

"Yes," I say softly. "That's what I meant."

"What's brought this up, or shall I say, *who* has brought this up? Although I can probably guess."

"It's just so different with Wyatt, and it's made me wonder what I had with Marcus. I loved him. I really did, but it wasn't like this."

"That's because he was your starter love. Wyatt is your forever love."

"Leave it to you to sum it up so perfectly."

"Listen, Dee... From what I hear, Marcus is very determined to put things back together with you."

"That's not going to happen. How can we make sure he knows that?"

"I could make sure his sister hears about you and Wyatt."

"How would you do that?"

"I could post a picture of you guys on Facebook with a caption that says something like 'cheers to new love.'"

"I like that idea. It would shut down any efforts to reconcile. I just can't bear the thought of him hunting me down to talk it out. What's there to say?"

"Absolutely nothing. Do you have a good picture of you and Wyatt?"

"I do."

"Send it to me."

"Should I text him first to ask if he minds if we go Facebook public?"

"He's moving here to live with you, Dee. He won't mind, and I won't tag him. We'll just be alerting the people here who need to know."

"You're diabolically brilliant, and I love you."

"I love you, too. I'm so, *so* glad to see you smiling again."

"It feels good, almost too good to be true."

"It's not. It's as true as it gets. He's crazy about you. We could all see that."

"I'm just as crazy about him. This week, since he left, has been sheer torture."

"I remember what that was like after I first met Austin, and he went back to Baltimore for a few days. It was brutal."

"That's a good word for it, even if I feel like I'm super dramatic. It's just that everything feels so urgent with Wyatt."

"I get that. You'll be with him soon enough and can get busy living."

"I can't wait. How're you holding up with Austin in spring training?"

"It's fine. The team is playing three games in Fort Myers this week. I just miss him when he's away overnight. I've gotten spoiled having him home all winter."

"I'd offer to keep you company, but I'm working tonight and tomorrow night and flying to Phoenix Sunday morning."

"Don't worry about me. I'm fine. Austin will be home late tomorrow night. Everly and I will try to come in for dinner tomorrow when you're working."

"I'll look forward to seeing you both."

"Send me that picture."

"I will. Thanks again, Mar."

"Anything for you. Love you."

"Love you, too."

As always, my older sister makes me feel better about whatever is weighing on me. It's always been that way with us. While other sisters we knew fought like she-cats, we never did.

I find my favorite picture of me and Wyatt, a selfie I took on the boat last weekend, and send it to Maria. He's shirtless, with his gorgeous chest and tattoo on display, and I'm in a cute bikini top. Anyone who sees that picture will have no doubt we're happy and in love.

It pains me to think of hurting anyone, especially Marcus, even after what he did to me, but he needs to know there's no hope of reconciling with me. Maria is right—a post on her Facebook will shut that down pretty quickly.

I don't have any time to waste on the past. Not when my present and future are looking so damned perfect.

At three, I head over to check on my parents before my waitressing shift. I find them in the family room, sitting in side-by-side recliners and holding hands while they watch TV. They're so damned cute, and all I want in this entire world is to be their age someday and still holding hands with Wyatt while we watch TV.

"Hey, honey," Dad says. "I just talked to Vincent, and he said your first training session went great."

"Glad to hear he thought so." I kiss them both and sit on the sofa.

Dad turns off the news.

"Did *you* think so?" he asks.

"It was good. I have a lot to learn, but I've got time. It's an exciting challenge, though. How're you feeling, Mommy?" I've already texted both of them today, but I still have to ask.

"I'm fine. Nothing to worry about. I have a checkup the week after next."

"I'm sorry it's been such an ordeal."

"It is what it is. I'm staying focused on all the positive things in my life, such as the happy glow on my youngest daughter's face because she's found love again."

I can't stop the smile from stretching across my face at the mention of Wyatt. "I really have. He's amazing."

"He seems like a special young man," Dad says.

"He is. I'm going to Phoenix on Sunday to meet Wyatt's parents and drive back with him. I'll be gone about a week. Carmen promised to help out if needed, and Maria said she could do extra, too, especially since Austin is traveling with the team."

"Don't worry about us, honey," Mommy says. "Go have a wonderful time with your Wyatt. You deserve a break. You've been working and taking care of us for months. We'll be just fine."

"You promise?"

"I promise," she says, smiling. Being sick has softened her rough edges, made her sweeter and more loving than she's ever been, even if she was always a wonderful mother.

"We've been doing some talking, too," Dad says, "and we're going to sell the business."

She's a lawyer, and he's an accountant. Their firm provides legal and financial services to hundreds of other local businesses. They're self-professed workaholics, so this is somewhat shocking news. "This is a big deal."

"It's time," he says, sighing. "Duncan and Gloria have done a brilliant job running the show since your mother's illness. We're negotiating a deal for them to buy us out over ten years, which will give us guaranteed income for the next decade. After that, we'll be able to tap into our 401(k), and Social Security will kick in."

I'm surprised by how far along they are in planning this, and it's the first I've heard of it. "Sounds like a good idea." All this change is a lot to absorb. "Do you think you'll miss it?"

Dad smiles. "If you'd asked me that six months ago, I would've said there was no way I could be away from it for this long. But now..." He looks over at Mommy, who gazes at him with love and affection. "Now, I couldn't care less about the business, which tells me the time is right to step aside. With Vincent and Vivian doing the same, we're hoping to do some traveling together."

"That sounds wonderful. I'm happy for all of you. You've worked hard your entire life. It's time to play."

"That's right. As soon as your mom gets the all-clear from the doctors, we're outta here."

I just hope she gets that all-clear sooner rather than later. I leave them to head to the restaurant for one of the busiest nights of the week. It's not unusual for me to make as much as three hundred dollars in tips on Friday and Saturday nights.

On Saturday night, I work on the Cuban side of the house, which I requested to see what's up with her and Mr. Muñoz. As I do my prep work before the rush, Abuela comes to help me roll silverware into linen napkins.

"Thanks for the help."

"No problem."

She's had her hair done, as usual for a Saturday, and looks particularly lovely in a champagne-colored dress. I take a closer look and notice she's wearing eye shadow that matches her dress.

"You look beautiful, Abuela."

"Oh, thank you, honey. I do what I can with what I've got left."

She makes me laugh every time I talk to her. "You've got plenty left."

We work together in contented silence for quite some time before it occurs to me that contented silence isn't Abuela's thing.

"What's going on with you?"

She looks up at me, seeming startled by the question. "What? Nothing is going on."

"Something is. You're quiet."

"All this talk of change has me unsettled," she says after a long pause, during which I'm not sure if she's going to tell me what's on her mind. "Vincent told me to think of something I've wanted to do while I used work as an excuse not to do it. I just have no idea what I'd do if I didn't have this place to come to every day."

"Maybe you should accept Mr. Muñoz's offer to join him for dinner. Although the poor guy would probably die of shock if you said yes."

Her face flushes with a blush that's adorable and shocking. "Hush."

"Abuela." I wait until she looks at me. "Do you *like* him?"

She shrugs. "He seems nice enough. He sure is persistent."

"He's been asking you out for how long again?"

"I don't know. Four years, maybe? Since about a year after his wife died."

"Have you heard of him going out with anyone else in that time?"

She thinks about that for a second before shaking her head. "I don't think so."

"Abuela... He's waiting for you to say yes to him. He's holding out for you."

"Don't be foolish. He is not."

"He *is*. He's waiting for you to say yes, and he's never going to stop asking until you do. What do you have to lose by having dinner with a nice man who likes you?"

"I can't do that here. Everyone would talk. It would be mortifying."

I stare at her, incredulous. "Is *that* why you haven't said yes to him before now?"

She picks up the pace of her silverware rolling, but the set of her shoulders gives away the truth.

"If you say yes to him, I'll personally make sure no one says a word about it. I promise."

"Good luck with that in this family."

"I'll put up a firewall around you. I promise, Abuela. No one will say a word."

"But they'll still know."

"That two consenting adults ate a meal together? What do you care if they know that?"

"I can't bear to be the center of attention and gossip. I just can't."

"I'll put out the word that the topic is off-limits. I'll make sure of it, Abuela. Or I'll ask Mr. Muñoz to take you somewhere else."

"Somewhere else," she says with a disdainful huff of laughter. "There is nowhere else."

The curse of owning and working for a family restaurant known for its outstanding cuisine has made restaurant snobs out of us all.

"Say yes to him, Abuela. Please say yes."

Before she can reply, we spot early birds showing up at the hostess stand, and she takes off to greet them.

We start to get busy, but I keep an eye on her and watch for Mr. Muñoz, who comes at the same time he does every week, says a few complimentary words to Abuela as she shows him to his table —always C32, from which he can see the hostess desk—and asks her to join him. From across the room, I watch him gesture to the chair across from his. The hopeful expression on his handsome face touches me deeply. *Please say yes, Abuela.* I'm not sure if I think it or say it, but I watch them so closely, I barely blink or breathe in the full minute it takes for her to pull out a chair and take a seat.

It's all I can do to contain the joy that fills me as she settles into her seat and drops the napkin we rolled together across her lap.

The stunned look on his face is priceless.

Vivian approaches me from behind, taking me by surprise. "What's going on?"

I use my chin to direct her attention to C32. "Look."

She gasps at the sight of her long-widowed mother sitting with a man.

"You can't say anything about it to her. I promised her we wouldn't make a thing of it. Okay?"

"I, um, okay."

"Will you tell everyone else? I got the feeling she wanted to say yes to him but didn't want everyone teasing her about it. I promised her we wouldn't."

"I'll put out the word."

"Are you okay with it?"

"Oh, honey, of course I am. She's been alone for such a long time. After my dad died, I always hoped she'd find someone else, but she was so stubbornly determined to stay true to him. What do you suppose made her finally say yes?"

"I think it was Vincent telling her and Nona that they needed to find something to do besides work. And when I promised her I wouldn't let anyone tease her, that seemed to help make up her mind."

"That's wonderful, Dee. Well played."

"I'd better get over there and take their drink order before she starts critiquing the service."

Vivian laughs. "Good idea."

"You'll tell everyone to play it cool?"

"Yep. I'll take care of it, and I'll cover her hostess stand."

"Thanks, Auntie V." I head over to C32, where Abuela and Mr. Muñoz are engaged in animated conversation that stops when I get close to the table. "Hi there, welcome to Giordino's. I'm Dee, and I'll be taking care of you tonight. Can I offer you a cocktail?"

I know their drink orders by heart, but I play the role anyway.

Mr. Muñoz gestures to Abuela. "Marlene, what are you having?" His eyes sparkle with pure delight that makes my heart happy.

"I'd like a vodka Collins, please, with Absolut and two cherries."

"Coming right up. And for you?" He always gets Maker's Mark bourbon with branch.

"I'll have the same," he says, smiling at her. "That sounds delightful."

She blushes furiously.

Could they be any cuter? I go to the bar to get their drinks. When I return, his arms are on the table, and he's hanging on her every word. After placing their drinks on the table, I run through the list of specials and take their order. She orders the ropa vieja, and he requests the picadillo.

"I'll be right back with salad and bread." As I start to walk away, Vivian brings another party to a nearby table without so much as a glance in her mother's direction.

Perfect.

Over the next couple of hours, they enjoy dinner, dessert and a bottle of champagne Vincent sends over.

Abuela is giggling and smiling and generally having a wonderful time. It's the best thing I've ever seen. They're still there when we begin to clean up for closing.

"Are we going to have to kick them out?" Vivian asks.

"Maybe."

But before we can do that, Mr. Muñoz stands to help Abuela out of her seat.

I walk over to say good night.

He hands me his credit card.

"Vincent said to tell you it's on the house."

"That's very nice of him. Please thank him for us."

"I'll do that."

He puts his card back in his wallet, withdraws a hundred-dollar bill and presses it into my hand. "Marlene tells me you're going to Phoenix to help your new boyfriend move to Miami. Use this for dinner one night on your trip."

"Thank you so much, Mr. Muñoz. Can I call a cab for you two?"

"I already ordered an Uber. I'll see Marlene home safely."

I kiss Abuela and whisper in her ear, "Don't do anything I wouldn't do."

She sputters and smacks at my arm, but as she walks away with her hand tucked into his bent elbow, she's as happy as I've ever seen her as if she's finally done something she's wanted to do for a long time.

I'm still high off the success of Abuela's "date" when I get home and jump in the shower. I throw in a load of laundry and pack for the trip to Phoenix before I settle in bed to call Wyatt.

He immediately accepts my FaceTime call. "Hey, beautiful. How was your night?"

"It was so great. You won't believe what happened." I tell him all about Abuela and Mr. Muñoz and how she finally said yes to him. "She was *so* happy. It was the sweetest thing I've ever seen."

"You did a good thing giving her a push."

"I know what it's like to have everyone up in my business and how uncomfortable that can be. If all it took was a promise for no one to tease her, it was worth it. I'm so happy for both of them. He's just the nicest man. Vincent treated them to dinner, but Mr. Muñoz gave me a hundred dollars to take you to dinner on our trip."

"Very nice of him. I'll make sure you get some awesome Southwest food while you're here."

"How many more hours?"

"About seventeen."

"I'm not going to make it."

"Don't give up on me yet. We're almost there. And the good news is we're going to sleep through most of those hours."

"I'm so excited. How will I ever sleep?"

"You need to be very well-rested when you get here."

His words send a shiver of longing down my spine that lands in a tight knot of need between my legs. I've never craved someone physically before. Not like this. "I can't wait."

"Me, either, sweetheart."

CHAPTER 18

WYATT

I'm at the airport two hours early. The word is out among my family, friends and colleagues that I'm moving to Miami. My phone has been buzzing with texts all week that I haven't answered yet. I'm waiting for Dee to get here to take a new selfie of us together that I'll send to everyone wanting to know what's in Miami that we don't have in Phoenix.

Overall, people seem to be taking the news well. Even my mom has been somewhat restrained this week, checking on me only once since I saw them on Monday, rather than the usual three or four times. I suspect my dad advised her to go with the flow after seeing how intent I am on having this life with Dee.

I can't remember the last time I was more excited about anything than I am to see her. Thank God her flight is on time. A delay would send us both over the edge today.

The anticipation is killing me until they finally announce the arrival of her flight from Miami. Another half-hour goes by with no sign of her—pure torture.

By the time I see her coming toward me, I feel like I can't wait another second for something I thought I didn't need. She was right. It would've been a damned shame to miss out on ever feeling the pure joy that overtakes me at the sight of her beautiful, smiling face. She walks into my outstretched arms like she's coming home, and in a way, we both are.

She hugs me as tightly as I hug her. "So happy to see you."

"Me, too. I was about to spontaneously combust, waiting for you to get here."

"Don't do that. I need you all in one piece."

I let go of her only long enough to take her backpack and the handle of her suitcase. I put my arm around her again to walk out of the airport. When we leave the air-conditioned airport, we step into a hot, sunny day in the desert. "What did you think of the view from the air?"

"It's so different from Miami."

"It looks like Miami in need of a glass of water."

She laughs at my description. "Just a different climate. I can't wait to see more."

"I wish we had time to go to Sedona and the Grand Canyon. We'll do that when we come back to visit. You'll love Sedona. It's the most beautiful place."

"I can't wait to see it all."

When we get to my SUV, I stash her bag in the back and hold the passenger door for her.

"This is nice," she says about the car.

"Thanks." Because I can't wait for another second, I lean into the car to kiss her.

Her hand cups my face, and her mouth opens to my tongue. Just that fast, I'm completely lost in her. "Hold that thought," I tell her when I finally withdraw from the kiss to walk around to the driver's side. Once in the car, I reach for her again, and we pick right up where we left off, both of us straining to get closer.

"Please tell me we don't have any plans today."

"I have one plan that involves you in my bed for many, many hours."

"Let's get to that."

"Yes, ma'am." I drive us home as fast as I dare, giving her a windshield tour of Phoenix as we go.

"I love the cacti! We need to get some to take home to Miami for our new house."

"We can do that. Speaking of our new house, what's the latest?"

"The Realtor set us up with appointments at both for a week from Tuesday. She said they've been on the market for a while, so it's probably safe to wait. She asked the listing agent to let us know if they get other offers."

"I told you—if there's one you like better than the other, it's okay to make the offer."

"I want you to see it first."

"As long as you're there with me, I could live in a tent and be happy."

"That's crazy. You can't buy a house without ever seeing it."

"Yes, I can. Carpe diem. Isn't that our motto? If you like one of them better than the other, make the offer."

Her nervous laughter fills me with a lighthearted, breathless feeling I'm beginning to recognize as joy. It's the best thing I've ever experienced.

"Are you sure? Like a thousand percent sure you want to buy a house without seeing it?"

"I'm ten million percent sure. Pull the trigger, babe."

"Gulp." She gets out her phone and calls up a listing on Zillow that she shows me at a stoplight. "This is the one I liked the best." In the time it takes for the light to change, she gives me a tour of the house I've seen once before online. "The kitchen is to die for, with two ovens, a gas range and top-of-the-line appliances. I like that it has two master suites, so if your parents come to visit, they'll have their own space."

"That'd be perfect because I told them they ought to consider wintering in Miami."

"They totally should. There're also four bedrooms and two bathrooms upstairs, a media room and an office we can share."

"There's no one I'd rather share an office with than you. Show me the pool again."

She flips to the picture of a fenced-off pool surrounded by lavish, mature landscaping and palm trees.

"I loved that one, too. That pool is gorgeous. Text the agent. Tell her we'll take it."

Again, she laughs, but there's a higher tone to it that tells me she's excited but nervous. I love that I already know these things about her. "Are we really doing this?"

"We're really doing this, and it's the very best thing to ever happen to me. Buy the house, Dee. Let's make a home there together."

Her eyes are bright with excitement when she shows me the asking price at another stoplight. "What do you want to offer?"

"Full price, so they'll take it."

"No one offers full price, Wyatt. We're not doing that." She shaves a hundred thousand off the asking price and sends the offer by text to the Realtor before dropping her phone into her lap like it's suddenly too hot to handle.

"You're not going to puke, are you?"

Smiling, she looks at me with gorgeous eyes filled with happiness. "I don't think so, but I reserve the right to puke later."

"It's all good, love. I'll get a pretty penny for my place here, and I've been smart with money. We'll be fine."

"Plus, we have my new job, too."

"That's right."

"I know it's nothing compared to what you probably make—"

I lean over to kiss the words off her sweet lips. "It's *not* nothing. It's fantastic, and you're going to be the best general manager in the history of GMs."

She rolls her eyes. "If you say so."

"I say so. There's no way your aunt and uncle would've asked you if they weren't as sure as I am that you'll be great at it. They have a lot on the line entrusting their very successful business to someone. You can bet they gave it a ton of thought before they asked you."

"I'm sure they did."

"They asked the best person for the job. No question."

"As I've told you before, you're very good for my ego."

"If you knew how often I thought of you this last week, your ego would be too big to fit in this vehicle."

"Is that right? So how many times are we talking?"

"You want, like, a number?"

"A number would be good."

She's been here fifteen minutes, and already everything is better. The sun is brighter, the sky is bluer, and my heart is lighter than air. "Maybe, like, a thousand?"

"Hmm."

"What? Is that too low?"

Her laughter delights me. "Of course not. Were you thinking of me when you were doing surgery?"

"Yep."

"Is that safe?"

"For who?"

"The patient!"

I lose it laughing. "Some of these surgeries I do so often, I could do them in my sleep, even if every one of them is different in some way or another. It's safe for my mind to wander to thoughts about my favorite person."

"I'm your favorite person?"

"Hell yes, and you were before last weekend. I've never

thought more about another person in my life than I have about you since the day we met. The whole time I was on the flight to Miami, I was telling myself to stay far away from you, because if I saw you again..."

"What?" she asks, sounding breathless.

"I was afraid I wouldn't have the willpower to do what was best for you, and it turns out I was right about that."

"No, you weren't. What's best for me is more time with you, as much as I can get for as long as I can."

"And you wonder why you're my favorite person."

"You're mine, too."

"You don't have to say that. You've got a lot of people in your life."

"But there's only one you, and you're my new favorite. I thought of you nonstop this last week, too. I thought Sunday would never get here."

I push on the accelerator, dying to get her home so we can spend the rest of the day in bed.

"Is there a reason you're speeding?"

"Yep."

"Are you going to tell me?"

"I'd rather show you."

CHAPTER 19

DEE

I've never felt anything even close to what happens when I'm with him. During the long week apart, I had a few moments of concern about whether I'm doing the right thing, diving into this thing with him without any of the usual care and concern I'd typically put into such a big decision. The sense of urgency attached to his situation has caused me to skip right over the due diligence my accountant dad taught me.

Due diligence is about doing my research, making sure the decision is sound and practical, that it makes sense in the context of the rest of my life.

Dad and I did a cost-benefit analysis before college in New York and then another when I decided to stay after graduation. We made a list of all my expenses and came up with a salary range I needed to live there independently. He says I have the mind of an accountant with the way I analyze everything to death.

This is what makes my behavior with Wyatt so out of character.

I don't care about due diligence. I haven't spent one minute trying to track down a social media presence for him or looking beyond the initial google searches I did before I knew his whole story. I don't care about who he's dated before or who his Facebook friends are.

I only care about being with him.

Nothing else matters, except my new job and my family, but even they suddenly matter less than he does.

I ought to be scared out of my mind. I ought to be questioning everything. I ought to be panicking.

I'm not. I'm too busy feeling fully alive for the first time in my life to worry about things such as due diligence.

As I take in the desert topography out the window, I just want him.

My belly is full of butterflies. The giddy anticipation reminds me of Christmas morning as a child when the excitement threatened to consume me. This is just like that, only better. So much better.

By the time he pulls into his condo complex, I'm practically bouncing in my seat.

While he grabs my bag, I wait for him in the blistering sun that feels so much hotter than it does in Florida, even though the temperature is comparable. He takes my hand and leads me up the stairs to the front door of a white townhouse with a blue door.

"Just a heads-up that my mom and sister helped pick out the furniture, and anything that's even kind of nice is thanks to them."

"Good to know before I give you credit for your lovely home."

"I don't deserve any credit."

While the furnishings are mostly neutral colors, it's the artwork that catches my attention. "I love the art."

"It's from a local artist who specializes in desert landscapes."

"It's beautiful."

"I'm glad you like it. We'll pick a few favorites to bring to Miami."

"I want to see your artwork, too."

"I'll show you everything." He drops my suitcase by the stairs and puts his arms around me. Staring down at me, he smiles and says, "Hi."

"Hi."

"Welcome to my place."

I curl my arms around his neck and go up on tiptoes to kiss him. "Thanks for having me."

"Definitely my pleasure. Can I get you anything? I got some of that iced tea you like."

"That's very sweet of you. I'll have some later." I look to the stairs. "What's up there?"

"Bedrooms."

"Show me."

"Happy to." He keeps one arm around me and picks up my suitcase with his free hand as we go up the stairs. "To the right."

We pass two other bedrooms and a bathroom on the way to the master, including an en suite bathroom.

"Nice crib, Doc."

"I liked it a lot until I saw that house in Miami, and now I can't wait to live there with you."

"I'm still trying to believe this is happening. You're moving to Miami, and we're buying a house together. Someone, please pinch me. I must be dreaming."

His hand slides down my back before he pinches my ass. "Not dreaming, although it feels like a dream in some ways. How could something this amazing be real? But it's so real, and you were right. It would've been tragic to miss out on this, so thanks for making me fall in love with you. It's the best thing I've ever done."

"I enjoy being right."

"Haha, I'll be sure to remember that going forward."

"See that you do." I love who I am with him. I say whatever comes to mind and never take even so much as a second to ask myself whether I should say it. There's no self-editing, no worries about him taking something the wrong way. It's so freeing. "Can I tell you something?"

He puts my suitcase down next to his dresser. "Anything."

"When I was with Marcus, I used to worry about what I said to him and how he would take it. I don't have to do that with you, and it's a huge relief to me. I thought you might like to know that."

"I love knowing that, and I feel the same way. Being with you is easy like breathing."

"I realize that's the way it should be."

"It's everything," he whispers in the second before he kisses me.

While I'm in his arms, the whole world fades away until there's only him and me and us and this room. The afternoon sun filters in to cast a warm rosy glow over the king-sized bed. This, right here with him, is the single best moment of my entire life so far. As we slowly and reverently undress each other, I have a feeling we'll top this many times over.

Wyatt lowers me to the bed and comes down on top of me, all without breaking the kiss that makes every other kiss I've ever had, even with him, seem shabby by comparison. His tongue tangles with mine. I strain to get closer to him. I want everything, and I want it right now. That sense of urgency makes the desire sharper and more intense than it's ever been before.

"Easy," he whispers as he breaks the kiss to focus on my neck.

His lips against my sensitive skin send shivers down my spine and heighten the need to almost unbearable levels.

He cups my breasts and teases my nipples with his tongue and fingers. "So fucking sexy," he whispers against my nipple.

I grasp a handful of his hair, needing something to hold on to, while he seems intent on kissing me everywhere. How can something so elemental be so different with him than it was with the man I used to love? It's almost confusing that with Wyatt, I feel like I finally understand what it means to make love.

His hands, lips and tongue take me to the edge of release before backing off and starting over. He does this several times, leaving me a trembling, quivering mess by the time he pushes into me and triggers an orgasm that rockets through me like an out-of-control wildfire.

I think I scream, which has never happened, except with him.

Good thing he lives in an end unit, which is my first thought when I come down from the highest of highs to discover he's still hard and moving in me and not at all finished. Holy crap, he's going to kill me with his stamina. Heart problems? What heart problems?

I flatten my hands on his back and slide them down to cup his muscular backside, giving a squeeze that makes him groan. "Turn over."

"Hmm?"

I give his shoulder a gentle push.

He reaches under me, and with his hands on my ass, he turns us over without losing our connection.

I sit up and push my hair back from my face. "Impressive."

His eyes go hot with desire as he stares at my breasts. "You liked that?"

Nodding, I pivot my hips and draw another deep groan from him.

"God, that's so good. It's so fucking good." His fingers dig into my hips as I move on top of him.

Since his eyes are closed, I take him by surprise when I lean forward to bite down gently on his nipple.

He comes with a shout as he surges into me.

I land on his chest, and he wraps his arms around me.

"I really, really love you, Dee Giordino."

"I really, really love you, too, Wyatt Blake."

"That makes me happier than anything ever has."

"Me, too."

We shift to our sides, so we're facing each other. The ceiling fan sends a steady stream of cool air over us that makes me shiver as my body recovers from the exertion.

Wyatt pulls a blanket over us, snuggling up to me with an arm around my waist and a leg between mine. "Comfy?"

"Very. I may never want to leave this bed again."

He runs his fingers through my hair. "I'd be fine with that."

I'm suddenly exhausted after getting up before five to make my seven o'clock flight. My eyes won't stay open, but sleep is the last thing I want to do after counting the minutes until I could see him. I open my eyes to find him watching me. "Sorry. I'm super sleepy all of a sudden."

"Take a nap. We've got all the time in the world."

I really hope that's true.

CHAPTER 20

DEE

The time in Phoenix is filled with joy in every possible way, except for one—the chilly reception I receive from Wyatt's parents when we go there for dinner Wednesday night. While he wraps things up at work, I've been working during the day to pack up the clothes and personal items he wants to take to Miami.

We're tired from staying up way too late every night and excited to start our life together in Miami, but minutes into the get-together with his parents, I feel deflated. His parents are polite, but it's obvious they don't approve of Wyatt's plans or my influence on him.

It's nothing they say or do. It's more the vibe his parents put out.

They don't ask about me or my life or make any attempt to get to know me. They mostly speak to him and act like I'm not even there. Wyatt keeps drawing me into the conversation, but it's awkward and stilted.

As the four of us sit at the table to eat dinner, it's all I can do to choke down a few bites around the massive lump in my throat. I'm so afraid his mother will be offended if I don't eat that I force myself to chew and swallow.

It doesn't help that the AC on deep freeze mode, which has me shivering. I'm a Floridian. AC doesn't usually bother me, but their chilly reception has me so rattled that I'm cold to the bone.

After dinner, Wyatt takes me upstairs to show me his childhood bedroom. I'm so relieved to be away from his parents that my legs feel shaky. I'm not used to being disliked on sight before I even get to say a word in my defense.

When we're in his room, he immediately puts his arms around me. "I'm so sorry. Please know that had nothing to do with you and everything to do with me."

"It felt rather personal to me."

"I know, babe, and I feel awful. I hate that they acted that way, but it's not about you. They're upset about me moving. I told you that."

"Yes, you did, but can we please go soon?"

"Of course. I'm sorry they made you uncomfortable. They're not like that. Once they get to know you, they'll love you as much as I do."

I'm sure he wants to believe that's true, but since they made no effort whatsoever to get to know me, I'm not optimistic. For the first time since Wyatt and I hatched our wild plan, I have serious doubts. His parents dislike me simply because he's moving away from them to live with me.

As Wyatt shows me the treasures from his childhood, I'm so upset, I can barely focus on him or what he's saying.

"I love these Rock 'Em Sock 'Em Robots. I played them with everyone when I was in the hospital. An orderly named Oscar showed me how to win every time, and after that, no one could beat me."

"What will happen to the stuff you still have here?"

"I guess I'll put away things like the robots for my future nieces and nephews."

"What about your kids?"

He puts the robots back on the shelf where they live and turns to me, looking stricken. "What kids?"

Suddenly, I'm cold all over once again, albeit for entirely different reasons. "The ones we're going to have together."

"I, um... I'm not having kids, Dee. How could I do that, knowing I may not live to see them grow up?"

I'm going to be sick. That's the only thought in my head as the meager contents of my stomach come rushing up. I run for the bathroom in the hallway, managing to shut and lock the door before I bend over the toilet and vomit.

WYATT

Fuck. This night has been a goddamned disaster. Watching Dee sprint from the room and hearing her retching in the bathroom breaks my heart. Is this going to screw up everything? It can't. I won't let that happen. I go to the bathroom and knock softly on the door. "Let me in, sweetheart."

"No."

"Please?"

Several minutes later, the lock pops, and the door opens. I step into the scent of the air freshener Dee sprayed to hide the smell of vomit.

Her face is ghostly pale, and her eyes are big and full of tears that gut me.

"Dee, honey..."

She takes a step back from me, not that there's far she can go in the small bathroom. "Don't. Please. I'd like to go home, please."

"To my place or Miami?" I can barely breathe as I wait for her to reply.

"To your place for now."

For now. Have two words ever carried more weight?

I find a washcloth in the linen closet, wet it with cold water and wipe the tears from her face. "Please don't cry. I can't bear that."

"I'm sorry." She makes an effort to pull herself together, running her fingers through her hair and pinching some color into her cheeks. "Will you please tell them I'm not feeling well so we can go?"

"Yeah, sure, and don't apologize for being upset."

As we head downstairs, I'm full of fear that everything has changed with Dee in the matter of one disastrous evening. I've never been in a situation like this, in which someone else's happiness means more to me than my own. I'm pissed with my parents, but apparently, they're pissed with me, too, which makes everything awkward as we say our goodbyes.

"Will we see you before you leave?" Dad asks.

"I don't think so. We've got a lot to do to get ready for the movers."

"So, when will we see you again?"

"I'll come back to visit in a couple of months, and you're always welcome in Miami. Our house has a guest suite that's all yours." Although, after tonight, how can I subject Dee to having my parents staying in our house when they barely spoke to her? I'll take that up with them on my own when she's not there to be further hurt by them.

"Thank you for dinner, Mr. and Mrs. Blake," she says in a stiff tone that's so far removed from her usual warmth that it might as well be coming from a stranger. "It was very nice to meet you."

"You, too," Dad says.

Mom says nothing.

I want to scream at them. *Don't you realize this woman means everything to me?* That she's the love of my life, the same life they weren't sure I was going to get to have for a very long time? I'll say all that and more when I call them tomorrow. But for now, I have to get her out of here and deal with the other issue that arose upstairs.

I hug them both before I follow Dee out the door. "I'll call you."

Dee's already in the car when I get in and look over at her, stunned to see tears rolling down her cheeks.

"I'm so sorry that was such a disaster in there."

"It's fine."

I've never had a girlfriend before, but one thing I know for sure is if a woman is in tears and says everything is "fine," it most definitely isn't. I start the SUV and back out of the drive-way, navigating the first streets I ever drove on, after the transplant when the whole world opened to me. Learning to drive and getting my license had been at the top of my list.

I want to tell her that, but I'm not sure I should say anything until we address the elephant sitting between us. I think back over every conversation we've had, and no, we never did talk about kids, which I can now see was a significant oversight on my part. I should've told her I don't intend to have kids, but I sort of assumed she'd know that.

That was a huge mistake, one I'm not sure can be corrected at this point.

She says nothing to me on the twenty-minute ride to my place, which is a marked contrast to the usual nonstop chatter between us. We never run out of things to talk about, and the silence sits like a heavy weight on my chest.

I can't fuck this up with her. After having been loved by her, I'd be devastated to lose her.

Back at my place, she goes straight upstairs to shower and change into pajama pants and a long-sleeved T-shirt of mine. It's the first time she's put on clothes for bed since she got here, and it makes me sad. I love sleeping naked with her.

I give her a half hour to herself before I go up to check on her. I bring her a glass of the iced tea she loves and put it on the bedside table on what's become her side of my bed. I sit on the edge of the bed and reach for her hand, which is icy cold. "Can we talk about it?"

"Which part? The one about your parents taking an instant dislike to me or the part about you not wanting kids and waiting until now to tell me that?"

"It's not that I don't want kids, Dee. If everything were normal for me, I'd want a bunch of kids, especially if you were going to be their mother. But how do I do that to them or you, not knowing what the future holds for me? Do you want to wake up a single mother to however many kids we have when my heart suddenly gives out?"

"What I would've liked, about two weeks ago, was to know how you felt about this subject. I made the mistake of thinking when you said you were all in, that meant *all* in."

"I'm all in with you. I love you. I want everything with you, but I don't want to bring kids into this uncertain reality of mine."

To my great dismay, she begins to cry so hard that sobs shake her body.

I reach for her, but she puts her hand up to stop me. "Dee, honey…"

"Don't. Please don't."

I've never felt so helpless. "I can't stand that you're upset because of me."

"It's my fault." She uses the tissue I hand her to wipe away tears and blow her nose. "I dove in without doing my due diligence. I should've asked you about kids before I agreed to go all in. I should've told you how I've waited my whole life to be a mother. When we talked about my miscarriage, I should've said how important it is to me to try again someday."

The sinking feeling that overtakes me fills me with the kind of desperation I haven't experienced since the days when I expected to die at any moment. "I never want you to be upset because of me, but can't you see, even a little, why I feel this way? What would your life have been like if your dad had died when you were a little kid?"

"It would've been very different, but I would've known how much he loved me because my mom would've told me every day. I'd get to have a life because he gave that life to me."

"But you'd be sad to have lost him, especially if you didn't even remember him."

"Yes, but that wouldn't have stopped me from going on to live a very satisfying life." She accepts a second tissue from me and wipes her face again. "When you said you wanted to experience every part of being in love, I thought that extended to kids."

"I'm sorry I didn't say otherwise."

"So am I."

I feel like I'm going to be sick myself. "What does this mean for us?" I'm terrified to ask that question.

"I don't know. We were impulsive. We jumped in so quickly. Maybe we made a mistake."

"This wasn't a mistake." I've never felt so desperate about anything as I do about fixing this with her. "I don't want to lose you, Dee. I love you so much. You've been the best thing to ever happen to me."

Her chin quivers and new tears spill from her gorgeous brown eyes. "I love you, too. I really do, but…"

I stop breathing, waiting for her to finish that thought.

"You're asking me to sacrifice one dream for another, and I just don't know if I can do that, Wyatt. Even for you." She takes a deep breath and lets it out. "And your parents are so upset about you moving. Maybe you shouldn't do that to them."

"I'm not going to live what's left of my life for them. I want to live for myself and you."

"I want kids."

Three little words have never packed a more significant punch than those do. "I don't have life insurance, Dee. I can't get it, which means I'd be leaving you without any kind of cushion other than the house and the money I've managed to save, a big chunk of which will go toward the house. My savings is decent, but it's not enough to help you raise a family on your own in an expensive city like Miami."

"I have a good job now. I can do it on my own if I have to. Maybe we won't live in a fancy house, but they'll have what they need. I'd make sure of it, and my family would be there to support me. I wouldn't be alone."

My guts have twisted into knots, but I feel a tiny spark of hope. "The thought of having children that might never know me is so… It's overwhelming to me. Can you understand that at all?"

"Of course I can, but it goes back to what we talked about at the beginning of all this, about not living in fear of a future we can't control anyway. You have no idea whether you'll die young or live to be an old man, and I don't know that for myself, either."

"You'll never be an old man."

For the first time in more than an hour, she cracks a small smile. "I don't know if I'll live through tomorrow any more than you do."

"Please don't say that. You're going to live a good long life."

"And you might, too. That's my point. We don't know what's going to happen, so why not live to the fullest while we can?"

"You make excellent points. Could I have some time to think about it?"

"How much time? You're supposed to move to Miami in two days. If we're at an impasse on this topic, maybe…" Her voice catches. "Maybe you shouldn't move."

I draw in a deep breath and release it on a long sigh. "This is why I had rules I never broke. I never wanted someone to look at me the way you are now as if I've disappointed you profoundly."

"It's not your fault. We both did this. We dove in headfirst without taking even a second to make sure we were doing the right thing."

"Nothing in my entire life has felt more right to me than this has, than you have." When I reach for her this time, she lets me.

When her arms encircle me, I'm full of relief to have her back in my arms, even if I know our problems are far from solved.

CHAPTER 21

DEE

I barely sleep that night. I'm a wreck after the last few hours and fearful that everything has changed between Wyatt and me—and not for the better. He tosses and turns, too, and has dark circles under his eyes when he comes to kiss me goodbye before he leaves for his second-to-last day at work in Phoenix.

"Should I... um, keep packing?" What was definite only yesterday has now been thrown into complete uncertainty.

"Yeah, I mean, I quit my job here. Miami-Dade is expecting me the week after next. We made an offer on the house in Miami. This place is going on the market this weekend. It's all in motion."

Everything else is in motion except our relationship, which hit a major roadblock last night.

"We'll talk tonight," he says, kissing me again. "We'll figure this out. I promise. I wish I didn't have to go, but I've got back-to-back surgeries today."

"I know."

"I love you, Dee. No matter what you're thinking or feeling, please remember that."

"I love you, too."

"As long as we have that, the rest will fall into place. I believe that, and you should, too."

I can tell he honestly doesn't want to leave me but pulls himself away to go to work. After I hear the door close downstairs, I reach for my phone to call my sister. She's at work by now, but she'll take the call if she can.

The call goes to voice mail, and I leave a message asking her to call me when she can.

I bring the phone with me when I go to shower and then downstairs to make coffee. I feel awful, almost as bad as I did when I found out Marcus married a stranger. The sick feeling, aching eyes and pervasive hopelessness are far too reminiscent of that awful time in my life.

I never wanted to feel like that again, and here I am. Even in the short time I've been with Wyatt, I already know he's way better for me than Marcus ever was, but I'm discovering that heartache feels the same no matter who causes it.

Maria calls me back an hour later, when I'm in Wyatt's room, putting the last of his clothes into boxes.

"Hey," she says when I take the call. "How's it going?"

"It was going great until last night."

"What happened?"

"Do you have a minute?"

"I have thirty minutes. It's lunchtime here."

"Oh good. I might need all those minutes. Wyatt took me to meet his parents last night, and they were super chilly to me. He says it's got nothing to do with me. They're pissed he's moving. But it sure felt personal to me."

"Yikes, I'll bet it did."

"I was so uncomfortable the whole time. I felt like they were blaming me for his decision to move or something. I don't know. It was just so screwed up."

"I'm sorry that happened."

"Me, too, and that's not even the worst part. Wyatt took me up to the bedroom that'd been his growing up and was showing me some of the stuff he kept for future nieces and nephews. When I asked him what about his kids, he gave me a blank look and said he's not having kids of his own and figured I knew that."

"Oh *shit*," Maria says on a long exhale. "What did you say?"

"I was so shocked to hear him say that I didn't know what to do. I threw up in the bathroom."

"Ah, Dee."

"I know. It was awful. Later, when we were back at Wyatt's place, he told me he doesn't want to bring kids into the world, knowing he might not be there to raise them. He doesn't think that's fair to them or me."

"I can sorta see where he's coming from. Can you?"

"Of course I can, and I blame myself for not bringing this up with him sooner. I made the mistake of assuming all in meant *all in*. He also told me how he couldn't get life insurance because of his condition, so he wouldn't be able to leave me with a financial cushion if the worst should happen."

"Those are very valid concerns, Dee. Raising kids is expensive, and if you were doing it on your own, it'd be tough."

"I know."

"No, you don't know. Neither of us can know the truth of it. We think we know, but the reality is probably far more difficult than it seems from the outside looking in. He's protecting you. You have to see that."

"I do, but is it going to be a choice between him or having kids? Because I don't know how I'd ever make that choice. I've always pictured myself with kids."

"I know you have."

"I love him, Mar," I whisper. "I know it happened fast, and you guys are probably questioning my sanity, but I love him."

"We're not questioning your sanity. I promise we're not. We're concerned about you getting hurt—maybe not right now, but down the road, if the worst should happen. But anyone with two eyes can see that you two are crazy about each other."

A tear slides down my cheek, and I brush it off. "We are. It's the best thing to ever happen to me, and he says it is for him, too."

"You have to ask yourself if you could ever be happy again, knowing he's out there somewhere without you. I hate the idea of you giving up your dream to have kids, but it may come down to a choice."

"I hate feeling as if someone punched me in the stomach."

"I know that feeling, and it's awful. I'm sorry that what should be such a happy time for you guys has been messed up this way."

"Dad would tell me it's because I didn't do my due diligence."

Maria laughs. "Yes, he would, but you know the important stuff about Wyatt. You know he's a really good guy, and he's wild about you. It made me happy to see the way he looks at you and how you glow around him. I've missed seeing you happy like that since it went wrong with Marcus."

"I was so excited about everything with him, and now..."

"Now, it's gotten real, and that happens to everyone at some point."

"Has it happened for you with Austin?"

"The last few weeks have been kind of real, with him back to work after being home for months. I got used to having him here all the time, and now he's gone for days at a time. We're so lucky to have his parents helping with Everly, but I miss him so much when he's not here."

"It's good to know that reality strikes for everyone, even perfect couples like you two."

"We're not a perfect couple," she says, laughing. "We fight about how Austin leaves his crap all over the place and how I clog the shower drain with my hair. It drives him crazy that I'm such a neat freak. Neither of us *ever* wants to go to the grocery store, and we never agree on what to watch on TV. He likes *horror* movies. I mean, seriously? And don't even get me *started* on his love of heavy metal."

I'm truly stunned to hear they ever disagree about anything. Austin and Maria seem so in sync all the time. "I had no idea."

"Nothing is ever perfect, Dee, but Austin is as close to perfect for me as I ever hoped to find in this lifetime. And if Wyatt is your Austin, be careful drawing lines in the sand and making ultimatums that'll leave you miserable without him. His situation is unique, and I think he's wise to plan for worst-case scenarios. I give him major points for being concerned about things like not having life insurance and the financial impact of him being gone and you having to raise kids on your own. Those aren't small concerns, and you should be thankful he cares enough to worry about that stuff."

"I'm so thankful for the way he cares about me, and I'd be miserable without him after what we've had so far."

"Then find a way to make it work, even if you don't get everything you want."

"Not having kids is a big deal to me, Mari. I'm not sure I can do that."

"Then maybe you can get him to compromise on having one."

"I'd hate to have my child grow up alone, though."

"He or she would *not* be alone. Your child would have Everly and the other kids Austin and I hope to have together, and Car's kids and Nico's and Milo's kids someday. They'd be surrounded by surrogate siblings the same way Carmen was with us."

"That's true." I release a deep sigh. "Thank you for this. It helped to talk it out with you."

"Keep breathing and keep talking to him. I'm sure you guys can find a way to compromise. I never again want to see you hurt the way you were after Marcus, and I have a feeling if this doesn't work out with Wyatt, it'll be worse."

"It would be. He's my one. I know it."

"Then do whatever it takes to make it work."

"I hear you."

"I'm here if I can help."

"You already have. More than you know."

"Keep me posted, okay?"

"I will. We're supposed to leave tomorrow afternoon after the movers leave."

"Can't wait to have you both back in town to stay. Text me later and let me know how you are?"

"Yeah, for sure. Love you."

"Love you, too. Hang in there."

"I'm hanging."

I end the call with my sister feeling a thousand times better than I did before I talked to her. She always has that effect on me. No matter what's bothering me, talking to Maria makes it better.

For a long time after we end the call, I sit on Wyatt's bed thinking about every minute we've spent together since we met at Carmen's rehearsal. I think about the first night I spent with him and how I discovered something new and special with him.

I think about how Wyatt texted me frequently after that night, even though we both knew it couldn't go anywhere with him in Phoenix and me in Miami. I liked that he kept in touch even after we slept together. A lot of guys would've moved on after getting "the milk," as Nona would say. But not Wyatt. He liked me from the start and having sex with me only made him like me more.

I stepped wildly out of character to have that one-night stand with him in the first place, and I did that because I already knew, even then, that I could trust him. The fact that he's Jason's good friend helped, but it was more than that. We had a connection from the beginning, something I've never had with anyone else. The first time I saw him again when he came back to Miami, I knew for sure that connection was real.

Nothing has ever been more real than Wyatt has been, and I don't want to go back to the life I was living before he was part of it. With that in mind, I download the Instacart app, create an account and order what I need to make dinner for him from a local grocery store. When he gets home tonight, we're going to talk, and we're going to work this out.

I'm not willing to consider any scenario that doesn't include him right next to me where he belongs.

CHAPTER 22

WYATT

*T*oday has been the most miserable day I've had in years. I lost a patient during a routine stent procedure when the guy suddenly coded. We did everything we could to get him back, but nothing worked. I had to tell his wife that the procedure had gone wrong and her husband was dead. I'll be hearing her heartbroken wails in my dreams.

I know there was no negligence on my part, but since the procedure ended badly, I wouldn't be surprised if there's a lawsuit. Thank goodness for malpractice insurance.

The heart is a tricky, unpredictable organ in more ways than one. Mine has been aching all day over the disaster that unfolded last night on multiple fronts. After more than ten hours away from her, I'm prepared to give Dee six kids if that's what it'll take to keep her happy and with me where she belongs. I had a very long day to ponder the rest of my life without her, and I'm not down for that. We're going to make this work, no matter what has to happen that wasn't in my plans.

Even kids.

My heart does crazy things at the thought of having babies with Dee. It's as if all the emotion inside me is too big to fit in the available space. It's a feeling unlike any other I've ever had, and I'm officially addicted to the high of being in love with her.

I'm almost to a clean escape from my last day of work when my colleagues waylay me with a going-away party that adds another hour to this endless day. But I go through the motions with the people I've worked with for years, accepting their good wishes for me, my new girlfriend and our life in Miami. A few of them know what I've been through in my life, and they're incredibly happy for me.

I just hope it's not already over, and not knowing where things stand with her has my anxiety spiking to dangerous levels.

When I'm finally on my way home, an hour later than usual, I put through a call to my dad on Bluetooth. I've had all day to think about what I want to say to him. I chose him because he tends to be easier to deal with in situations such as this one. Not that I've ever been in any situation quite like this one.

"Hi there," Dad says when he picks up the call. "Didn't expect to hear from you today."

"Yeah, so, about last night."

"What about it?"

"Where should I start? How about with the way you guys were super rude to the woman I love?"

"When were we rude?"

"When you completely ignored her and took the fact that you're pissed with me out on her."

"We didn't do that."

"Yes, you did, Dad! You made her feel like shit, which makes me feel like shit. I know you don't want me to move, but aren't you the slightest bit happy that I'm in love for the first time in my life?"

249

"We're happy for you, son, but what we don't understand is why you have to move there. Why can't she come here where your doctors are and where you have the support of family and friends?"

"There're doctors in Miami, and she can't come here because, as I've already told you, her mother is battling breast cancer, and she's just been offered a fantastic career opportunity running her family's business. I certainly won't be alone there. I'll have Dee, her family, Jason."

My dad has no reply to that.

"I know this isn't what you want, and I get why you feel the way you do. But you and Mom fought so hard for me to get the chance to *live*. That's what I'm doing. You have to let me, and you have to be nice to Dee, or there's going to be trouble between us. I don't think you want that."

"I don't want that, and neither does Mom. We've been upset since you told us you were moving."

"I'm sorry to upset you, but that doesn't give you the right to treat Dee the way you did last night. I was mortified. You never asked her a single thing or talked directly to her. Do you know how awkward that felt for us?"

"I… I'm sorry, son."

"I'm not the one who needs the apology. I'm going to send you Dee's number. I want you guys to text her and tell her you're sorry for the awkward night and that you look forward to getting to know her better, and anything else you can think of to smooth this over. You got me?"

"Yeah, sure. We'll do that. I hope you know… It's not about Dee."

"I know that! *You* know that! But how in the hell do you think she felt when my parents would barely look at her because they blame her for a decision I made completely on my own? That's unacceptable, Dad."

"Yes, it is. We'll fix it with her."

"Please do, and sooner rather than later. I'm happy than I've ever been with Dee. I want you guys to be happy for me."

"We are. We can see that you care for her."

"I want you to be part of this and not left on the outside looking in. But if you force me to choose, I'll choose her. I want this thing with her more than I've ever wanted anything."

"I understand."

"And you'll talk to Mom?"

"I will."

"Thank you. I hate that you guys are upset about this. I hope you'll eventually see that this move was the best thing for me, that *she* is the best thing for me."

"We want you to be happy, son. It's hard for us to let go of the worry we've lived with for so long. I hope you can understand that a little."

"I hope I never know what that was like for you guys, and I have no doubt I wouldn't be here without you fighting for me every step of the way. But we *won*, Dad. *I* won. I have this chance to truly *live*, and I'm going to take it."

"I, ah..." He sniffles, which makes me realize he's in tears. I'll never forget the first time I saw him break down when the doctors first told us how dire my situation was. I'd insisted on knowing everything that was happening, and seeing my strong, stoic dad in tears left a permanent mark on me. "I want that for you, son. All I've ever wanted was for you to have everything. You've made us so proud with your tenacity and your incredible career."

"That means a lot to me, but I never felt like I truly had it all until I met Dee. Now it's like someone has opened a secret door and shown me how much *more* there is to discover, and I want it *all*."

Even things I thought I'd never want, like children.

My dad agrees to text Dee, and I sign off with him feeling like he understands where I'm coming from. Hopefully, he can get my mom on board, too, because I want them to be part of this new life I'm creating with Dee.

When I'm at a red light, I send her number to him. I drive faster than I should because I want to get home to her so badly. I just hope she's still there.

CHAPTER 23

MARCUS

*R*ehab sucks. All we do is talk, talk, *talk* all day long about our problems, our feelings, our addictions. I'm so sick of talking and listening to other people I don't care about go on endlessly about shit that doesn't matter.

In the meantime, I'm acutely aware of time getting away from me where Dee is concerned. It's been more than a year since I fucked it all up, and that's a lot of time for someone like her to build a new life for herself that doesn't include me.

Desperation, the likes of which I haven't felt since I first came to in that hotel room in Vegas and learned I married the wrong woman, has overtaken me in the last two days. I have to get out of here. And I have to get out now.

After another group session, I return to my room and get my wallet from under my mattress. I jam it into my pocket and go to the front office to request my daily allotment of five minutes with my phone.

I sign for the phone and go to the main lobby to check my

messages. There's one from my sister, another from my mother and two from friends, all checking on me, letting me know they're thinking of me, etc. I appreciate the support from the people in my life, but the only person I truly care about is the one I haven't heard from in far too long.

I wait for my opportunity, and it appears in the form of a UPS man arriving with two big boxes that distract the receptionist and give me the chance to walk out the main door without anyone seeing me go.

Once I clear the parking lot right outside the facility, I take off running for the main road, stopping only to summon an Uber that will take me to my sister's. I need someone to talk to, and Bianca is my first choice.

In the Uber, I vibrate with tension. The desperation is so intense that it makes it hard for me to breathe or swallow or do anything other than stare out the window at the familiar city. Where is she? Home with her parents or back in New York?

All at once, I remember that we used to be able to track each other's phones. What if Dee never turned that off?

I find her in my contacts and click on the info button, waiting with breathless anticipation for it to tell me where she is.

What the fuck is she doing in *Scottsdale, Arizona?*

Because I can't wait the fifteen minutes it'll take to get to Bianca's, I call her.

"Marcus? How are you?"

"Why is Dee in Arizona?" Her long pause sends my heart rate soaring. There's an excellent chance I'm going to stroke out any second. "Bianca! *What is she doing there?*"

"She's met someone else, Marcus."

"No, she hasn't. There is no one else for her but me."

"You have to listen to me."

My head begins to pound, and my mouth goes dry. "I don't want to hear this, and how do you even know that, anyway?"

"Maria posted something on Facebook."

I put the call on speaker and fumble around on my phone until I find my Facebook app. I search for Maria and click on her name. Sure enough, the first post is a picture of Dee with some dark-haired guy, the two of them smiling like fools.

So happy for my sweet sister, Dee, and her new love, Dr. Wyatt! You two are so cute together! No one deserves to be happy more than you guys do. Xoxo

I'm having a heart attack. Dee has got someone else. The guy's a doctor, and even someone who's not into guys can see he's a good-looking dude. But more than anything, the blissed-out expression on Dee's face is what hits me the hardest.

I've never seen her look at me the way she's looking at him.

"Marcus."

I've all but forgotten I was on the phone with Bianca.

"Are you there?"

"I'm here."

"Did you see the post?"

"Yeah."

"What can I do for you?"

"I'm on my way to your house."

"Marcus! What're you doing? You can't just leave rehab."

"I just did."

"I'm not at home, but Tara is there. She's staying with me for a while. I'm in the Keys for Destiny's bachelorette."

Fucking great… Bianca's best friend from forever has always had a massive crush on me that I couldn't do a damned thing about because my sister would've neutered me if I so much as looked at the girl.

Tara is the last thing I need right now, but since I can't very well hide out at my place until I figure out my next move, I don't redirect the driver. I'm such a fucking mess that I'm sure Tara will feel only pity when she sees me for the first time in a couple of years.

Besides, she's probably moved on, too. Everyone does.

"Do you want me to come home, Marcus?" Bianca asks.

"No. Don't do that."

"I'm worried about you."

"I'm okay." I say what she needs to hear because I don't want to interrupt her good time.

She promises to check on me later, and we end the call.

I'm sure she's texting everyone we know to let them know I've busted out of rehab and am not in a reasonable frame of mind. There was a time I would've cared about people knowing my business. That time is long in the past now.

I stare at the picture of Dee and her "new love," Wyatt. I hate the guy on sight. What right does he have to look at her that way? I want to call Dee and tell her she's making a huge mistake with him, but I can't do that because I've still got the presence of mind to know she isn't the one who made the huge mistake.

And then I'm sobbing in deep, gulping wails that has the driver watching me in the rearview mirror, probably concerned for his safety.

The worst part of realizing your life is a fucking disaster is knowing you have only yourself to blame for the wreckage scattered all around you.

"You all right, man?" the driver asks.

"Yeah, sorry. Got some bad news."

"Condolences."

"Thank you."

The bad news is the love of my life, the one whose heart I shattered by marrying a woman who meant nothing to me, has found someone else to love. I've been blessed not to have much experience with grief in my life, but that's the only word I can think of to describe the awful feeling that's sunk its claws so deep inside me, I might never be able to rid myself of it. You don't move on from this kind of pain. It's permanent.

I'm sadder than I've ever been while I continue to stare at the photo of Dee and Wyatt as if I don't already have every detail memorized.

Dee has someone else. Dee is *in love* with someone else. She's never coming back to me. There's nothing I can do or say to fix things with her, and suddenly, there's no point to rehab. It was all for her. Everything was for her.

What does it say about how fucked up everything is that even in the fog of grief and despair, I'm able to recognize this as the lowest point in my entire life? This is worse than everything that's come before. Knowing I have no hope with Dee is a kick in the gut that takes the breath right out of me.

As long as she was out there somewhere, I had hope. But now, knowing she's moved on and is happy with someone else...

I'm done.

The Uber drops me at Bianca's complex, but I lack the energy to walk up the two flights of stairs to her place. I fall onto a bench out front that has no protection from the blisteringly hot sun that beats down on me. I can't find it in me to care that I might be getting badly sunburned. What does that matter?

What does anything matter?

I have no idea how long I sit roasting on that bench before someone says my name. I pull myself out of the pits of despair and look up at Tara gazing down at me, brows knitted in confusion. She's holding a brown bag, and her light blonde hair is up in a bun.

"What're you doing here?"

"I, uh... I don't have anywhere else to go."

"Does Bianca know you're here?"

"Yeah."

"Do you want to come in?"

I don't. Not really, but what else can I do? Broil in the sun until I have a third-degree sunburn to add to my litany of problems? "I guess so."

She extends her free hand to help me up. "Come on."

I take a good long look at her hand before I raise mine to take it, hoping I'm not replacing one set of problems with another by letting her, of all people, help me.

CHAPTER 24

DEE

*W*yatt texted to tell me he was running late, which gave me more time to make sure everything was perfect for the night I've planned for us. Nona sent me the recipe for her famous seafood casserole, which I cooked with a tiny bit of olive oil rather than the usual ton of butter in deference to Wyatt's avoidance of cholesterol.

I have just enough time to worry that maybe he doesn't like seafood other than salmon, or perhaps he's allergic to shellfish. I wonder if I should've even bought seafood in freaking Arizona, which isn't exactly close to the ocean. I've worked myself into a full-on anxiety meltdown by the time I hear his key in the door.

He comes in and stops short at the sight of the table set, lit candles and me in a black dress and heels that I packed in case we went anywhere that required such a thing.

I spent time on my makeup and hair, which cascades over my shoulder in long spiral curls.

He drops his work bag and keys right inside the door and

comes to me, sliding his arms around me and holding on as tightly to me as I do to him. "I'm so glad you're still here."

"Where else would I be when you have my heart? I can't leave without that, without you."

Pulling back, he looks down at me for a long moment before he kisses me with almost twenty-four hours' worth of pent-up desire, despair and fear. His tongue brushes up against mine, and my knees go weak from wanting him.

He has me pressed so tight against him that there's nothing I can do but surrender to the desperate need for a lifetime of feeling just like this.

"Dee." His lips skim lightly over mine. "I love you. I want you. I want *us*, but more than anything, I want you to be happy. If you need babies to be happy, we'll have babies. We'll figure it out. As long as I have you, I have what I need."

I'm overwhelmed by relief at being back in his arms and hearing his sweet words. But I've learned to be wary of situations that resolve themselves too quickly. "We should talk."

He hugs me even tighter. "Let's do this for another minute first."

We hold each other in the soft glow of the candles I placed on the table.

When he finally pulls back from me, he says, "You look beautiful, and something smells incredible."

"I made dinner."

"How'd you do that when there's almost no food in the house?"

"Instacart."

"Ah, very industrious."

"Are you hungry?"

"Starving, as always, but let's talk first. I need to get some stuff off my chest."

"Let me just turn down the oven, and I'm all yours."

Before he releases me, he kisses me again, softly this time. "I want you to be all mine forever."

I place my hand on his handsome face. "I am all yours. I had a very long day to think about going back to my pre-Wyatt life and concluded there's no going back to before you. There's only forward *with* you."

"I feel the same way. Turn down the oven, and let's talk about it."

After I see to the oven, I pour a glass of chardonnay for myself and seltzer for Wyatt and bring them with me to join him on the sofa.

He's looking at his phone but puts it down when I sit next to him.

"Everything all right?"

"I lost a patient today during a fairly routine procedure. Hell of a way to end my tenure there."

"I'm so sorry, Wyatt. That must be horrible."

"Having to tell family members that a routine procedure led to death is the worst part of my job, especially when there's no good explanation for it. Sometimes things just happen that we can't control or explain."

"Do you worry about getting sued when that happens?"

"Always, but we have pretty airtight consent forms that spell out all the possible outcomes of heart surgery. And I always, *always* tell the patients I'll give them my very best, but I can't promise anything. It just sucks when it happens, and I wouldn't be surprised if they sue."

"Ugh, that's awful."

"It happens. That's why we have malpractice insurance. This is the first time in my career I've lost a patient during what should've been a routine stent procedure, but I witnessed similar scenarios two other times during my residency. Both times it happened the same way. Everything was fine until it wasn't."

"I'm sorry it happened today when you should be celebrating the end of a successful time here and the start of a new adventure."

"Thanks. It was a bummer of a last day, for sure. But my colleagues had a potluck going-away party for me at the end of the day, and they all signed a card. They made it a nice sendoff."

"I'm sure they'll miss you."

"Enough about me. Tell me what's on your mind, and then I'll tell you what's on mine."

I roll my lip between my teeth, trying to find the words I need. "I heard what you said before about having as many babies as I want, but just last night, you were pretty adamant about not having any. I'm worried you're going along with what I want, but maybe you still feel the same way."

"I'm trying to pivot to this new anything-is-possible mindset you've taught me. For the longest time, I limited myself out of fear of what *might* happen. You've helped me see that's no way to live, and while I still have the same concerns about leaving you alone to raise kids without a financial cushion that life insurance would provide, I, too, had a long day to think about returning to life before Dee."

He turns to face me and takes hold of my hand. "I can't do it, either. You've ruined me for anything other than being with you. I still have major concerns about bringing kids into this world and maybe leaving them far too soon, but I also heard what you said last night about them having a life because of me, even if I'm not there to enjoy it with them. That's not nothing."

"No, it isn't. And our kids would be surrounded by a big loving family and men like my dad, my uncles, my brothers and friends like Jason and Austin. It wouldn't be the same as having you, but they'd be okay. I'd make sure of it. And it would leave me and everyone who loves you with a piece of you here with us forever."

"That's true," he says with a small smile. "I feel better about it when you remind me you wouldn't be alone, and neither would they. They'd have my family, too, and speaking of them, you should have a text from my parents."

"Really?"

He nods as he gets up to retrieve my phone from where I left it in the kitchen. He brings it back to the sofa and hands it to me.

Sure enough, there's a text from a phone number I don't recognize. I glance at Wyatt before I read it.

Hi Dee, this is Gary Blake, Wyatt's dad. I'm here with my wife, and we wanted to apologize for the way we behaved last night. It's not like us to be unwelcoming to our kids' friends, especially one who's as important as you are to Wyatt. We're upset he's moving and worried about him for reasons you can certainly understand. However, none of that is about you, and we hope you'll forgive us for a dreadful first impression and give us another chance. We're happy you and Wyatt have found each other and that he is getting to have this experience with you. He seems very happy, and we're determined to be happy for him. Anyway, we're sorry, and we hope to see you again soon. Gary and Dawn

"Wow, you must've given them one hell of a talking-to."

He smiles, which makes his eyes twinkle. "My dad and I had a *conversation*."

"Thank you for smoothing things over with them. I hate to get off to a bad start."

"You didn't. They did, and my dad sounded genuinely remorseful about it. I can't promise there won't be more bumps with them because they worry about me at extremely unhealthy levels. But he promised they'll make a genuine effort to get to know you and to be part of this."

"I suppose I can't ask for anything more than that, and I understand they're overprotective after what you all went through."

"Overprotective isn't a strong enough word to describe

them. Again, I remind you my mom texted me when I was in Miami to make sure I was taking my antirejection meds."

Although he's seriously annoyed, I can't help but laugh at that.

"It's not funny!"

"It's kinda funny."

He shakes his head. "Not even a little funny."

I pinch my fingers together. "A tiny bit."

"Just don't you get any ideas about making sure I take my meds."

"I'll refrain from nagging you about that as long as I'm allowed to nag you about everything else."

"Nag away, baby."

"So, we're good?"

"We're fantastic."

"I want you to know I appreciate the way we dealt with this like two adults and didn't turn it into a multiday nightmare that undermined all the good stuff."

"Is that how it worked for you in the past?"

"Sometimes. Trust me, this is way better." I glance at my phone. "Let me respond to them, so they know there're no hard feelings."

Thank you for your message. I appreciate it, and I hope you can visit us in Miami soon. I promise to do my best to make Wyatt happy and to take very good care of him. It means a lot to me that you reached out. Thank you again. Dee

I show it to him. "Is that good?"

"It's lovely and more than they deserve after the way they acted."

"They're frightened parents, Wyatt. We can't hold it against them. That could be us someday. You just never know what might happen." Another thought occurs to me that I should've had before now. It's so big it takes my breath away for a second. "The condition that led to the transplant. Is it hereditary?"

"No, it's not. My issue was determined to be a rare birth defect that led to damage to my heart. My siblings and parents don't have it, and there were no genetic links, either."

"Well, that's a relief."

"Indeed. If it were a hereditary thing, kids would've been a hard stop no matter what. I'd never want to subject a child to what I went through, but our kids will need screening. If they have a defect, we can correct it before it causes damage. The damage had already occurred when mine was discovered."

"Would they need heart surgery if they have it?"

"Yes, but it's a pretty basic procedure that would prevent a world of problems down the road."

I swallow hard as I try to imagine my child having heart surgery.

"It bodes well for our kids that no one else in my family had the same issue, so we shouldn't worry about that until we need to. Hopefully, we'll never have to." He tips my chin up so he can kiss me. "All good?"

"All good."

"Now about this dinner you made. It smells fantastic, and I'm starving."

"Then let's eat."

Hours later, I'm lying in Wyatt's arms, watching him sleep and marveling at how much my life has changed in a few short weeks. My one-night stand has become my once-in-a-lifetime, and I couldn't be happier to know we get to be together from now on, for as long as we can. Maybe it'll only be a short time. If it is, I'll be thankful forever that I knew him and was loved by him.

Giving your heart into someone else's care isn't something any of us should do lightly. It's a big deal to give someone the power to hurt you. I learned that lesson the hard way, but I already know I'll never have to worry about Wyatt wanting someone other than me. He's sowed those so-called wild oats with his history of fleeting encounters with women. We're both ready for something more lasting.

"What're you staring at?" he says in a low grumble.

"You."

"Do I have something on my face?"

"Yep, a whole lot of handsome."

The side of his face that I can see lifts into a smile. "You need to sleep. We've got a long day tomorrow."

"I don't want to sleep. I want to look at you."

His eyes open, and he draws me in closer to him, our bodies intertwining as if we've been doing this for years. "You've got a little line between your brows. Right... here." He leans in to kiss the spot. "What's that about?"

"I'm not sure."

"Are you scared, sweetheart?"

"Of what?"

"Of all the unknowns and what-ifs?"

"Maybe a little, but it's nothing I can't handle."

"I really, *really* hope I never break your heart, but if I do, I want you to know that loving you made my life whole. We're just getting started, but I already know that everything before this was leading me to you."

"I love you so much," I whisper. "I never knew things like this could happen, and then there you were at my cousin's wedding, too handsome to be believed. You have no idea what it meant to me that day to have a guy like you paying attention to me after what I'd been through. You lifted me so high."

"You dazzled me at the wedding. I felt like a tongue-tied teenager around you."

"No way."

"I swear! I was tripping over myself to keep you talking to me and dancing with me."

"I would never have known that if you hadn't told me. I was in a horrible place that day, and you made everything better."

"I'm glad to hear it." He runs his hand up and down my back, making soothing circles. "Do I need to thank your ex for that first night we spent together?"

"How do you mean?"

"If he hadn't put out the word that he regretted what he did and wanted you back, do you think you would've had your first one-night stand after the wedding?"

I think about that for a minute before I speak. "That might've had a tiny bit to do with loosening my inhibitions, but I can assure you, it never would've happened if I hadn't felt a connection to you." With my hand on his chest, I look into his eyes. "And if you hadn't kept texting me, none of the rest of this would've happened. Every time I heard from you after our night together, I got the same lift you gave me at the wedding. Your texts made me so happy during a rough time with my mom. I started to look forward to them."

"I was like an eighth-grader with a new cell phone waiting for you to reply to me. I was checking it obsessively, every chance I got. One of my surgical nurses asked me one day if I had a girlfriend, and that shocked me." He mocks a shocked expression. "That was how I looked at her."

"What did you say?" I ask him, laughing.

"I told her I didn't have a girlfriend, but for the first time in my life, I thought I might want one. She said, 'Ah, so you've met *the one*, have you?' I had no idea what to say to that. It was the first time I understood that maybe you were my one, and after that, all I could think about was getting back to Miami as fast as I could. And then the very next day, Jason called to tell me about the opening at Miami-Dade. He made a joke of it, saying if only I were interested in moving, we could work together again. I took that as a sign from the universe and asked him to send me the info on how to apply, even as I told myself to stay away from you because it wouldn't be fair. I just couldn't stay away."

"That's amazing. I loved getting your texts, but I had no idea you were thinking of me so much."

"I thought about you *all the time*. I've never thought of anyone more than I've thought of you."

"I'm thrilled you came back to Miami."

"So am I."

"The bad stuff from before I met you seems like a lifetime ago as if it happened to someone else. It doesn't even matter anymore."

"It still matters because it's part of your story, but I'm glad I could help you move on from something that caused you so much pain."

"You did help. I thought I was doing so great moving on from it until that night of Carmen's bachelorette, and suddenly, I was right back at day one."

"That must've been an awful feeling."

"It was! I was home for a happy occasion. My beloved cousin, who'd been through so much after losing her first husband, was getting married again to a great guy. I was ready to celebrate, and then I heard what Marcus had been saying." I blow out a deep breath. "It just sucked the life out of me to hear that about him."

"Did you think about seeing him or getting back together with him?"

"God, no. Never. My love for him shriveled up and died the second I heard he married someone else. But the hurt… That took a lot longer to go away. The rough part was thinking I was over it and had moved on, only to be right back in that painful space the second they told me what he was saying. That was the same weekend we found out my mom was sick, too."

"That's a lot all at once."

"It was, but I shouldn't be talking about him with you."

"Why's that?"

Smiling, I tell him, "I know this is your first official relationship, so you may not know that talking about your ex to the new guy is frowned upon."

"You can talk about anything with me, even him. He doesn't threaten me. At least I don't think I need to be threatened." He gives me a playful side-eye. "Right?"

"You don't need to be threatened by anyone. You're in a class all by yourself."

He kisses me, and as all kisses with him seem to do, one thing leads quickly to another, and he's on top of me, pushing into me, making me crazy the way only he can. At times like these, when he's so vital and alive, I find it easy to forget about the threat to his health that'll be part of our life together.

I don't want to think about that or anything else coming between us, not when everything about this feels so damned good.

CHAPTER 25

WYATT

*T*he movers are quick and efficient and have the truck packed by noon. After we close on our house in Miami, they'll deliver the furniture from my house. Dee packed up everything in my kitchen, calling it our starter kit. I'm not much of a cook, but she says we can get the rest of what we'll need when we're ready.

This is really happening.

I'm leaving Phoenix to make a life with Dee in Miami.

A few weeks ago, none of that would've seemed feasible to me, but now she's shown me anything is possible. All I have to do is believe it. Maybe we're both being naïve and unrealistic about what's probably ahead for me—and us—but I'll be damned if I can find the wherewithal to care inside the happy bubble with her.

My parents surprise us with lunch. They both hug Dee, which helps to repair the damage they did the other night. My sweet girl is so forgiving, so loving. She treats them like old friends, even after the way they behaved at their first meeting.

"Did you guys leave work to bring us lunch?" I ask as we stand around the kitchen island to eat the salads they brought.

"We did," Dad says. "We wanted to see you before you left."

"I'm glad you did."

Mom gets a little emotional at the sight of my empty living room. "Wow, you're really moving."

"I'm really moving, and I can't wait until you guys can come to Miami and meet Dee's awesome family and eat at their restaurant. It's the best food you've ever had anywhere. And wait until you see the house Dee found for us. It has a second master suite that's all yours anytime you want to come to visit."

"That sounds very nice," Mom says.

I know her well enough to understand she's making an effort for my sake and maybe Dee's, but she's still heartbroken about me leaving.

"It has a pool, and it's right near a golf course, Dad."

"You're speaking my language."

We visit with them for another half hour. They leave with hugs for both of us and promises to come to Miami as soon as we're settled in our new house.

"Please check in often, or I'll worry," Mom says when she hugs me a second time.

"I will. I promise."

Dee and I walk them out and wave to them as they drive away.

"It was nice of them to come," she says.

"It was. I'm glad you got to see the Mom and Dad I know and not that weird version of them from the other night."

"I am, too."

We have a quick meeting with the Realtor who's listing my place so I can sign the agreement that puts it on the market. And with that, it's time to go.

At two o'clock, we load suitcases, backpacks and other things we'll need on the road, including an entire bag devoted to my medication, into my SUV. We take one final walk-through to make sure we didn't miss anything. As I shut and lock the door on my Phoenix home for the last time, so many emotions overwhelm me.

Chief among them is excitement for what's ahead, and that, in and of itself, is such a welcome feeling. Ever since I passed the eleven-year mark, I've been living in this odd state of suspended animation, waiting for the sky to fall. There's not much room for things like hope or excitement inside that mindset.

Dee has changed everything for me. She's shown me a different way, a better way, and as I go down the stairs to the parking lot, I don't look back. I only look ahead to Dee, who's standing by the car waiting for me. With the sun streaming down on her, she looks like an angel sent from above to show me what it means to truly live rather than just exist.

I surprise her when I go to her rather than the driver's side of the vehicle. "Before we leave, I just want to say thank you."

"For what?"

"For showing me another way to live."

"You like this better?"

Nodding, I kiss her softly. "So much better. Thanks for all you did to get ready for the move. I never would've gotten it done without your help."

"We make a good team."

"Yes, we do."

"Should we get this show on the road?"

"Absolutely." I hold the passenger door for her and wait until she's settled to steal another kiss. "Let's go home."

MARCUS

I sleep better than I have in weeks and wake up twelve hours later to sunlight pouring into my sister's bedroom. Since she's out of town, I slept in her room after talking to Tara for hours about everything that's happened since we last saw each other.

Unlike Dr. Stern and the people at rehab, Tara listened to me without interrupting. She let me talk until I had no words left, and then she asked what I needed.

"I don't know. I just don't know."

"Maybe you should sleep on it and see how you feel in the morning."

I was utterly exhausted after seeing Maria's post about Dee and talking it all out with Tara, so I took her offer of a place to stay for the night and slept like a dead man.

I feel a little better today, but I'm so sick of myself and my never-ending litany of problems. I've made a God-awful mess of my life. That's about the one thing I know for sure.

In Bianca's bathroom, I "borrow" an unopened toothbrush and take a shower.

Wearing yesterday's clothes, I leave the bedroom to figure out what I'm going to do next.

Tara is in the kitchen standing watch over something on the stove. "Coffee?"

"Sure, thanks."

She pours coffee into a mug and puts it on the counter along with cream and a sugar bowl. "How'd you sleep?"

"Really well for once."

As I watch her move around in the kitchen, I have the same thought I had last night. The cute young girl who used to follow me around like a puppy has grown into a beautiful woman. I haven't seen her in years, and the change in her is remarkable. "Sorry to make it all about me yesterday. I never even asked where you've been since I saw you last."

"I was in Ecuador for three years with the Peace Corps."

"Oh wow. That's amazing."

"It was great. I taught English as a second language to elementary-aged kids. I loved every minute of it. I got back two weeks ago, and I'm moving into my new place at the end of the month. Bianca was nice enough to let me crash with her in the meantime."

So while I was drinking my way into oblivion and making a full-on disaster of my life, Tara was off saving the world. "That's really cool. I'm impressed."

She smiles, which makes her eyes light up. "Thanks. It was fun, but now I have to figure out what's next. I've applied to a bunch of places, and I'm just waiting to hear something. The waiting is making me crazy. I always need to have a plan."

When she retrieves plates from the cabinet, her T-shirt rides up on her back, revealing two sexy indents at the base of her spine. Not that I have any business noticing Tara's sexy indents. *Drink your coffee, Marcus, and keep your eyes off your sister's friend.*

Tara serves scrambled eggs, turkey bacon and buttered toast.

"Thank you so much for everything, Tara. I really appreciate it."

"No problem." After refilling my coffee, she joins me at the bar, and we eat in silence until she puts down her fork and looks at me. "What're you going to do?"

"I don't know. I just don't know."

"May I offer a suggestion?"

"Sure. After all, you listened to my bullshit last night. I'm interested in your opinion."

"You need to go back to rehab and finish what you started there."

That's the last freaking thing I want to do.

"Everything you talked about last night comes back to one thing—you need to deal with your alcoholism before you worry about anything else."

She's right. I know she is, but I still don't want to go back there, even if I know I have to. They've called six times since I left, but I've declined the calls and haven't listened to the messages from them or Dr. Stern, who's called three times.

"I can give you a ride if you'd like."

I want to say *no, thank you*. I want to tell Tara I'm not going back there, but she looks at me in such a way that lets me know my bullshit isn't going to fly with her. "I've been unfair to you."

That seems to surprise her. "How so?"

"When we were younger, I always felt like you were maybe into me, and I spent hours last night talking to you about Dee and how upset I am that she's found someone new."

"I was into you."

"Oh."

"So into you, it wasn't even funny," she says, laughing. "But you were always with Dee."

"I'm sorry if I was clueless."

"It's fine. I got over it."

For some strange reason, I'm sad to hear she got over me, which is ridiculous in light of everything else I've got going on.

"I'm sorry you had to hear that Dee's moved on from a Facebook post."

"That was more than she got from me when I married someone else."

"True. That wasn't your finest hour."

She's cute, funny, intelligent and insightful. If things were different, I'd want to sit here all day and talk to her about anything and everything.

"I know you're beating yourself up over everything that went down, and while you should feel bad about what happened with Dee, you don't need to carry that around with you for the rest of your life. It happened. It's over. She's moved on. You're moving on. Life goes on. You need to work on forgiving yourself for things that happened when you were dealing with an illness."

"I'm not sure I'll ever forgive myself for what I did to her."

"You have to, Marcus."

"I feel like I need to see her for that to happen."

Tara shakes her head. "No, you don't. That's not what she needs. She's moved on. Seeing you wouldn't be good for her."

I blow out a deep breath as it finally registers with me that there's nothing I can do where Dee is concerned besides leave her alone and wish her well. My phone rings with yet another call from the rehab. I decide to take this one.

"Hello."

"Marcus, this is Dr. Stern. We've been trying to reach you."

"I know. I'm sorry. I had some stuff to take care of."

"We'd like you to come back to the facility. Do you have a means of transportation?"

I look at Tara when I say, "Yeah, I do."

"Can we expect you back today, then?"

I take a deep breath and release it. "Yes, I'll be there."

"I'll look forward to seeing you soon."

After we end the call, I put the phone on the counter.

"You're doing the right thing," Tara says. "You can't worry about anything else until you're healthy again."

"That's easier said than done." I glance at her. "We'd probably better go before I make another bad decision and talk myself out of going back."

"I won't let you do that." She clears the plates and puts them in the sink. "I'll be ready in a minute."

After she disappears into the other bedroom, I force myself to sit there and wait for her when everything in me wants to bolt. For whatever reason, I feel like that would disappoint Tara, and I don't want to disappoint her or anyone else. I've done enough of that.

Tara comes out wearing leggings and a tank that clings to her full breasts. She blossomed from an awkward girl to a gorgeous woman since I saw her last. And the best part is she's beautiful on the inside, too.

As she drives me to the rehab facility in her silver Hyundai Sonata, we're both quiet.

I watch the scenery go by—palm trees, strip malls, colorful flowers and ponds with fountains in front of apartment complexes. It's all so familiar and yet so foreign, too. When was the last time I bothered to pay attention to the scenery? When was the last time I had the bandwidth to think about anything other than getting drunk or fixing things with Dee? It's been a long, long time.

Tara pulls up to the main door at the rehab and puts the car in park. "Unlock your phone and let me see it."

I do as she asks, even if I'm not sure why.

She taps at the screen and then hands it back to me. "I programmed in my number. If you need a visit or a care package or a friend to talk to, call or send a text."

"Thank you, Tara. You'll never know what you did for me just by listening."

"I'm glad I was there when you needed a friend."

I eye the main doors apprehensively. "Well, here goes nothing."

"No, Marcus." She puts her hand on my arm and looks at me with warm, hazel eyes. "Here goes *everything*."

She puts a huge lump in my throat with that.

"Thanks again," I manage to say before I get out of the car and head inside without looking back. If I look back, I suspect she'll still be there, making sure I'm inside before she leaves.

It's the strangest thing. Yesterday, I found out Dee had someone else and nearly lost my mind. I ran from rehab, landed at my sister's and found an old friend who provided just the support and comfort I needed. Today, I find myself wondering when or if I'll get to see Tara again.

I really hope I do.

CHAPTER 26

DEE

Since we get a late start, we drive six hours to Albuquerque the first day and arrive around nine p.m. And yes, we know Albuquerque is out of the way, but neither of us has ever been there, so we take a detour to the north to check it off the bucket list of all the places we want to go together that we made during the ride. We hold out for dinner at a local restaurant and stumble into a hole-in-the-wall place next door to our hotel that has some of the best food I've ever tasted outside of Giordino's. We walk back to the hotel and fall into bed, exhausted from the long day.

In the morning, we take a couple of hours to explore Albuquerque. We wander around Old Town, and Wyatt buys me a gorgeous bowl from one of the galleries we visit and two small cacti for our new home. However, I take a pass on his suggestion to check out the Rattlesnake Museum.

"I can't believe you don't want to learn about rattlesnakes," he says with a playful pout.

"I'd have nightmares for days if we went there, especially when we're driving through rattlesnake country."

"If you're gonna be that way about it."

"I'm gonna be that way about it."

Since our goal today is to make it to Austin, Texas, we don't linger for long in Old Town and hit the road shortly before ten for the eleven-hour drive to Austin.

Wyatt seems tired after doing all the driving yesterday, so I insist on taking the first shift.

We have the windows down and sing along to the eclectic selection of music he plays on the Bluetooth. Everything from Lil Wayne to CCR to Eminem to Tim McGraw to Selena. He's impressed when I sing the Selena song to him in Spanish.

"Your musical taste is all over the place," I tell him.

"I like songs, not genres. If a song speaks to me, I add it to my playlist. I don't care who sings it or whether someone my age ought to like it. My grandfather is a huge Rat Pack fan. He had me listening to Sinatra and Dean Martin and Sammy Davis Jr. when I was a little kid. I knew all the words to their songs by the time I was eight."

"That's very sweet."

"This is his favorite." He plays "My Way" and sings along.

He's got a great voice, which I learned about him that night in Miami when we stayed up all night listening to music. Since we left Phoenix, I've also learned he wants to stop at every cheesy tourist trap we pass on the road, which has me calling him Clark W. Griswold.

"If you don't want to see the world's largest mud hut, I'm not sure we can make this relationship work."

"I'll take my chances."

We laugh and joke and tease and sing and eat the healthy trail mix he buys from the convenience store when I would've gone for chocolate and chips. I can already see his influence is going to be good for me.

Being on the road with him is the most fun I've ever had in my entire life.

Much later that night, we're driving through the ghost town that's West Texas when we see a sign for a bus stop that cracks us up.

"Who in the hell is coming out to the middle of nowhere to catch the bus?" Wyatt asks.

He took over the driving when we rolled into Texas a few hours ago, and I'm manning the playlist.

I've added some of my favorite salsa and hip-hop songs to keep things interesting as we drive for miles without seeing another car.

"I could put the cruise control on ninety, put my feet up on the dash and take a nap, and we'd be totally fine," he says.

"Except you're not going to do that."

"But I could. Have you ever been on a more desolate road in your life?"

"I don't think so." I keep checking my cell phone to make sure we still have service out here. So far, so good, but I wouldn't be surprised to lose service at some point.

We drive for what feels like forever before we see headlights coming from the other direction.

"Check it out!" Wyatt bounces in the driver's seat. "Someone else survived the zombie apocalypse!"

"That's such a relief. Maybe we can form a new community with the other survivors."

As the vehicle approaches, the bright lights blind us after so much darkness.

"What the hell's he doing?" Wyatt asks as the other car closes in on us.

The car seems to be partly in our lane, or it appears to be. "I can't tell if my eyes are playing tricks on me or what."

Wyatt slows down and inches closer to the far right side of

the road as the other vehicle comes so close to us, it nearly side-swipes us. He has no choice but to wrench the wheel to the right, which sends us careening off the road into the brush.

I scream as I grab the handle above the passenger door window and hold on until the car comes to a jarring stop about ten feet from the road. Thankfully, the airbags don't deploy.

Behind us, we hear a loud boom as the other vehicle crashes.

"Are you okay?" Wyatt asks, his expression panicked.

"I think so. Are you?"

"Yeah, the seat belt didn't feel good against my chest, but otherwise, I'm okay. I should check on the other driver." He throws the SUV into reverse, drives up onto the road and heads back to where the other vehicle landed. "Try calling 911 and see if there's service out here."

As I make the call, I realize my hands are shaking. Thankfully, the call goes through, and I can report the accident, although I have no idea where we are.

"We'll use GPS to locate you, ma'am," the operator says. "Just keep the line open."

"My boyfriend is a doctor. He's going back to check on the other driver."

Wyatt parks our car and turns on the hazard lights before getting out to jog over to the other vehicle. He returns a few minutes later. "Just grabbing the first aid kit. His head is bleeding. He says he fell asleep and is all apologies."

When I realize how close we came to a devastating crash, I can't stop shaking as I convey the new information to the 911 operator.

Help arrives fifteen minutes later in a helicopter that lands right on the road.

After I tell the operator the chopper has arrived, we end the call, and I get out of the car to watch. In the bright lights coming from the helicopter, I can see Wyatt talking to the paramedics. I wonder if the other driver knows he got lucky by nearly crashing into a car driven by a doctor.

With the paramedics on the job, Wyatt returns to our car, holding the first aid kit.

"Is he going to be okay?"

"Yeah, he might have a concussion and some broken ribs, but he'll be fine." He tosses the kit inside the car and then puts his arms around me. "That was scary."

I cling to him as the adrenaline seems to leave my body all at once. "Sure was. You did a good job avoiding the accident."

"All I could think about was what I'd ever do if something happened to you."

"I'm fine. You're fine. We're fine."

"Keep reminding me." He brushes the hair back from my face. "You referred to me as your boyfriend."

Laughing, I say, "Well, you are."

"That's a first for me. I need a minute to enjoy it."

"I'll say it every day if you want."

"That'd be good."

We stand there, holding each other until the chopper departs, leaving us once again alone in the dark.

"Come on," he says, "let's get going." He holds the door for me and closes it after I get settled.

When he gets in the car, he looks over at me. "You sure you're not hurt at all?" He rubs his chest as he asks.

"I'm fine, but are you? Should we get your chest checked?"

"I don't think we need to. It's just bruised from the seat belt."

"Are you sure?"

"I'm sure. I don't take any chances in that area. Nothing to worry about." He turns the car back toward Austin, and we set out, both of us subdued after our close call.

"You know," I say a while later, "this was a sign."

"What do you mean?"

"Nona is a big believer in the universe sending us signs, like the one you got when Jason called about the job in Miami. Think about what just happened. We're out in the middle of nowhere, not another car in sight, and the one car we encounter nearly hits us head on. One or both of us could've been killed. It's proof we're doing the right thing."

"I'm glad we're doing the right thing—and PS, I already knew that—but I'm not sure I follow how it's a sign."

"We could've died right here on this lonely road in West Texas, Wyatt. We're all going to die someday. You might go sooner than the rest of us, but it could've been me today if that car had hit us just right."

"Don't even say that. I can't bear to think of anything happening to you."

"I can't bear to think of anything happening to you, either, but it will. Someday. In the meantime, we have to soak up every single moment of happiness and joy out of the time we do have without spending another second worrying about when it all might end."

"It sounds so simple when you say it like that, but for so many years, I just didn't think that was possible."

"That's because you were planning for worst-case rather than living best-case. You just needed me to show you that."

He surprises me when he pulls the car over and turns on the flashers.

"What're you doing?" I ask him.

Reaching for me, he tips my chin up to receive his kiss. "I'm so, *so* thankful I found you, and you showed me how to live."

I place my hand on his sweet, handsome face and return the kiss with a bit of tongue that makes him gasp. "Have you ever done it in the desert?"

"Not in the Texas desert."

That makes me laugh even as I continue to kiss him.

"As much as I'd love to christen the Texas desert, I'd be afraid of someone hitting us."

"Good point."

We reluctantly separate, but he takes hold of my hand and doesn't let go.

I hope he never lets go.

EPILOGUE

DEE

*W*e're moving into our gorgeous new home today, and the entire family has come to help us. Wyatt had his first week at Miami-Dade and loves his new coworkers and patients. He thinks he's going to be very happy there, which is a huge relief to me. I want him to be happy in his new hometown. I want him to be as happy as I am since we came home to Miami to stay.

Ever since the night in the desert, when the universe sent us a sign, Wyatt hasn't once mentioned any worries about the future. We're too busy loving the present to spend any of our precious time being concerned about things we can't control.

Maria told me Marcus is making progress in rehab, which is good news. Despite what happened between us, I want only good things for him.

When my parents come to help us move in, my mom hands me a letter sent to their house. I can tell it's from Marcus, but I haven't opened it yet. Today is about new beginnings, and I don't want to bring my painful past into it. I'll read it later.

"Where do you want this box?" Milo asks, carrying one of the many boxes my cousin Domenic sent from my former apartment in New York.

"In the kitchen, please."

"You got it."

Jason and Austin help Wyatt and Nico move the sofa from Phoenix to three different locations in the great room before I find the perfect spot.

"Thank God," Nico says, scowling at me.

"What? I wanted to get it right while we have the help." I'm worried about Wyatt doing too much, but I'd never say that to him. He wouldn't appreciate it.

We arrange the furniture from his place in Phoenix, put away the items we've purchased locally in the last week and unpack boxes from my New York apartment. Nona and Abuela take over the kitchen, and I happily defer to the experts. My mom and Aunt V make our bed while Uncle V and my dad put together Wyatt's desk from Phoenix in the room we're planning to use as an office.

My mom is feeling much better since she ended her course of antibiotics. She insisted on coming to help today, and I'm thankful she felt up to it.

Carmen and Maria help me set up the master bathroom and put away the towels from his house and my apartment.

"It's cool that your towels match his," Maria says, noting that the pattern in mine complements the navy in his.

"Is it normal to be so happy that you feel like you're going to burst?" I ask them.

"Entirely normal," Maria replies. "I still feel that way with Austin. Like it's too much to contain inside one heart."

I'm relieved to have her put it into words for me. "Yes, it's just like that."

"For me, too," Carmen says. "When I'm with Jason and even

when I'm not. That's how I knew at the beginning that he was special."

"Are you going to read the letter from Marcus?" Maria asks.

I had to tell them about it. "Eventually. I'm sure it's another apology, which is nice, but it's all in the past now."

"I heard Bianca's friend Tara has been to see him a few times."

"I remember her! She's a nice girl."

"I suppose he deserves a nice girl after being married to the skank," Maria says begrudgingly.

We share a good laugh, and it amazes me that a conversation that would've hurt so much not that long ago has no impact on me whatsoever. I've found my happily ever after with Wyatt, and I want Marcus to find his. Despite the pain he caused me, I'm rooting for him and his sobriety.

It's a long day, but we make a considerable dent in turning our house into a home.

At dinnertime, Wyatt passes his phone around for a massive takeout order for all our helpers. We eat Mexican outside by the pool, sitting on furniture he put together last night after it arrived in six different boxes.

I'm thrilled to have my family at *my* house for dinner. That they seem to love Wyatt as much as I do makes the first day in our new home one of the best of my life.

"We should all do a weekend away somewhere," Carmen says as she sips her second margarita. She and Jason brought the drink mix and tequila along with a super fancy blender as a housewarming gift.

"Oh, we should," Maria says. "Before Austin's season starts."

"My season has already started, babe," Austin says.

They left Everly with his parents today so they could help us.

"I know, but not the regular season. You'll have at least one weekend free between now and the official start, won't you?"

"I'll see what I can do."

"Where should we go?" Jason asks.

"Key West," Carmen says. "Or Islamorada. Either would be awesome."

"I'm down with that," Wyatt says. "We need a vacation after moving."

"I wanna go," Milo says.

"Me, too," Nico adds. "I'll bring Sofia and Mateo. He'd love to play with Everly."

I can't believe Nico drops that so casually, as if him bringing Sofia and Mateo on a getaway wouldn't be a big deal.

"Just when we thought we'd hired our way out of working all the time, she's already planning a vacation," Vincent says with a teasing smile.

"Jeez, I never even thought of work," I tell him.

"It's so hard to get good help these days," Vivian says, and we all share a laugh.

"I promise I'd make sure everything is fully covered if I took off for a weekend," I tell my new "bosses."

"We're not worried about it, honey," Vincent says. "It'll take a while for us to get used to not working all the time. We're around."

"You guys are taking the trip to Italy this fall, though, right?" Carmen asks her dad.

Her parents and mine booked the trip for September, with everyone hoping my mom's treatments will be completed by then. They need something to look forward to, other than Maria and Austin's wedding in November, and we couldn't be more excited for them.

"Hell yes. It's on. Two weeks in Tuscany, a week at Amalfi and another week in Sicily."

"I'm so jealous," Wyatt says. "That sounds amazing."

I decide right then and there to start saving up to take him to Italy as soon as possible.

"I have big news." When Nona has everyone's attention, she smiles as big as I've ever seen her smile. "I start my flying lessons tomorrow afternoon."

"That's great, Nona," Carmen says. "We're so proud of you."

"I don't know about this." My dad glances at Vincent. "Are you sure about this, Mother?"

"I'm very sure," Nona says. "I can't *wait*."

"Leave her alone and be happy for her, Lorenzo," Abuela says. "She's wanted to do this for as long as I've known her."

"How do you know that, but her sons don't?" Vincent asks.

"Because she told me, and she didn't tell you because she didn't want you to worry about her doing something that'll bring her joy."

"This is all your fault," my dad tells Vincent. "You decided everyone needed to get a life outside of work, and now our mother is taking flying lessons."

Vincent laughs at his brother's good-natured jab. "I'll take the blame if it makes her happy."

"Thank you, Vincent," Nona says. "I haven't been this excited about anything in years."

"That's sweet, Nona," Milo says. "I can't wait to see you fly."

She smiles lovingly at him. We joke that he's her favorite. "Thank you, honey."

"Speaking of getting a life, how's Mr. Muñoz, Abuela?" Carmen asks.

Abuela gives her a withering look. "Mind your own business."

"Since when is your business not my business?" Carmen asks with an innocent expression.

"Since she started dating Mr. Muñoz," I say, earning a scowl from Abuela.

"Where did we go wrong with these children?" Abuela asks our parents. "They're so impertinent."

"That's her vocabulary word of the week," Nona says.

Ever since Carmen's parents took Abuela and her sister back to Cuba for a visit that'd broken their hearts, Abuela has been determined to speak only English. She's accepted she's never going "home" again.

"It's funny how it's impertinence when we want to know her business, but it's *not* impertinence when she wants to know ours," Maria says, making everyone laugh.

"Talk about someone else." Abuela waves her hand. "Nothing to see here."

"Where there's smoke, there's fire," Jason says.

"And here I thought I liked you," Abuela says, making us howl with laughter.

The family leaves around eight with promises to be back tomorrow after brunch to help us finish unpacking. I head for the shower with every muscle in my body aching after working nonstop for most of the day.

When I emerge from the shower, I find a gift bag on the counter that Wyatt must've put there. I look around the corner into the bedroom, but I don't see him. There's a card in the bag that I open first. It says, "Congratulations on your new home! May you know only love and joy as you make new memories."

We're so, so, SO happy for you and Wyatt, and we wanted to help you enjoy your first night in your new home. We love you so much, and we're thrilled to have you here with us where you belong! Love you both! Car and Mari

I have tears in my eyes as I pull the tissue paper out of the gift bag to find a sexy silk nightgown in the palest shade of pink, a scented candle and a bottle of champagne.

My girls are the best, and I couldn't be happier to be living close to them again. I put on the nightgown and bring the candle and champagne with me into the bedroom where I find another gift, this one a big white box with a red ribbon on it.

"Wyatt?"

He comes into the bedroom and stops short at the sight of me standing next to the bed, his eyes gone hot with desire. "*What* have we here?"

I strike a pose. "This old thing? Just a gift from my sister and cousin."

Walking toward me, he flashes the warm, sexy grin I love so much. "Have I mentioned how much I *adore* your sister and cousin?"

"I do, too. They also gave us this yummy-smelling candle and a bottle of champagne."

He kisses me. "Stay put. I need to grab a shower, and then I'll find a lighter and some glasses."

"What's in that box?"

Over his shoulder, he says, "You'll have to open it to find out."

"I didn't get you anything."

He stops and turns to me, looking at me in a way that makes my knees go weak. "Please, Dee. You've given me *everything*."

"Right back atcha."

"Don't go anywhere."

"Nowhere else I'd rather be than right here with you."

After he goes into the bathroom to shower, I push the box toward the center of the bed and discover it's lighter than expected. I get into bed and wait for him, taking a look around at the big, beautiful room we'll share. I can't believe this is my home, that this is my life, that *he* is my life.

While I have a second to myself, I decide to read Marcus's letter. Not that it matters what he has to say, but since he took the time to write it, the least I can do is read it. His familiar handwriting takes me right back in time to when I thought I was going to spend my life with him.

Dee,

*I'm sorry. If I say that a million times, it still won't be enough.
I'm deeply, profoundly sorry for what I did to you and us with
my thoughtless behavior. I'm sure you've heard by now that I'm
in rehab, getting treatment for what became full-blown alcoholism over the last few years. And yes, I hid that from you. I
never wanted you to know how messed up I was. I'm trying to
fix that now and also trying to accept that I can never fix the
mess I made with you, the most precious person in my life.
I'm sorry for what I did, that you had to hear it from others
and that I never reached out to you. I was so appalled and
ashamed of myself that I couldn't bring myself to contact you. I
was a coward, Dee. I couldn't bear to know how badly I
must've hurt you.
I heard you met someone else, and you're happy. That's all I've
ever wanted for you. I hope if we see each other again someday,
we can be friends or at least be cordial. That might be more
than I deserve, but I'll hope for it anyway.
Please accept my apology and know that I love you very much.
I always will.
Marcus*

I'm deeply moved by his heartfelt words and relieved to hear
directly from him about how he feels about me and what
happened. It doesn't change anything, but it's nice to hear after
all this time. I put the letter in my bedside drawer and return
my focus to the present, where it belongs.

Ten minutes later, Wyatt comes out of the bathroom with a
towel wrapped around his waist. "Stand by for fire and glass."

"Standing by."

He returns with the glasses and a fire striker we bought
when we went to Home Depot for batteries, trash cans and
other household necessities. While he opens the champagne, I
light the "Home Sweet Home" candle that puts out a sweet,
spicy scent.

Wyatt sits on the edge of the bed and hands me a glass. "Here's to home sweet home and happily ever after."

I touch my glass to his, more than willing to drink to that.

He surprises me when he takes a sip of champagne.

"Are you breaking another rule?"

"Just one sip to be polite." He puts his glass on the table and takes mine to put it next to his. "Open your present."

I reach for the box and bring it toward me. "When did you do this?"

"The other night when I had to 'work late.'"

"Ah, so you're already lying to me, huh?"

His grin is big and goofy and adorable. "Yep."

"I'll allow it anytime gifts are involved." I pull the bow off the box and open it to find nothing but tissue paper that I pull out until I uncover another smaller package wrapped in shiny silver paper. I'm all thumbs as I try to get the paper off, and my heart nearly stops when I reveal a navy blue velvet box. "Wyatt..."

He takes the box from me, gets down on his knees next to the bed and takes hold of my hand.

My heart is beating so fast that I fear I might hyperventilate. "Wh-what're you doing?"

Wyatt kisses the back of my hand. "I was so thrilled when Jason asked me to be in his wedding. He's one of the best friends I've ever had, and I was looking forward to sharing his big day with him. But I had no idea whatsoever how that weekend in Miami would change my life forever. I spent one day and one night with you, and all I knew was I needed more of you. When Jason told me there was an opening at his hospital, he was joking around. Wishful thinking, he said. He never expected me to jump on it and ask him to get me an interview because he didn't know yet that I'd fallen hard for his wife's cousin."

"Wyatt." I use my free hand to wipe tears from my face.

"You can't begin to know what you've done for me, Dee, how you've given me things I never dared to dream possible for

myself. Before I knew you, I was living half a life, and now…"
His voice catches, and he takes a second to deal with his
emotions. "Now, my new heart doesn't have enough room for
all the love I have for you and the life we're building together.
When I said you gave me everything, I meant it. You've shown
me that the things I denied myself are the very best things, the
things that make life worth living. I know it's all happened fast,
but as you said, we have no time to waste. I already know what I
want, and that's to spend the rest of my life with you. Will you
marry me, Dee?"

"*Yes!* Oh my God, Wyatt! Yes, yes, yes, a million times *yes.*"

Smiling, he pushes himself up and onto the bed to kiss and
hug me so tightly, I can barely breathe. "Thank you for everything. I can't wait to marry you."

I pull back so I can see his gorgeous face. "You say I've given
you so much, but you've done the same for me. When I think
about the place I was in that Friday night when you came back
to Miami, that seems like another lifetime after everything
that's happened since then."

"None of it would've happened if you hadn't been the
strongest, most courageous person I've ever met. You never
blinked an eye when I told you about my situation. You just
grabbed me by the hand and demanded I live as fully as possible
for as long as I can."

"And you… You've restored my faith and put me back
together."

He shakes his head. "You did that on your own. That's why
you were ready for me when I came along."

"I like the way I look to you."

"I *love* the way you look to me." Flashing a dirty grin, he runs
his hand down my back to cup my ass and pulls me in tight
against his erection. "Wait! We forgot the ring!"

I dissolve into laughter. Once upon a time, the ring might've been the most important part of this moment. Not anymore. Not with him.

He finds the velvet box and opens it to reveal a stunning diamond ring that he slides onto the third finger of my left hand, holding it up to admire how it looks. "What do you think?"

I can't believe we're engaged or how gorgeous the ring is. "I love it, Wyatt. Almost as much as I love you."

"Carmen and Jason helped me pick it out."

"She knew about this and didn't tell me?"

"I swore her to secrecy. I wanted us always to remember the first night we spent in our new home."

"Safe to say I'll never forget it."

"Let's make sure, shall we?"

When he kisses me, I wrap my arms and legs around him, wanting him and our life together more than I've ever wanted anything. For however long it may last, being loved by him makes me feel like the luckiest woman who's ever lived.

Thank you for reading *How Much I Love*! I hope you enjoyed this new installment in my Miami Nights Series. I'm having ALL THE FUN with this family and these stories. I hope to continue this series with more books, so make sure you're on my newsletter mailing list at marieforce.com to hear about future books. Also, keep an eye on the Miami Nights Reader Group at facebook.com/groups/MiamiNightsSeries for information about upcoming books, and join the How Much I Love Reader Group at facebook.com/groups/howmuchilove/ to discuss Dee and Wyatt's story with spoilers allowed. We have some fun Miami Nights merchandise in the store, including series boxes offered with and without the books. Check out the collection at http://bit.ly/MiamiMerch.

I loved what my beta reader Dinorah said to me in her note about the book: "Thank you for this amazing series. You had me crying, laughing and feeling hopeful all in just a few hours. I think this is a great book for everyone to read, especially during what everyone has just gone through with this pandemic. We need to remember that we need to live each day to the fullest and not worry too much about what may or may not happen. The future is not ours to see. Que será, será." I'm so glad she took that message from Dee and Wyatt's story because it's the truth. As Dee says, all we have is right now. If this last year has taught us anything, it's that we have to enjoy every moment to the best of our ability.

It takes a village to write and publish books, and I'm incredibly thankful for mine. A big thank you to Dan, Emily and Jake for always championing my author career, as well as the team that supports me every day: Julie Cupp, Lisa Cafferty, Tia Kelly, Jean Mello, Andrea Buschel, Ashley Lopez and Nikki Haley, as well as my wonderful editors, Linda Ingmanson and Joyce Lamb. Kristina Brinton, thank you for the gorgeous covers for the Miami Series. I love them!

I'm thankful to so many people who help me behind the scenes. Mona Abramesco, a long-time Miami resident, helped me figure out a fun day for Dee and Wyatt that led to their fishing outing from Black Point Marina. Sarah Hewitt, family nurse practitioner, was a huge help in making sure I got the particulars of Wyatt's situation right. I did tons of research into the experiences of heart transplant patients and read so many inspiring stories. I'll probably never again take a healthy, beating heart for granted after having written this book. A huge thank you to my first-team beta readers Anne Woodall, Kara Conrad and Tracey Suppo, and to the Miami Series betas Mona Abramesco, Dinorah Shoben, Miriam Ayala, Emma Melero Juarez, Carmen Morejon, Stephanie Behill and Angelica Maya.

And to the readers who follow me wherever the muse may

take me, even to South Florida, thank you so much for coming along for this wonderful ride. You make everything so much fun, and I appreciate every one of you!

Xoxo

Marie

ALSO BY MARIE FORCE

Contemporary Romances Available from Marie Force

The Miami Nights Series
Book 1: How Much I Feel (*Carmen & Jason*)
Book 2: How Much I Care (*Maria & Austin*)
Book 3: How Much I Love (*Dee & Wyatt*)

The Gansett Island Series
Book 1: Maid for Love (*Mac & Maddie*)
Book 2: Fool for Love (*Joe & Janey*)
Book 3: Ready for Love (*Luke & Sydney*)
Book 4: Falling for Love (*Grant & Stephanie*)
Book 5: Hoping for Love (*Evan & Grace*)
Book 6: Season for Love (*Owen & Laura*)
Book 7: Longing for Love (*Blaine & Tiffany*)
Book 8: Waiting for Love (*Adam & Abby*)
Book 9: Time for Love (*David & Daisy*)
Book 10: Meant for Love (*Jenny & Alex*)
Book 10.5: Chance for Love, *A Gansett Island Novella* (*Jared & Lizzie*)
Book 11: Gansett After Dark (*Owen & Laura*)
Book 12: Kisses After Dark (*Shane & Katie*)
Book 13: Love After Dark (*Paul & Hope*)
Book 14: Celebration After Dark (*Big Mac & Linda*)
Book 15: Desire After Dark (*Slim & Erin*)
Book 16: Light After Dark (*Mallory & Quinn*)

Book 17: Victoria & Shannon (Episode 1)

Book 18: Kevin & Chelsea (Episode 2)

A Gansett Island Christmas Novella

Book 19: Mine After Dark *(Riley & Nikki)*

Book 20: Yours After Dark *(Finn & Chloe)*

Book 21: Trouble After Dark *(Deacon & Julia)*

Book 22: Rescue After Dark *(Mason & Jordan)*

Book 23: Blackout After Dark *(Full Cast)*

Book 24: Temptation After Dark *(Gigi & Cooper)*

The Green Mountain Series

Book 1: All You Need Is Love *(Will & Cameron)*

Book 2: I Want to Hold Your Hand *(Nolan & Hannah)*

Book 3: I Saw Her Standing There *(Colton & Lucy)*

Book 4: And I Love Her *(Hunter & Megan)*

Novella: You'll Be Mine *(Will & Cam's Wedding)*

Book 5: It's Only Love *(Gavin & Ella)*

Book 6: Ain't She Sweet *(Tyler & Charlotte)*

The Butler, Vermont Series

(Continuation of Green Mountain)

Book 1: Every Little Thing *(Grayson & Emma)*

Book 2: Can't Buy Me Love *(Mary & Patrick)*

Book 3: Here Comes the Sun *(Wade & Mia)*

Book 4: Till There Was You *(Lucas & Dani)*

Book 5: All My Loving *(Landon & Amanda)*

Book 6: Let It Be *(Lincoln & Molly)*

Book 7: Come Together *(Noah & Brianna)*

The Quantum Series

Book 1: Virtuous *(Flynn & Natalie)*

Book 2: Valorous *(Flynn & Natalie)*

Book 3: Victorious *(Flynn & Natalie)*

Book 4: Rapturous *(Addie & Hayden)*

Book 5: Ravenous *(Jasper & Ellie)*

Book 6: Delirious *(Kristian & Aileen)*

Book 7: Outrageous *(Emmett & Leah)*

Book 8: Famous *(Marlowe & Sebastian)*

The Treading Water Series

Book 1: Treading Water

Book 2: Marking Time

Book 3: Starting Over

Book 4: Coming Home

Book 5: Finding Forever

Single Titles

Five Years Gone

One Year Home

Sex Machine

Sex God

Georgia on My Mind

True North

The Fall

The Wreck

Love at First Flight

Everyone Loves a Hero

Line of Scrimmage

Romantic Suspense Novels Available from Marie Force

ABOUT THE AUTHOR

Marie Force is the *New York Times* best-selling author of contemporary romance, romantic suspense and erotic romance. Her indie-published series include Gansett Island, First Family, Treading Water, Butler Vermont, Quantum and Miami Nights. She's also the author of the Green Mountain and Fatal Series.

Her books have sold more than 10 million copies world-wide, have been translated into more than a dozen languages and have appeared on the *New York Times* bestseller more than 30 times. She is also a *USA Today* and *Wall Street Journal* best-seller, as well as a Spiegel bestseller in Germany.

Her goals in life are simple—to finish raising two happy, healthy, productive young adults, to keep writing books for as long as she possibly can and to never be on a flight that makes the news.

Join Marie's mailing list on her website at *marieforce.com* for news about new books and upcoming appearances in your area. Follow her on Facebook at *www.Facebook.com/MarieForceAuthor* and on Instagram at *www.instagram.com/marieforceauthor/*. Contact Marie at *marie@marieforce.com*.

Made in United States
North Haven, CT
28 June 2022

20709534R00189